# TRUSTING YOU

## A SMALL TOWN ROMANCE

Havenport Series Book 1

## DAPHNE ELLIOT

# CONTENTS

Published by Melody Publishing, LLC

Editing by Happily Editing Anns

Cover design by Kari March Designs

daphneelliot.com

*To my babies, G and T. You inspire me every day.*
*I wrote this book to show you that you are never too old and it*
*is never too late to pursue your dreams.*

# PROLOGUE
## CECELIA

I NEVER INTENDED TO BE A TOTAL FAILURE. IT certainly wasn't part of my grand life plan. But even with the best intentions, I still ended up back here. Maybe I could become a motivational speaker? Speak to high school kids about my failure to adult properly? Launch some kind of self-help empire for the chronically underachieving? I would think about that later. Now, I just had to breathe.

It takes a special kind of underachiever to wind up back in your hometown with no job, no boyfriend, and no apartment at age thirty-one. It wasn't as if I was ashamed of my recent breakup or layoff. I knew deep down that neither was a good fit. And I'd had enough jobs and boyfriends to know how to pick myself up and dust myself off when things went south. But things were different this time. Because I was faced with the very unsettling realization that after thirty-one years on this planet, I had very little to show for myself. I didn't love my career as a pharmaceutical marketing executive. I didn't even like it most days. And I certainly had not loved Xavier, my creeper ex. I didn't love my harried, anxious life in New

York. My life was just devoid of passion and fun and excitement. And that was a far bigger blow than losing a mediocre job and a mediocre guy. So, in addition to being single and unemployed, I was also in the middle of a Grand Canyon-sized rut.

If I was capable of getting out of my own head, I would have seen the beautiful views, smelled the salty sea air, and realized that it actually was nice to be back. Instead, I was just living in my own doom spiral of shame.

My heart rate rose as I crossed the bridge over the swelling Haven River. The large "Welcome to Historic Havenport, founded in 1685" sign greeted me as my car crossed over into town.

So here I was. On the other side of thirty with not a clue what was going to come next. But I knew one thing for sure. I was done with men. For good.

# 1

LIAM

It was time to face the truth. My business was floundering.

I took a deep breath. "So what you're saying is that I should close?" It was the last thing I needed to hear today.

"Of course not. What I am saying is that you need to find some ways to generate more income so you can keep brewing amazing beer."

"But if I can't do that in the next few months then I have to close?" I was well and truly screwed. And not in the fun way.

Callum, my older brother and financial advisor, sighed deeply. "I'm just saying. Your building is worth a lot now. The south side of town is experiencing a huge boom and I know there are many developers who would love to convert it into luxury condos."

"I hate luxury condos."

"I know you do. I'm just saying. As your financial advisor, you have a very valuable asset. If you need to shut down you will land on your feet."

"But what about as my older brother?"

"As your older brother, I want you to keep brewing

and build your empire. But if you want to keep the brewery going, you need to change things up a bit. I don't know, maybe accept some fucking help once in a while."

I let out a big sigh. "Okay, thanks."

"I know you don't want to hear this. But you need more support. You need to take on investors and focus on new areas of growth. And you also need to hire someone who can handle the marketing side of things, social media, events, that kind of thing. You are an incredible brewer, but the greatest beer in the world still needs to be marketed and sold."

He wasn't wrong.

"I've said it before and I'll say it again. You need to hire a marketing and social media person. Promotion is eighty percent of the battle and you don't have the time or the knack for it, bro."

"But I don't even have the time to advertise and interview applicants. Not to mention, who wants a part time job that pays shit right now?" As much as I needed help, I couldn't take my eye off the ball for one minute right now if I was going to save this place.

"Hey, keep your chin up. You are doing great and this is a temporary blip." Cal was always such a good motivational speaker. "Who knows? The perfect person could walk in the door tomorrow."

I had heard this song a thousand times over the years. My family was incredibly generous and supportive, but they were not shy about calling me out on my shit. Callum was a financial genius and one of my biggest supporters, and I knew he was right. I just wasn't sure what to do about it. "Okay. I gotta run, bro. But I will see you tomorrow night."

I hung up and rubbed my temples. The conversation was basically the same one we had every week. I needed to be making payments on my loans, I needed to diversify and come up with some new revenue streams, and brewing award-winning beer was not enough if you weren't a fucking hashtag or distributed around the world. And I would love to hire someone, but finding someone who could handle this shit show for very little pay was basically impossible. And as attractive as outside investors would be, I was not yet ready to give up control of this operation. I had been burned in the past, and Binnacle Brewing was my baby and I didn't want too many cooks in the kitchen. I was generally a laid-back guy. I was the youngest, the peacemaker, the one who could be counted on to crack a joke when things got tense. But when it came to my business, I was a dictator. The stakes were too high and I had worked too hard to risk screwing anything up.

I leaned back in my chair as I surveyed my desk. My laptop was open, my inbox screamed for attention, and the piles and piles of paperwork mocked me. It was only eight a.m. on a Monday morning. I had thought I could do this. I had thought I could handle things, and I had thought I could scrape by. But each day it was looking more and more like this was just another epic failure.

Opening a brewery had been my dream since college. A dream I had carefully and slowly worked toward. I got my degree in microbiology and then took every internship, apprenticeship, and fellowship I could find. I traveled the world learning about the craft of beer, visiting Belgian Monasteries and German hop farms. My first venture went bust a few years back due to some bad luck and poor management, and I picked myself up, dusted myself off, and scraped and saved until I could try again.

A timely inheritance from my grandmother gave me the opportunity to buy this old warehouse and get my brewery set up, and for the last four years, I have been busting my ass to make it. I have worked seven days a week, sometimes twenty hours a day to brew, distribute, and market my product. It was exhausting, but it was my dream.

I loved this town deeply. It was strange and fun and downright weird sometimes, but it was home. Havenport is a pretty quirky place. We had a storied history of great thinkers, revolutionaries, artists, and rebels. The town had been through so many transformations over the years, what was left was a melting pot of artists, activists, yuppies, fishermen, and working families. In the eighties, Havenport emerged as a friendly hub for LGBTQ folks fleeing discrimination elsewhere. In fact, Havenport elected America's first openly gay mayor in 1989. Burt, who had retired after serving four terms, was now a sort of town mascot and could be found riding his Vespa around town. I wanted Binnacle Brewing to succeed so badly. Both for myself and for this unique and crazy town.

The irony was that I had actually had some success. My beer was good. Really good. Binnacle got some recognition in the trades and had placed well in a few regional competitions. So the product was strong, and I had some interesting specialty beers. With some more revenue, I could expand our brewing capacity and open up new areas for growth. The problem was that the craft beer market was insanely oversaturated, especially in New England, and it was hard to break through. Binnacle was carried in a lot of local restaurants, and our cans were sold in liquor stores across New England, but we lacked the "hook" to really take it to the next level. And given how expensive the equipment and real estate was to brew beer, if I didn't make it to the next level soon, the brewery would be toast.

It felt like we had been on the precipice of the next level for a while, and I just couldn't figure out how to get us there. It was not enough to brew good beer, you also needed a huge distribution network and catchy marketing. You practically needed Banksy to design your cans and have millions of Instagram followers to pay your bills. I was working day and night trying to figure it out, but I could only do so much on my own.

Between brewing and selling and distributing and dealing with the taproom and everything else there wasn't much time for business strategy. Maybe if we could get someone in to help, maybe a marketing person, that could take a few things off my plate. The irony was that I couldn't really afford to pay anyone, but I couldn't succeed in taking these additional steps without more help.

I took my Binnacle brewing hat off and ran my fingers through my, admittedly, very dirty hair. I thought about pouring myself a beer but settled on a half-eaten protein bar that I found lying on the desk. It looked fine, and I hadn't had a real meal or showered in days, so my standards were pretty low. I decided to go in search of sustenance.

Unlocking the loading dock door, I looked up to see Trent, my oldest friend and loyal employee. He gave me a big grin and reached out for a fist bump. "I love the smell of hops in the morning," he exclaimed with a spring in his step.

Trent was one of those amazing people that always had a smile on his round face. He's an assistant brewer and cellerman, which meant he was responsible for cleaning and sanitizing the fermentation and conditioning tanks and transferring the beers from tank to tank. He kept all the machinery working at top capacity and had become an excellent brewer and our resident coffee guru. He was also my best friend, my sounding board, and one of the most loyal human beings on earth. The thought that he might lose his job, a job he loved, because I couldn't get my shit together made me feel even worse.

I smiled at Trent. How could he be so chipper so early? He looked me up and down. "Rough night, Liam?" He winked at me and then his face fell, taking in my disheveled appearance. "I see. Someone hasn't had their coffee yet. I'll get started, boss."

I clap him on the shoulder. "Good man, Trent." I needed to get some coffee and start thinking about how I was going to right this ship. Now, coffee was not just coffee. We were beer guys, which means we geeked out over the science of brewing and crafting beer. Same went for coffee. Because we brewed and canned in shifts 24/7, a lot of coffee was consumed. And because we were all science nerds at heart, we got extremely technical about the beans, roast, and grind of our coffee. We even had competitions to see who could make the best coffee. Trent was the reigning champion, which was just one of the reasons his schedule always seemed to match up with mine.

A bit later, Karl walked in rubbing his back. Karl was a retired brewmaster and chemist from Vermont who moved to Havenport with his wife a few years back to enjoy his retirement. He previously worked for a large national brand and ran an entire brewing and distribution plant. He was old and cranky, but he was an incredible mentor. His wife got sick of him hanging around the house and told him to get a hobby. Since the man couldn't stay away from beer, he instead came here and convinced me to hire him. His wife was an amazing baker and always sent him in with delicious treats. It's like she knew we needed to be bribed to keep him around. Today he was carrying two enormous trays of muffins. I secretly thanked her for thinking of me and grabbed two before heading back to my office.

"Karl," shouted Trent, who was carrying two Yetis

filled with strong black coffee across the brewing floor. "Can I get you some coffee, freshly made?"

Karl gave Trent a look. He liked to pretend to be annoyed by Trent's boundless optimism, but I knew deep down he adored him. "Okay, kid. But skim milk for me. My wife says no more cream."

"Roger that," Trent said, handing me my mug. I rolled my eyes at him and headed to my desk to continue the workday that had started sometime around four a.m.

Today was one of those days where I had to take a minute and be proud of what I had built. After years of dreaming and saving and some serious catastrophes along the way, I had done it. I had achieved my dream. And it had thoroughly kicked my ass, but I had loved every single day. I just hoped I could keep things going. Because as stressed as I was, and as much as the pressure felt crushing sometimes, I was still proud and happy to be here every day. Working with my friends and making something amazing that people all over New England would enjoy was a privilege.

So it was more important than ever to come up with a plan and quick. Crunching the numbers with Callum, I knew I needed to increase revenue significantly in the next few months. The fastest way to do this would be to leverage what we already had, which was the taproom and event space. I just needed to find someone, a perfect unicorn employee who was creative and energetic and could help us increase revenue, to see the potential in this place. If things didn't improve in the next few months, my dream would be over.

# 2

CECELIA

As I pulled into the driveway flanked by blooming wildflowers, I couldn't help but notice the chipped paint and wood rot on the garage. Once a great beauty, my mother's house was slowly but surely falling into disrepair and losing its vibrancy and charm. Despite her wear and tear, she was a grand home and had been filled with a lot of love and adventure over the years.

The state of our family home used to make me sad. These days, it makes me feel validated. The old girl had been through some hard times and was showing her wear and tear.

My parents had bought it for pennies in the early eighties when Havenport was a dingy fishing town, before it underwent a massive revitalization into the commercial and tourist hub it was today. Over time, they lovingly fixed it up and made it their own. This house had seen generations of families, births and deaths and weddings and graduations, and still she stood, proud but a bit humbled by age. I could have learned a thing or two.

I was halfway through my cleansing breaths when my

mother burst out the back door, a blur of flying scarves and jangling bracelets. "Cecelia! My love. Get over here and give me a hug." Where I was quiet and thoughtful, my mom was loud and energetic, always moving at high speed to the next thing on her to-do list. Her waist-length raven hair was streaked with gray and woven into an intricate Game of Thrones style braid. Dangly amethyst earrings highlighted her long, graceful neck, and she was, of course, barefoot.

She embraced me with her skinny but deceptively strong arms, and I was engulfed by the smell of sandalwood. "You look gorgeous, honey. I am so thrilled you are here." She squeezed me tighter and took a big breath. "I love you so much and I am so proud of you."

I pulled back a bit, feeling smothered. "Mom, I do not look gorgeous. I have most of my earthly possessions in this car because my life has completely blown up. I am broken out, sleep-deprived, and have been eating nothing but Ramen for the last two weeks." I did not add that I was so bloated my Toms barely fit on my feet right now and my hair hadn't been washed in a few days. My mother's unwavering love and support could get old at times, especially when I just wanted to wallow and eat ice cream. Having her tell me she was proud of me when I was not proud of myself was a bit of a blow.

My mother smoothed an unruly curl out of my face. I did not inherit her height, her build, her green eyes, or her zany energy, but I did get her wild hair. Our hair was thick and curly and resistant to any scientific advances in hair care. It grew quickly and in every direction, and I spent a small fortune to try and keep it under control. *Thanks, genetics.*

"Cecelia Marie Leary, I do not allow negative self-talk in my house. You are a gorgeous butterfly, and you just need to get a little break so you can spread your wings and fly. Now let's get you unpacked. I'm hosting moonlight meditation tonight. You're gonna love it."

"Mom, I don't think I'm up for meditating tonight. I just want to be alone."

"Nonsense, Cecelia," she says, crossing her arms and tapping her foot—oh my God, this woman cannot keep still—"you just got back and I want to spend time with you. I have to pop over to Lucy's—she just had surgery and I made her some freezer meals today, vegan and gluten free, obviously—and then I have to stop by Burt's and return the book he lent me and then we can make some dinner and meditate. It will be just like when you kids were little." I forgot just how fast my mom speaks. My head was spinning. I just wanted to sleep and maybe watch some Bravo.

"Mom, I need to be alone right now and lick my wounds."

My mom smiled at me and gave me a pitying look. *Oh shit. Here it comes.* "Darling, I love you. You are the light of my life and I think you are amazing." She reached out to gently squeeze my cheek, and her eyes turned steely. "But if you think I'm going to let you wallow in despair under my roof then you are sorely mistaken." With that, she bent down, grabbed a suitcase, a backpack, and a cloth shopping tote, and walked through the slider into the kitchen.

*So I guess wallowing is off the table...*

———

After some cathartic ice cream and a forty-five minute full moon meditation with my mother and some of her friends in the backyard, I was feeling much better.

I looked around, savoring the feel and smell of my childhood home. The sunroom was our favorite place growing up and it had not changed over the years. It was filled with light and plants and shelves stacked with board games. In one corner was an ancient couch, and on the other side was an enormous, battered wood table and eight mismatched chairs surrounding it under a Victorian-era chandelier. As kids we always wanted to eat dinner in here to see the sunsets through the giant windows. So, one weekend, mom went out and found a table and some mismatched chairs at a yard sale and the kitchen and dining rooms hadn't been used since. We ate many meals and played many games in here, first as a family of four and then a family of three after my dad died. Not that it mattered to my mom where we ate—she made sure we were always laughing, having fun, and loving one another.

I had spent a lot of time judging my mom's meditation group, but it was actually a pretty cool group of people made up of some neighbors, some of my mom's teacher friends, and my aunt Joyce. It was all women except for Burt, who never went anywhere without his Yorkie, Coco Chanel.

After meditation, everyone retired to the sunroom to lounge and drink wine. My aunt Joyce droned on about her crystals while I zoned out for a bit and attempted to enjoy myself. How long had it been since I had enjoyed the company of other women? How long since I had meditated or practiced yoga or done any self-care? *Way too fucking long.*

I took a long sip of my wine and settled into the old armchair, happy to just fade into the background. This was actually not a terrible way to pass an evening. Of course it was not meant to last. Probably desperate to get off the topic of crystals, Emily turned to me. "So Cece, are you going to stay in town long? It is so nice to have you here."

Emily was a beautiful, eccentric soul who had married her college sweetheart and popped out three kids before hitting thirty. She never wore makeup and had the kind of shiny, shampoo-commercial hair that made you instantly hate a person. She was a preschool teacher turned stay-at-home mom and was a genuinely kind, lovely person. But at this moment, when the chatter hushed and I felt multiple sets of eyes on me, I wanted to slap her.

I took a deep breath. "Well, I'm not sure. I needed a break, so I decided to come home and spend some time with my family"—I exhaled, while scanning the inquisitive faces in the room—"and I am so glad to be back." I pasted on a fake smile and hoped the topic was closed.

Aunt Joyce leaned over the arm of the old sofa. Her oversized sweatshirt was covered with kittens and matched the giant dangling kitten earrings in her ears. "Are you still working? Your mom told us you sell drugs?" Oh Jesus, Joyce, she knew what I did for a living. She was my aunt, for Chrissake.

"I don't sell drugs," I said through clenched teeth. "I am a pharmaceutical marketing executive. I was laid off a few weeks ago when the company I worked for stopped manufacturing the product I sold. I am looking for a new opportunity."

"There are so many marketing jobs up here, away from the city." My mom's friend Ronnie added.

Belinda Wilson, my fourth grade teacher, nodded. "Oh yes. I know lots of people who are hiring."

"I think I'm fine for now. Thanks."

"Actually," Mrs. Quinn piped up. Annie Quinn was a tiny, wiry woman who terrified me. She was my mom's best friend and one of those women who could silence you with a glance. I wasn't fooled by her batik-print tunic and linen pants. Behind the new age facade was a fierce woman. She was married to Captain Quinn, a local fishing tycoon, and was the mother to three boys. She held my mom's hand after my dad died and helped her pick up the pieces. For that I will always be grateful to her, but she still scared the shit out of me.

"You know, my son Liam owns Binnacle Brewing. He is doing very well and is super busy right now. Just last weekend he was over for Sunday dinner telling us how he needs some help with marketing. I bet he could use a creative, successful woman like you to help him!"

Huh. Liam Quinn. I remembered him from growing up. We used to play all the time when our moms were together. I remember when he and his brothers built a bike ramp in their backyard and dared me to do it. My older sister, Maggie, refused, but I was nine and criminally stubborn. I went off the jump, flipped over the handle bars, and wound up in the emergency room getting stitches. It hurt like hell, but definitely earned me some street cred with the older kids. Our childhoods had overlapped - he was only a grade above me in school, but after high school we lost touch.

She stared at me over the top of her wineglass, as if daring me to defy her. "Thank you, Mrs. Quinn. I need to be back in New York in January, so I'm not staying."

"And," I added, hoping to nip this conversation in the bud, "I'm not sure I'm qualified to work in a brewery."

"Why not?" *Shut up, Aunt Joyce.* "I've been over there and it's fabulous what Liam has accomplished. It would probably be really fun for a bit."

"You know," said my mom, totally betraying me, "Joyce is right. What a fun thing to try! And Liam is such a close family friend, it would be so great if you could help him out temporarily while you are staying in town. You have so much marketing experience."

"The brewery is adorable. Industrial chic," Burt added.

Mrs. Quinn looked at me expectantly. "The taproom is only open on weekends. It's quite fun. We all pitch in sometimes. My boys Callum and Declan help out when they can."

I just stared, trying to think of some polite excuse.

"I'll text him and tell him you're available to interview tomorrow." She reached for her phone.

The room was silent while I felt the weight of a dozens sets of eyes on me. I didn't know what to say.

"Thanks, Mrs. Quinn. It does sound like a ton of fun," I said, lying through my teeth and trying to figure out how to make my exit and escape to my room. "But I'm sure he doesn't want someone who knows nothing about brewing or beer."

"Oh no!" exclaimed Mrs. Quinn. "He will be thrilled for the help. The fall is very busy with all the town festivals, and you are a childhood friend and sooo accomplished." She gave me an encouraging smile. "He starts brewing early in the morning. I would get there around nine a.m. and see if it's a good fit."

The entire room was smiling and nodding and encouraging me. Including my turncoat mother who just a few hours ago had held me while I cried and fed me ice cream.

Emily squeezed my shoulder. "This sounds so exciting! I can't wait to come see you there." God, she was so damn sweet.

I looked around the room at all the kind, excited faces. I didn't have the heart to tell them that the last thing I wanted was a pity job. "Okay," I say, raising my glass to the assembled ladies, "I'll give it a try."

My mom raised her glass, "To new opportunities."

"To new opportunities," everyone echoed.

I took a deep gulp of wine, wondering just what the hell I'd got myself into.

# 3

## LIAM

I was knee-deep in a fermenting tank when my phone pinged. It was the security system I set up. After some break-ins last year, I decided to install some cameras. I had a really large space and work late nights, so it seemed like the responsible thing to do. I turned them off when the taproom was open, but since it was only nine a.m., I was a bit confused.

I pulled up the app on my phone. Someone was outside the loading dock entrance. It looked like a woman, all dressed up. Probably a rep trying to sell something. Since Trent was bottling, I decided to deal with it myself.

Climbing out of the tank and down the ladder, I trudged out to the door still wearing my rubber waders and boots.

The sunlight hit my eyes and I was temporarily disoriented. When I opened them, I was greeted by a strange sight. A beautiful woman, all dressed up, staring at me like a deer in headlights. She was wearing a power suit and sky-high heels while clutching an expensive looking leather tote, and her hair was severely pulled back into one of those huge donut buns at the nape of her neck. She looked like a business Barbie—if Barbie had sexy librarian glasses and a little more meat on her bones. I was momentarily stunned. Brewing was, unfortunately, a bit of a boys' club, and most of the people I dealt with were men. It was a bit unsettling to see a gorgeous woman hanging out behind my building. My eyes were drawn to her tight skirt which left nothing to the imagination. Damn. Those were some serious curves.

"Can I help you?" I tried to stand up straight and look authoritative, but I realized I just sounded like an asshole. I was so off my game right now.

*Get it together, jackass. You own this place.*

"Um, yes. I am looking for Liam Quinn."

I give her a quizzical look. "I'm Liam."

"Oh my God! Wow." Her posture relaxed, and a big smile spread across her full lips. "I'm Cecelia Leary. I don't know if you remember me from high school. I didn't recognize you with the, ah…" She gestured to my beard and strange outfit.

"Holy shit." I took off my baseball cap and then put it back on when I realized my hair probably looked insane. "Cece? It's been so long. My mom told me you were living in New York. You're so grown up now. It's great to see you." And I meant it. The Learys were our family friends for decades. Cecelia was a couple of years younger than me, but she was always around when we were little. I remember a small, determined girl with wild, curly hair and a pretty, chatty teenager with even more wild, curly hair. "Ah. What are you doing here?"

Her shoulders slumped, and her face fell. "Oh. Um. Sorry." She looked down at her shoes. "Um…I'm here for the job interview?"

"Sorry, what?" I had no idea what she was talking about. Why was this woman standing here all dressed up at my brewery, looking for a job?

Now instead of depressed, she looked thoroughly uncomfortable. "Oh my God, this is so embarrassing. Your mom told me you were hiring someone to help with marketing and said I should be here at nine a.m. sharp. I thought you knew." She stared at me with large, brown eyes, and I suddenly had an overwhelming urge to hug her. She seemed pretty shaken up by my confusion.

"Sorry. My mom can be a bit of a flake sometimes. I am sure she meant to tell me but forgot."

Her eyes widened even further and she shifted on those insane heels. "You look busy. I should go."

"No," I shouted, a little too forcefully. She should go. I don't know what my mom told her, but I guarantee she has no idea what we need here. "Come inside. I can show you around, and we can chat." My mouth kept saying things I knew I shouldn't say. I felt this strange pull toward her. I wanted to keep her here. Show her what I've built. Get to know her.

I gesture toward the door and repeated, "Come inside. I'll show you around."

She gave me a sheepish smile. "Are you sure? I don't want to impose. I feel like an idiot."

"No. Please." I begin to sound desperate. "My mom will kill me if she finds out I turned you away. You'd be doing me a favor." I needed to get it together and find my balls. I was basically begging this woman to hang around my brewery at nine a.m. on a Tuesday.

She relented and walked in. *Keep your eyes off her ass, Quinn. She is not a piece of meat. She is a family friend and potential employee.* But I was a weak man. And damn, she had a nice ass.

Clearly, I had no idea what I was getting into.

———

"So, what is it you do? What is a Field Marketing Director?"

Her face flushed. "Well, I was responsible for a large territory selling a pharmaceutical product for arthritis. I targeted rheumatologists and internal medical providers and blah blah blah."

"So you sold drugs?" I smirked, attempting a joke.

"Yes and no. I sold legal, FDA approved drugs that drastically improved the lives of patients all over the world. But if you want to trivialize the last eight years of my life, then yes—I sold drugs." *Way to go Quinn, you just insulted the overqualified job applicant. Awesome.*

Her attitude and the stormy look in those brown eyes made me sit up a little straighter. I liked that she wasn't a pushover. But there was a hint of sadness in her demeanor as well. As I stared at her across the table, I noticed that her eyes were hazel with small gold flecks. I let my gaze travel down to her mouth, and oh my God, she had the most pillowy, kissable lips I had ever seen. *Get it together and stop staring at her like a serial killer.*

"So, it sounds like you have quite an impressive résumé. What are you doing here?" I realized I sounded rude, but was completely taken aback by this drive-by interview. I wasn't on my game. I was getting distracted by her beautiful but sad eyes.

"I am in town for a bit, taking a break. And your mom said you needed help here, and I need a job to keep me busy for a while."

"Okay. Well, do you have any brewing experience?"

"No."

"Do you even like beer?"

She shrugged. "It's okay."

"Um, okay. Any bartending experience?"

"Yes, actually. I bartended during and after college at a

few different bars in Brooklyn. It was really high volume and super intense. Amazing tips, though."

Okay, I could work with that. I needed help, and here she was asking for a job. On paper, she was both over- and underqualified for this job. But I was desperate, and needed anyone with marketing experience. I knew I only had a few months to turn this place around.

Just as I was trying to think of something semi-intelligent to say, I heard my phone ping in my pocket. I didn't even have to look to know it was my mother texting me to demand I give this woman a job.

"Listen," she said, getting visibly uncomfortable, "it's not a big deal. Your mom and my mom just demanded I come down here. I don't want to force you to hire me. You can get back to your day, and I'll find something else."

I nodded, trying to figure out how to respond. I was busy trying to reconcile the Cece I remembered from childhood with the woman sitting before me. As a kid, Cece was bold and lively, always trying to keep up with the big kids. I remember her on the sidelines at high school football games, camera in hand, trying to get the best shots. This woman seemed defeated and a little shy, totally unlike what I remembered. What had happened to her since leaving Havenport?

"Your mom also mentioned that Declan may need some freelance marketing help as well. Maybe that's more my speed."

My blood instantly boiled at the thought of her working for Declan, my taller, handsomer, more successful brother. The brother with the man bun and gruff attitude that every woman in a ten-mile radius fell in lust with at first sight. That wasn't an exaggeration. Declan couldn't get his teeth cleaned without multiple women falling at his feet. He had some kind of masculine, scruffy charm that I could not figure out to save my life.

I was seized by the feeling that I did not want to lose her. She seemed smart and accomplished, and I could easily teach her about beer. My business was on the line, so I couldn't afford to let her slip away.

I rubbed my beard and stared at her. She seemed sad, which was a personal kryptonite for me. I couldn't deal with a sad woman. It made me want to just jump in and fix everything. And she was especially dangerous because she was sad and pretty. I had been burned before trying to fix things for pretty girls. Many times. But like the big dumb idiot that I was, I could not let her walk out the door without trying to help.

"Well. Here's the thing. We actually do need help. Now that summer is winding down, most of our seasonal staff are gone. This is a small operation. Everyone here pitches in when needed."

She nodded, taking notes in a fancy leather folder thing.

"It pains me to say this, but I need help with marketing, social media, and events. We brew great beer, and we have a limited but loyal commercial business. But I need to maximize this taproom and get our name out there more." I don't know what made me so honest with this relative stranger. The truth was we needed lots of help. We needed to really step things up or we would be closing eventually. I didn't say that, obviously, but it was on the forefront of my mind. I didn't want to give up my dream, so I was willing to take drastic measures. And Cecelia Leary was nothing if not a drastic measure.

"Well, that I can definitely manage. Your space is gorgeous. I'm already getting all kinds of ideas."

I grimaced. I could already see her coming in and bossing me around and telling me all the things I'd done wrong. Ugh. "This also includes managing the taproom. Thankfully, it's only open on Friday and Saturday nights.

It's easy. We only serve what we brew in here, so you just have to learn to properly pour beer and talk to customers about it. But it also means you will have no social life."

"Okay, I can definitely do that." She perked up and gave me an interested look. "Plus I have no social life at the moment."

"Well, tell your husband or boyfriend or girlfriend or whatever that your weekends are gone for a while." I pretended to be interested in the paper napkin I was folding and refolding on the table. I could not meet her eyes after saying that.

"There is no one to tell. I'm single and have no life. So I would be happy to bartend on weekends."

Suddenly, the collar of my shirt felt too tight, and I could feel my cheeks redden. Goddamn Irish heritage. Trying to establish control of this meeting, I decided to lean into my inner asshole. I frowned at her. "But this is a small operation, and sometimes we need all hands on deck. We need you to help out with the tanks, clean and sanitize stuff, and run errands and do grunt work too."

She nodded, taking notes in her fancy portfolio.

I could not shake the feeling that this was a mistake. But I couldn't pinpoint why. She wasn't the perfect candidate by any stretch, but she was here, she was willing, and she had some of the experience I needed.

I had to get my head out of my ass and focus on this interview.

# 4

CECELIA

*WHAT AM I DOING? WHY AM I TRYING TO CONVINCE THIS
guy to hire me? I am so unqualified to work in a brewery, and
I don't even like beer for Christ's sake. I am also way
overqualified for whatever they do here, and this will in no
way be a résumé boost.*

But that damn overachieving part of my brain would
just not turn off. I had never *not* aced a job interview.
NEVER. And I wasn't about to start. Truth was, I need
something to do. What I didn't need was this holier-than-
thou hot guy droning on and on about the magical powers
of beer. This is a dingy warehouse. Not the state of the art
office towers I was used to back in New York. I was not
going to let him talk down to me.

"I think 'selling drugs,' as you so eloquently put it, has
many practical real world applications. I have a deep
scientific acumen, and I can master and explain complex
concepts. I am used to rejection and dealing with difficult
people. I can stay on brand and on message through any
situation and am a very quick study."

"Listen," he said gently, "I think we got off on the
wrong foot. You are clearly very impressive, and I was

trying to be funny, not belittle your career. I was just trying to push you a bit because marketing beer is a bit different than marking arthritis drugs." He leaned back in his chair and crossed his arms, giving me a spectacular view of his biceps and forearms. He was giving off a very strong angry hot guy vibe, which was diluted a bit by the rubber pants.

I relaxed a bit. Maybe he wasn't an asshole. Maybe he was just awkward? "With all due respect, no, it's not. You manufacture a product here. And you market, sell, and distribute that product. I can help you market that product to the right consumer base."

Why was I pushing so hard? This seemed like an interesting place, but I should have been back home contacting recruiters and polishing up my résumé.

With my experience and contacts, I could have found another job quickly. Especially now that I was back in New England, which was a health care and Pharma hub. I was sure there were other arthritis drugs I could sell, or insulin, or, if things got really bad, I could always sell boner pills. But as I'd sat in my childhood bedroom with my laptop trying to update my résumé, I'd had no motivation to apply for anything. Every job description sounded just as bleak as the last.

I hadn't wanted to market pharmaceuticals. I went to college and got a business degree, not because I was passionate about business, but because I wanted to get a steady job that paid well. I pursued marketing because I wanted to be creative and to innovate. I had lofty goals about helping people connect and building communities. I loved art and psychology and business, and it seemed like a great way to earn a respectable living by doing something I enjoyed. The reality was far from my college dreams. I ended up in Pharma because of money—those student loan payments were not going to pay themselves. And I stayed because I climbed the ladder, got promoted, got stock options, and I felt the invisible handcuffs get tighter and tighter as I slowly lost all of my creative instincts and passion for my work.

It's part of the reason I was so attracted to Xavier. Not that I found accounting particularly hot, but he always seemed so steady, so responsible, and so upstanding. Despite his annoying habits and general snobbery, I liked being with someone like Xavier. I thought that I could hide my inner hot mess with a boring boyfriend and some designer purses. Turns out, your hot mess will show when you least expect it.

While the alpha dog overachiever part of my brain whirled around trying to convince this guy I could market his brewery in my sleep, the cavewoman part of my brain couldn't help but notice that Liam Quinn GREW UP HOT. And not pretty-boy hot either—dark, hairy, broody MAN hot. And I'd be lying if I wasn't a tiny bit distracted. It's all that thick beard, ropey forearm energy. My stupid lady parts were tingling, and my nipples were trying to poke holes through my bra.

He was tall and imposing and a little stern. Even wearing ridiculous rubber pants he exuded competence and manly vigor. My ovaries were throbbing, and it wasn't from the lack of ventilation in this weird-ass building.

It was pretty obvious he was not going to hire me. And why should he? I didn't have the background he was looking for. And this was certainly not the type of workplace I had become accustomed to. I doubt I would even fit in here. And I used to head up a pretty sophisticated sales organization. Mopping floors and pouring beer is probably not going to fulfill me professionally. So why was I pushing so hard? Why was I sitting here trying to get this grumpy—and admittedly very hot—guy to hire me for a job I was overqualified for?

I straightened up and looked him straight in the eye. "Listen. I am good at what I do. I am professional and work hard and have almost a decade of marketing experience. We both know that qualified candidates don't randomly show up at your door every day." There. I said my piece. Now I could leave with dignity and go home and eat some ice cream under a weighted blanket.

He sighed and gave me an awkward smile. "Okay. Let's give it a try. I need help ASAP, and when I woke up this morning, I had no idea a marketing expert would show up at my door. I'm not about to tempt fate. So let's discuss pay."

We went through the details. What he was offering certainly wasn't anywhere close to what I made before, but it was fair and, for a short-term gig, not terrible. I got the sense money was tight, so I appreciated his offer. I couldn't help but think about some of my friends from college who had built up their own marketing firms or those who did freelance work on their own terms. It was certainly attractive, being able to pick and choose my clients, take on meaningful work, set my own hours and expectations. Too bad I wasn't cut out for that kind of life. I liked a dependable paycheck, benefits, and two weeks' vacation. I was a worker bee, not a queen.

He scratched the back of his neck. "But this place isn't fancy. Please keep your business Barbie clothes at home and show up in jeans and sneakers Friday."

"Friday?" I squeaked, both surprised and terrified. *Oh, there goes my whole boss bitch act.*

"Yes. Nine a.m. Friday. You can shadow me for a few days, learn the brewing business. Then we can figure out where to best leverage your..."—his eyes graze over my body, lingering at my hips. I knew this skirt was too tight to wear. Damn my mother and her delicious vegan meals

—"talents." He exhaled, like this conversation was too taxing for him.

I stood up and offered him my hand. He looked up at me and gave me a bone-crushing shake. "Copy that, boss. I'll be here at nine, ready to learn and wearing practical shoes."

I gathered up my tote, my folder full of printed résumés and references, and what was left of my dignity, and did my best to calmly walk out the back door to my car.

I did it. I am a badass. I just walked in there and talked myself into a new job. A job where I get to wear sneakers. I shook my hips a bit as I unlocked my trunk. *Take that, life crisis!*

# 5

## CECELIA

Nora looked at me intently while unpacking a box of new merchandise. "So. That's it. You are here to stay?" It was Tuesday afternoon and I had stopped by to help Nora unpack her new deliveries.

"Not entirely. I just needed a break so I decided to come here. Mom is getting older—she needs me. And my sister Maggie is preoccupied with her practice and her kids." While I was not *technically* lying to my best friend, the truth was a lot more depressing.

"So you gave up that gorgeous apartment?"

"I sublet it. Xavier moved out, and the lease renews January first. I couldn't afford the rent on my own when I was working, never mind while being unemployed. So I'm going back in January when she moves out." I sighed. "Between now and then, I either need to find a higher paying job or a roommate."

I would miss that apartment. I had spent years trying to find the perfect place. Quiet and cozy, but with decent closet space and a terrace. The rent was insane, but I loved it. But it wasn't just the apartment. Xavier insisted we go on fabulous vacations to Hawaii, buy designer clothes and

accessories, and eat at the trendiest restaurants. The
luxuries were fun, but I didn't actually enjoy them that
much. But it became a habit. I would treat myself to a
new Kate Spade after a difficult week and indulge in spa
treatments when I was feeling down. Looking back, I was
clearly spending money as a crutch to deal with my shitty
relationship. I was so unhappy with my life I thought I
could buy happiness with designer purses.

"What do you think about these?" Nora held up a pair
of fuchsia jeans with massive tears across the thighs.

I shook my head. "Fun, but not my style." Nora
folded them neatly on the counter and opened the next
box of merchandise. After getting a fashion merchandising
degree at Parsons, she had come home to Havenport and
opened her store, Jeanious Bar, on Water Street. Her
philosophy was that there was a perfect pair of jeans for
everyone. She stocked hundreds of brands in every cut,
style, and size imaginable. It was her mission to help every
woman feel amazing in her jeans. What started as a tiny
hole-in-the-wall boutique had grown into a straight-up
emporium of denim. People came from all over New
England to have Nora measure them and find them their
perfect pair. She took great pride in empowering every
woman who walked through the door to look and feel her
best. She even had a part-time tailor, Lucille, who could
nip and tuck and make things totally perfect. In a time
when retail was failing, Nora had forged her own way,
finding her audience on social media and valuing diversity
and inclusiveness.

Despite the physical distance between us, we were able
to see each other a few times a year when Nora came to
New York for buying trips. We would amble around the
garment district together, looking at the latest fashions and
singing karaoke in Little Korea until sunrise. Between
these visits, we texted and talked every day, just as we had

since high school. I was grateful to have her while I was trying to figure things out. She was kind, loyal, and unflinchingly honest. And she always made sure I was dressed well. I had hit the best friend lottery.

She rummaged under the counter. "Did you learn your lesson though? You dated him for two years despite most of the people in your life ringing alarm bells pretty frequently." While I valued her loyalty, she also had this very annoying habit of calling me out on my shit. I admired her for it, but it didn't make being on the receiving end any easier.

I busied myself folding to give my hands something to do. "I know. I know. I was an idiot. I just wanted a stable boyfriend. And I wound up with a snooty asshole who was sending photos of his dick to every woman in the Tristate area." I suppose it could be worse. I could have been dumped. When in fact, I myself did the dumping. After two years of dating, I learned that Xavier had an active Tinder account and had the very disgusting habit of texting photos of his erect penis to women he connected with on the app. Thankfully I got to do the dumping, and while I could no longer afford my beloved apartment, I did gain some dignity. Not that dignity could pay my Verizon bill, but right now, I'd take any win I could get.

Nora paused and seemed to be choosing her words carefully. "Yeah. I never really liked the guy, but I didn't peg him to be the type to send dick pics. That's a plot twist. At least it makes him slightly less boring?"

"Trust me. Do you have any idea how humiliating it is to have wasted two years of your life on a man who sends unsolicited dick pics?" I shuddered. "I feel like I want to apologize to all those unsuspecting women who just glanced at their phone and got an eyeful of his junk."

"Tell me he at least has a nice dick. It doesn't make it okay, but at least it could explain why he is so proud of it."

I choked on my cold brew a little bit, uncomfortable with this line of questioning. "Um…not really. I mean, it's a dick. I never was particularly impressed by it, but then again, we were not exactly setting the sheets on fire."

"What do you mean? You didn't have sex?"

"We did. Just not that often. We both worked a lot, and tax season runs from January to April, so he was usually super tied up and busy and I didn't want to push it. And then summer came and we didn't really rekindle the passion. I guess that's why he cheated on me." That wasn't the whole truth. I suspect he cheated on me because I didn't really love him or pay attention to him. I know I am not responsible for his behavior, but I knew from the beginning we didn't really fit together. I thought what we had was good enough. Companionship, shared life goals, the same taste in TV shows—I thought these things could sustain a relationship. I knew that wild passion and romance were temporary and mostly overblown by movies and romance novels.

Nora dramatically banged on the table. "Don't you dare blame yourself because he's a creep!" Nora, while a lovely and supportive friend, was also extremely loud and loved to shout for emphasis. The sheer volume of her voice almost made me drop my coffee.

"Okay, fine. Also I guess it's not cheating, is it? I mean he didn't have sex with anyone. Just sent photos of his dick around."

"I'm pretty sure that is cheating. Especially if you have a live-in girlfriend. Regardless, I am here for you and I will help you heal."

"Thanks. You're the best. But I'm honestly fine. I'm just embarrassed and a bit ashamed of myself. How did I ever think he was a good choice? How did I settle for a relationship that was so, so…blah?" It was a rhetorical question. I had settled because deep down, that's what I thought I wanted. No risk, no drama—just an easy, dependable partnership. Unfortunately it turned out to be a relationship devoid of passion, friendship, and trust, so I clearly had no idea what I was doing.

"Stop it right there. You know I have no tolerance for negative self-talk."

I never thought Xavier would be the type to cheat. I guess there is no type really. Xavier radiated "good guy" energy. Friendly and outgoing, he was a successful accountant who did pro bono work to help homeless veterans and ran marathons for charity. He was meticulous about his appearance and went out of his way to be friendly to everyone. In hindsight, maybe he was really only "friendly" to attractive women under the age of forty, but at the time I found his energy and positive vibes really alluring.

He was sort of handsome, in a very clean-shaven, suit-wearing, bland way. He was medium height and medium build and had a good relationship with his mother. He was a decent boyfriend, and the relationship was fine. I definitely did not fall head over heels for him, but he was safe, stable, and we got along really well. I just assumed we would get married someday, and that would be that. Little did I know he was secretly swiping right behind my back with dozens of other women. When I demanded to see his phone, he showed me hundreds of dick pics he had sent over the two years we dated. I had to hand it to him, he certainly found flattering angles and lighting because in person, it was not that impressive. I dragged myself to the Ob/Gyn and humiliatingly asked for every STI test on planet earth just to make sure. I was already nuclear mad, but if that fucker had given me chlamydia then I really would have chopped his balls off.

I plopped down on a large fuchsia couch. Nora's store was enormous, but very charming and homey at the same time. The walls were covered in white shiplap and oversize colorful couches were randomly placed throughout. Large tables piled with denim were decorated with measuring tapes, and huge crystal chandeliers hung from the cathedral ceiling. It was industrial meets girly, and totally Nora.

"Regardless of the reason, I am thrilled to have you back for as long as you want. Or…forever?" She threw me a wink over her shoulder. "But seriously, are you okay?" She sat down next to me and put her arm around my shoulders. We sat for a few moments while Billie Eilish poured from the speakers. I leaned into her and felt overcome with gratitude for having this badass woman in my corner.

"Yes," I said unconvincingly. "I'm just having a crisis. My career, my relationship, my apartment, everything is gone and I'm starting over and trying to make better choices and not keep fucking up my life."

"You haven't fucked anything up. Don't be dramatic. You are just in a moment of transition. Embrace it."

"Really? Embrace my quarter-life crisis?"

"Well, sweetie, you're thirty-one."

"Oh Jesus. So I'm having a mid-life crisis?"

"No. It's more of a one-third life crisis. That sounds more mathematically accurate."

I smiled at Nora. She could always make me laugh. "Okay, okay. I'm not staying forever. But practically, I'm probably staying through the end of the year.

"Have you thought about finding a job?"

"Actually,"—I hesitated, not sure why I didn't want to tell Nora—"I found something."

"What?"

"I interviewed at Binnacle Brewing this morning, and the owner offered me a job doing marketing and helping out with some other stuff."

"And by owner, you mean Liam Quinn?"

"Yes." I busied myself folding so Nora wouldn't see me blush.

"Huh," Nora said skeptically. "That's so interesting. And he is in need of a seasoned marketing professional like yourself?"

I looked up and felt the blush creep across my face and neck. "Yes. It's definitely a new challenge."

She tapped on the table. "And did you happen to notice during your very professional job interview that Liam Quinn is stupidly handsome?"

I knew where this was going. Nora was relentless.

"I may have noticed. But it's not a big deal."

Nora laughed out loud. "Okay, sweetie, keep telling yourself that. We all know he is a Grade A mountain man hottie."

She wasn't wrong about that. I had a brief flashback to this morning and had to fight the urge to fan myself.

"It's fine. I'm just giving it a try to help out while I'm here. It's just temporary."

"That's what they all say," she mused as she headed into the fitting room.

She came out a few minutes later with stacks of merchandise to put away. I joined her at the large table and we started folding and sorting.

"I have a ton of work to catch up on, but let's go to the Whale on Thursday. First Moscow Mule is on me. I need to hear more about your new job." The Tipsy Whale was a Havenport institution, a dive bar that had opened in the seventies for fishermen and evolved over time to be the preferred hangout of Havenport locals.

"Ugh, fine, you can drag me out tomorrow. My mom is making me do yoga tonight. But since when does the Whale serve Moscow Mules? We're usually lucky to get Fran to open a bottle of wine for us."

"Oh girl, you are in for a treat. Ever since Christian invested in the bar, he got Fran to spruce the place up and start making specialty cocktails."

"Of course he did." Christian, one of Nora's five older brothers, made his fortune on Wall Street in his twenties trading bonds and then moved back home. He had invested in local businesses with his husband Dante, and they had been responsible for the revitalization of several local establishments.

"It'll be fun to get dolled up and have a night out. Actually, wait. Let me get you some jeans."

"No. I can't afford anything new right now."

"I'm not taking no for an answer. I just got this new line in, and I need to see them on someone with hips."

"Wow, thanks," I said sarcastically.

She swatted me with her hand. "It's a compliment. You have an incredible body—deal with it. You need to stop selling yourself short and realize what a brilliant, beautiful warrior you are. Who knows, you might find a new guy while you're here!"

She placed the folded jeans in my hands and patted me on the head like a dog. "These will make your booty look incredible. Now, be a good girl and try them on before I pants you in my store."

# 6

LIAM

"How many beers have you had? You should slow down. You are already on the fast track to a dad bod."

It was only my third round, which for a beer professional, was nothing. And after the week I was having, which included that difficult call with Callum, my older brother and financial advisor, and a meeting with the bank, I needed about twenty more. I gave Callum a withering stare and flipped him the bird. He shrugged his broad, dress shirt-clad shoulders and gave me a pitying look.

My other brother Declan jumped to my defense. "Leave him alone, Fabio, we are not all as vain as you." I gave Dec a head tip for the defense. Back in college, Callum did some local modeling jobs around Boston to help pay for school. Catalogs and that type of thing. We have never let him live it down, hence his family nickname. It is important to take him down a peg now and again.

Callum immediately clapped back at Declan. "Sorry, I couldn't hear you. The live animal on your face muffles the sound of your voice."

Declan took a long sip of his beer and then stroked his scruffy beard slowly. "What are you still doing here anyway, Cal? Don't you have to go home and iron your polo shirts?"

I drained the last of my beer and plunked my stein on the top of the bar, feeling energized enough to join in. "Nah, Dec. He's got to be up early for a regatta." We high-fived, and I moved behind the bar for refills.

Callum was the oldest Quinn brother. He was also hardworking, polite, and deeply invested in his family and his community. Despite working in Boston as a financial advisor for years, he had always lived in Havenport and volunteered and participated in life here. He ran every charity road race and coached the high school science team. He checked in on our parents, shoveled their driveway every snowstorm, and couldn't walk down the street without half a dozen people stopping to say hello. He looked the part too. Always clean-cut, freshly shaved, and pressed. He was infuriatingly perfect.

Callum rolled his eyes. "Sorry. I was just trying to help you out. I can't help it if I'm the tallest *and* the best-looking Quinn brother."

Declan looks him up and down. "Yeah, yeah. We've heard it all before. That 2005 JCPenney catalog really gave you an ego, huh, Fabio? You may be the tallest and the prettiest, but we all know you have the smallest cock."

I almost spat out my beer. We loved to give each other shit, but Declan had a special way of just going after Callum that I could never pull off. The three of us started laughing hysterically, and Callum started tugging on Declan's beard at which point Declan jumped off his barstool and put Callum in a headlock.

For brothers born eleven months apart, they could not have been more different. Where Callum was friendly and upbeat, Declan was a broody loner. He spent most of his time alone with his dog, Ginger, a standard poodle who hated people more than he did. Unlike Callum, who'd headed straight for the Ivy League after high school, Declan decided to follow in our dad's footsteps and had enlisted in the navy. He'd served for almost a decade before coming home and taking over the family fishing operation. Although he would never say it, he loved being a third generation fisherman and carrying on the work that my father and grandfather started. He spent most of his time out on one of his boats or in his office and he liked it that way. He built himself a gorgeous house on the outskirts of town right on a bluff and spent all his downtime there. We called it his fortress of solitude. I had been there maybe three or four times in the last five years.

Where Callum was usually wearing a suit, or at least a dress shirt, and never had a hair out of place, Declan was shaggy, grizzled, and tattooed. Shorter than Cal, he was broader and stronger, with a thick dark beard and his ever present baseball cap. He was always dressed in Carhartts and Timberland boots and sometimes reeked of fish guts, not that he cared.

He rescued Ginger from a kill shelter near his naval base in Virginia. He brought her home to Havenport, and she had not left his side since. She was tall, imposing, and hated everyone who was not my brother. She went out on the water with him and rode in the passenger seat of his truck. When the taproom was closed, I allowed her in, where she held court from the custom dog bed Declan bought her. He may try to be a nasty hard ass, but anyone who has seen him with his dog knows that he is a giant softy on the inside. Not that I would have ever said that to him. He would definitely have kicked my ass.

My older brothers were two of the most loyal, helpful

guys on the planet but they were also my older brothers so they spent the majority of their time messing with me. Despite their differences, Callum and Declan were best friends. They had been inseparable since childhood and always had each other's backs.

And then there was me, the youngest Quinn brother. Born three years later, I had been the odd man out since birth. It also didn't help that they were the handsome, athletic gods growing up, and I was a chubby science nerd. My entire adolescence was girls trying to befriend me so I would fix them up with my older brothers. I hit puberty and outgrew my chub, but the insecurities remained.

That's partially why I loved having them here in my brewery. It made me feel validated. Like the stupid kid brother actually did something good. They would come by and check on me and critique my beers and bust my balls, and I finally felt like I had done something for myself. That I was standing on my own two feet. Somehow, by hanging out here and drinking my beer for free, my brothers were acknowledging me.

"But seriously, Liam, you have got to get out there and snag yourself a girl before you lose your looks, kid. Mom really wants grandkids"—he gestured at Declan—"and we know this lug head couldn't pay a woman to procreate with him."

Declan raised his stein in salute. "Amen to that. Women are way more trouble than they're worth. Ginger and I are doing just fine." Ginger looked up from her dog bed and barked at him.

I tried to shift the conversation away from my nonexistent dating life. "What about you, Cal? I thought you were dating that realtor?"

"Yeah…no. That didn't work out. And shame on me. I need to remember not to shit where I eat. I see her around town all the time."

"What happened?"

"We wanted different things. She wanted to be Mrs. Callum Quinn, and I wanted to never see her again."

Declan punched him in the shoulder. "You are such a dick."

"I was nice about it. Since Becca, I just can't find anyone I click with." Callum had married his college sweetheart, Becca. We all loved her and welcomed her into the family. Five years into their marriage, she came home one night and told him she was moving out. That was two years ago, and he was still not over it. He had been man whoring around town a bit lately, and I worried about him.

Callum walked around the bar to refill his stein. "And dating is fun. I like meeting new women and getting to know them and having fun. I am clear with expectations. No one gets hurt, at least most of the time. This one just turned out to be way more clingy than I imagined."

"Maybe you shouldn't be so picky, Cal," Declan piped up. "You're not getting any younger."

"And," I threw in, "you're getting a bit of a reputation around town. One of these days mom is going to find out about your conquests and then you will be in deep shit." My mother raised three boys with a fisherman husband who would be away for weeks at a time. She ruled with an iron fist and did not let us get away with any shit. She raised us to be perfect gentlemen, and I could only imagine the tongue lashing Callum would get if she found out about his "dates."

Callum sighed, his perfect facade shaking a bit. "I had the great wife and the house and was planning on the kids. That didn't work out. So now I'm thirty-six and just trying to live my life. I'm having fun, and I'm honestly beginning to think I may not be cut out for the family man life." I can see the pain in his eyes. Pain we would not talk about because we were Quinns and the Irish stoicism ran deep. Instead, I started pouring another round so we could do what we do best—drink.

Sometimes I wish Cal was a dick so I could properly hate him. But I couldn't. My big brother was as generous as he was handsome. When I launched the brewery, he immediately offered to invest and help with the business side of things. Although I was too proud to take his money, I was not too proud to take his business and accounting advice. I was a brewer, not a businessman, and I needed all the help I could get launching this place and making it successful. So after giving me some tough love yesterday as my finance guy, he was here busting my balls as my older brother.

I was not like Callum, who had always wanted the wife, big house and 2.5 smiling kids. He was just born to be a family man. It was clear as day when he was bossing us around as kids and taking responsibility for everyone and everything. Declan, on the other hand, thought relationships were pointless and would rather be alone. He had always warned me that women would mess up my life and it was better to just focus on yourself. I was somewhere in the middle. I'd had a few relationships and a few flings, and figured it would certainly be nice to find a special lady someday.

Last year I dated Katie, a nurse at the hospital. She was great, but things fizzled when she would get mad about how much I worked. Before Katie it was Brooke, and before Brooke it was Meghan. All great, but all not enough to distract me from the brewery. These women didn't understand that the brewery demanded every minute of my attention. Getting this place up and going had been my sole focus for the past three years, and we were finally on the cusp of really breaking through a highly competitive and oversaturated market. I had so much work to do to grow this business so we could keep going. I couldn't possibly make time for a relationship. So rather than disappointing another woman or having the same conversation about work life balance over and over again, I had sworn off women. It had been almost a year, and I had to say, it was going pretty well so far.

Callum clapped his hands. "So let's talk about the elephant in the room. Tell us what you need, Liam? How can we help?"

Declan piped in, "Yeah. It would be a shame if you closed up shop. This is some damn good beer."

I hated having these conversations. "I am good, guys. Yes, things are hard right now. But we had a good summer and are going to build on this momentum. I do need help, as I have to be able to delegate some stuff so I can focus on the big picture."

They nodded. It was the same story I had been telling them for months.

"But," I added, "I actually hired someone today. A marketing expert."

"Shit, man, that's awesome. That will be a huge asset for the brewery." Callum looked relieved. As my financial advisor, he knew just how much help I needed.

"Do we know him?" Declan asked.

"Actually it's a her. Cecelia Leary."

"Cece Leary? From Havenport?"

"The daughter of our mom's best friend?" My brothers exchanged looks, and I didn't like where this was going.

"Yup. She was a big-time marketing exec in New York for a while and is back in town for a bit."

"This has our mother's fingerprints all over it," Callum mused.

"She totally set you up," Declan agreed.

"What are you guys talking about?"

"How did you connect?"

"Well she saw mom last night, and mom told her to come here to interview."

"Uh-huh." Declan raised his eyebrows expectantly. "And you hired her?"

"Yeah. She's smart and hardworking and has social media experience. I could do a lot worse."

"Of course you could. I don't doubt she's qualified," Callum explained. "But you know this is mom setting you up."

I sincerely hoped that was not the case. My mother tended to be quite vocal about her desire for grandkids. Now that we were all in our thirties she had become aggressive in her attempts to get us to settle down. I had mostly avoided it since I was the youngest, but my brothers had definitely planted a seed of doubt in my mind.

"No, it's not like that," I protested.

"Let me ask you a question." I hated when Callum got into prosecutor mode. "Is Cecelia Leary single?"

"I'm not sure." That was a lie.

"Really?"

"Okay, fine. She mentioned she didn't have a boyfriend and was available to work on weekends."

"Bingo." They high-fived while I felt my stomach sink.

"And is she pretty?" Callum asked the question like he already knew the answer.

She was more than pretty, she was beautiful, but I wasn't going to admit that to my brothers and give them more ammo against me.

"Listen. I am one hundred percent focused on building my business, okay? I do not have time for distractions." And it was true. If I was going to make this brewery a success, I had to spend every waking moment focused and working toward that goal. I had let my personal life derail me in the past, and I wasn't going to let it happen again.

"Yeah, right," Declan said, draining his beer. "Who wants pizza? I need to soak up this booze."

# 7

CECELIA

THE TIPSY WHALE WAS NOTHING LIKE I REMEMBERED it. Gone were the splintered wooden barstools and sticky floors, and now the bar featured a live edge oak bar and strategically dimmed recessed lighting. The walls were adorned by tasteful photography and charcoal prints by local Havenport artists. The formerly cracked and peeling booths had been reupholstered, and everyone was drinking out of actual matching glassware, not the cans, bottles, and plastic cups I remembered.

Going to the Whale on a Thursday night was kind of an event for locals. Since the town was filled with tourists and out-of-towners on the weekends, Thursday nights were sacred in Havenport. It wouldn't be just a quick drink with Nora. I would likely see many people I knew, a few people I was distantly related to, and at least three former classmates. The thought of having to tell people I was unemployed, single, and living with my mother made me want to vomit up the quinoa she had made me for dinner.

Per Nora's explicit instructions, I wearing the new jeans Nora gave me. I hated to admit it, but they were pretty amazing. Painted on and hugging every curve but so soft and comfortable. Some sky high red pumps, a black tank top, and red dangly earrings completed the outfit. I decided to skip the usual truckload of makeup in favor of some mascara and tinted moisturizer, and my hair was down and sort of behaving. But while I may have looked put together, on the inside I was a mess.

Nora waved from her wrought iron barstool. "Over here, sweetie. I saved you a seat." I sidled up next to her and hopped on the stool, stashing my purse underneath. "Wow," I said, looking around and taking it all in, "this place looks incredible."

Fran, the no-nonsense bartender and owner of the Whale, made her way over. Nora pushed my hand away and declared, "Cece will have a Moscow Mule and I'll have another—you can put it on my tab."

"Is that an actual copper mule glass?" I said, marveling at Nora. "What happened here?"

"Oh sweetie, Christian happened here. Or I should say Christian and Dante happened here." They approached Fran about investing—she turned them down multiples times first, of course—and then they helped her renovate and market the place, and business has been booming. This place is full seven nights a week."

As I sipped my delicious cocktail, Nora gave me the lay of the land. "Whitney Fields…oh my God, girl, stay away from her. She is an MLM zombie. If you make eye contact she will start shilling her weird ass protein powder and you will never escape. I'm surprised she isn't handing out samples right now in this bar. Fran has kicked her out a few times for trying to make people shakes on the sidewalk outside. And don't look to your left. It's Lance Reynolds."

"What? Lance from high school?" I crane my neck

around to get a better look. I can't believe he still lives here.

"Oh yes. And he is still as weird as ever. He comes here once every few months to prowl around and make women uncomfortable. One time I was here alone, and he came up and said to me, 'you have the body of a stripper who let herself go.'"

I almost spit out my mule. "You can't be serious. What does that even mean?"

"I think he honestly thought it was a compliment. Maybe he was hitting on me? But I told him to fuck off and left. I should have kicked him in the balls, but now that this is a classy joint, Fran gets mad when people start fights."

I nodded, wiping my mascara and still laughing. "It's crazy to see how much has changed and how much is still the same." I was really worried about coming out tonight. But it was turning out to be fun. I had missed this place.

"How has it been so long? I feel like I see you all the time but always in the city."

"Well, Xavier didn't like it here. He said the town was weird, and he really didn't like my mom. So we didn't come up much. And I always told myself that I'm a big city girl and wanted to spend all my free time there." And that was the truth. Deep in my heart I knew I was a city girl. But I did miss my hometown. Looking back, I should have come home for holidays and to visit in the summer. I missed my mom. I missed Maggie and Josh, and their kids. I could have left Xavier in New York, or better yet, kicked his ass out months ago.

"I get that. And I go to New York so frequently for buying trips that I guess I never stopped to think to invite you here."

I was about to respond when I felt a commanding presence next to me.

"Cecelia Leary. So glad to see you again." I looked up and was momentarily stunned by the piercing brown eyes and chiseled cheekbones of Lucas Kim.

His smile faded as he turned his attention to Nora. I watched his eyes slide up her body with a predatory gleam. "Nora." He gave her a stern head nod and turned his attention back to me.

"Are you visiting up from New York?"

"No, I'm here to stay for a bit, hang out with family, decompress."

"Well, we are thrilled to have you back. I am hosting a fundraiser for the women's shelter this weekend at the Yacht Club. I hope you can come. The Haven Fire will be playing and we are raising money for such a good cause." He gave me a panty-melting smile.

Originally opened in the 1930s during the depression to house women and children with nowhere to go, the Havenport Family Crisis Center had evolved over time into a full-service organization that offered housing, financial support, job training, and education to women and children who were survivors of domestic violence. My mother had been volunteering there for decades, and the community frequently rallied to help upgrade the plumbing or hire additional counselors whenever needed. Havenport threw birthday and graduation parties for the children who lived there. Our former mayor Burt always dressed up as Santa and handed out gifts at Christmas. I was a bit taken aback and impressed that someone like Lucas Kim was involved.

I gave him a friendly smile. "That sounds really fun, Luke. Since my mother will very likely not take no for an answer, I will most definitely be there. Nora, are you going?"

Nora looked up from her phone, which she was pretending to be fascinated by. "I wasn't invited."

Luke rolled his eyes and gave her a piercing stare. I fought the urge to fan myself. "Nora, everyone is welcome. Even you."

"I'm probably busy."

He took another step closer to Nora, putting them inches apart. "Too busy to help families in crisis and survivors of domestic violence?"

It began to feel more and more like Luke and Nora were the only people in the room and I was looking in through a fishbowl.

Nora didn't respond. She just sat there shooting eye daggers at Luke. She sighed dramatically, making her ample bosom heave. It did not escape Luke's notice. They were engaged in some silent, sexy war I did not understand.

I shoved her to snap her out of it. "We'll be there, Luke. It sounds like a great cause. Havenport is lucky to have you."

He leaned in, gave me a peck on the cheek, and disappeared back into the crowded bar.

Nora went back to pretending to be fascinated by her phone. "Um…are you going to tell me what that was about?"

Nora attempted to give me a blank stare, but I was not buying it so I pressed her further. "Is there a reason you are feuding with the Mark Zuckerberg of Havenport?"

Nora rolled her eyes. "He is no Mark Zuckerberg," she scoffed.

"Well, true," I replied. "He is nothing like Zuck in that he is unbelievably hot." I paused to take a sip of my mule. "And apparently very charitable." I gulped. "Remind me why you hate him?"

"He thinks he's hot shit. He wrote some fancy computer code and got rich. Who cares? All he does is parade around town trying to get people to love him.

With his good looks and his charming personality. Ugh. He makes my skin crawl." Nora was obviously mad, and her face was very red. I could not figure out why she was so fired up about a random guy.

Recognition dawned on me. "Oh, shit. Did you guys hook up? Oh, you so did." I felt giddy. Nora was unapologetically sexual and had enjoyed some incredible flings over the years. She was one of those people who could have fantastic sex with someone for a while and then just move on with no hurt feelings. Actually, I shouldn't say that. Several of the men had some very hurt feelings when she wasn't interested anymore. She was definitely a hit it and quit it type. I respected the hell out of her for prioritizing her pleasure and her needs but was honest enough to know that was so not my style.

The look on Nora's face could have frozen lava. "We most certainly have not hooked up. How could you think that?" She took a dramatic gulp of her mule. Her indignation was hilarious. "We have some mutual friends and see each other from time to time. And I don't like him. Also the feeling is mutual. He hates me too."

"I didn't see hate. It looked like he wanted to drag you into the bathroom and bang your brains out. Or more likely he wanted to motorboat you." I laughed to myself. Nora was in the position of having a very round set of F cups that had been known to cause whiplash once in a while. Some men were drawn to them like moths to a flame.

"Gross. I would not touch that jerk with a rented vagina. He is a man whore. He comes in my store all the time with a different willowy model type on his arm. Spends tons of money buying them fancy designer denim in size zero and flaunts his wealth and his stable of dumb dates."

I was loving this. Nora was usually so cool when it

came to guys. She was protesting way too much. "So what you are saying is that he is not just an upstanding member of the community but also a loyal and generous patron of your small business?" I slapped my forehead. "Of course. You're right, Nora—he's a monster."

Nora rolled her eyes at me and signaled Fran for another mule. "He's a dick. You just don't know him."

At this point I was on a roll. "You're right, Nora. He is probably terrible. Do you think his house is filled with adorable rescue kittens?"

Nora glared at me. "You are supposed to be my bestie. Do not poke the bear when it comes to Luke Kim. I will not play."

"Okay, okay. I got it." I held my hands up in surrender. At some point we would have a longer discussion about this lust feud. I had never seen Nora so worked up about a guy before, but I also knew it was probably time to let it go for tonight.

But of course she beat me to it. "So let's talk about your love life, Cece. Xavier was clearly not giving you the goods on the reg so you need to find yourself a boytoy to have a fling with while you are here in town. Get some vitamin D, and you'll feel better in no time." She tossed me a saucy wink. "Always works for me."

Ugh. "Trust me, the last thing I need is guy drama." I could do with some mind-blowing orgasms, that's for sure, but they would have to be battery generated for the time being because the thought of dealing with men at the moment made me want to vomit. "I have so much to figure out right now. My life is nowhere near where I thought it would be, and I don't even know if I'm actually sad about that fact. The last thing I need is a complicated penis in my life."

"Well, yeah. You don't need a complicated penis."

"Precisely," I said, clinking her glass with relief, "you get it."

"What you need instead is a GIANT penis," Nora shouted. Oh my God, I forgot how loud she gets after a few drinks. I quickly turned around to scan the crowded bar to see if anyone heard and find myself staring smack-dab into the soulful blue eyes of my new boss.

He held my eye contact as he walked a few steps over to where we were seated. Nora elbowed me hard in the ribs. "Speaking of giant penises."

"Hi, Cecelia. Hello, Nora. Nice to see you both."

He nodded at Fran, who immediately started pouring him a Binnacle IPA.

I was so dizzy with vodka and lust I didn't know what to say to him. "Good to see you too. Why are you drinking here when you can drink your own beer at the brewery?"

"I'm meeting some friends." He reached for his wallet as Fran placed a pint glass in front of him.

I pushed his hand away. "I'll buy. It's the least I can do after I forced you to hire me."

He laughed and his eyes crinkled. "Well, don't forget about the trespassing too."

"I'm pretty sure it's only a misdemeanor. Don't get your boxers in a twist."

A group of guys entered and waved at Liam. He collected his beer and looked me dead in the eyes.

"Thanks for the beer."

"You're welcome. I'll see you tomorrow?"

He nodded and then headed off to see his friends. I liked him. I liked his cocky grin and his mischievous eyes. I liked how passionate he was about his business. It was a good thing I had sworn off men, because Liam Quinn was trouble.

# 8

LIAM

"You ready to train, Leary?" She looked ready. All fresh-faced and cute. She was carrying a notebook and pen, which made me like her even more.

"Yes, sir. I can handle anything you throw at me."

"Okay, because we have a ton of work to do."

She smiled at me. "Awesome. I hate being bored."

And we were not bored. Fridays are usually crazy at the brewery because we have to prep for the taproom being open on the weekend and make last-minute deliveries to local bars and restaurants. We also have to test and catalogue ongoing batches and wrap up our brewing activities for the week. It's a lot.

Cece kept up with me all day, asking insightful questions and jotting down notes in her notebook. She was sharp and smart and clearly invested in learning about the brewery. To keep her on her toes, I kept quizzing her on the names of various pieces of equipment, and she actually got some right. Brewing was a complex science, and I was impressed by how much she absorbed on her first day.

She was especially interested in the canning and

distribution processes. "So why do you can your beer and not bottle it?" she asked. "Isn't bottling classier?"

I laughed and scratched my beard. It was getting a bit shaggy, and I should probably start paying more attention to my appearance. "Well first, cans are more popular and sell better. We want to give the customers what they want. Craft beer of this type is normally sold in canned four packs."

She scribbled some notes in her notebook.

"And," I continued, "because cans limit exposure to both light and oxygen, the beer stays fresher and flavorful longer. Aluminum cans don't impact the taste of the beer and are better for the environment because they are more easily recycled. It's also far easier to get recycled aluminum or partially recycled aluminum than glass."

"Yeah. That makes sense. Everyone recycles cans, probably more so than bottles."

"Yes. And sustainability is one of our core values here. We recycle our water and have solar panels on our roof. We're not perfect, but we are trying."

She stuck her pencil back in her wild, messy bun. "I can respect that."

———

"So," I said, carrying the tiny tray with a freshly poured tasting flight on it, "you survived your first day."

Cece let out a sigh and smiled at me. "I did."

"And you listened to me drone on about beer all day. So now we finally get to drink some."

"Yay. I've been waiting all day for this." She rubbed her hands together enthusiastically and shimmied her shoulders. "Now mama needs a drink."

She was adorable. I had spent the entire day with her, and she had proved to be a major distraction. I kept getting whiffs of her lavender-scented shampoo every time she bent her head down to scribble in her notebook. She was conscientious and detail oriented. I liked it. I also liked her smile, her eyes, and her luscious ass. *Employee! Employee! Stop it, Liam.*

Good thing I wasn't interested. Especially because she showed up to work looking like a completely different person. Her wild hair was pulled back with curls escaping around her face and she wasn't wearing heels or ten tons of makeup. I could see a healthy dusting of freckles across her nose, I was such a sucker for freckles.

I also spent the day trying not to check out her body. She was wearing tight jeans, Chuck Taylors, and a tiny Boston Red Sox T-shirt that left very little to the imagination. She was a girl-next-door fantasy come to life. All hair and hips and curves and freckles. *Stop looking and focus. She is an employee.*

She was easy to talk to and smart as a whip. But as much as I would love to get her naked, I couldn't do that. She was my employee, and I had to keep it professional. And she was clearly not a one-night girl. She was the type you take home to mom and marry. And I couldn't handle a relationship right now. I couldn't disappoint another woman by not giving her the attention she deserved. I couldn't commit to anything beyond this brewery. I couldn't lose focus.

"Oh my God," she squealed. "These tiny glasses are so cute."

I rolled my eyes. "This is a tasting flight. It is a small sample of several of our beers so you can compare and contrast. So the golden rule of beer flights is that you start with the lightest and end with the darkest." I placed the trays down on the large table and took a seat.

We started to sample and talk about each beer.

"This next one is All Hops on Deck. It's our signature New England style IPA."

"What does that mean?"

"IPA stands for India Pale Ale. At the height of the British Empire, there were British ships, sailors, and soldiers all over the world. All of whom wanted to drink beer. It was too hot in India to brew, so brewers in England brewed a beer with more hops and a higher alcohol content than regular ale. The extra hops and alcohol acted as preservatives for the long voyages from London to India so the beer wouldn't spoil by the time arrived. Thus, India Pale Ale was born."

She started scribbling in her notebook again. "That's awesome. I can't wait to try it." She held the small glass up to her nose and breathed in the aroma. "It certainly smells hoppy." She took a small sip and left a tiny bit of foam clinging to her lush upper lip. "Yum. That is really good. Crisp, refreshing, with a hint of citrus."

I smiled. "I am impressed by your palate." I take a big swig to keep myself from potentially saying something stupid.

"So what makes this New England style?" she asked, taking another big, satisfying sip.

I never thought it would be such a turn-on to see a beautiful woman enjoy beer that I had brewed, but it was becoming my favorite fantasy. "We dry hop the beer so it's hazier and has a fuller body and smoother flavor. This style is generally less bitter and hoppy than a traditional IPA."

She drained her glass and looked at me. "That was great. Unique and fruity and just different than anything I've ever had before."

"I'm glad you like it."

"I do. I never really liked beer. But I also never really tried good beer. I mean, I drank Coors Light in college like everyone else." I shuddered visibly. But she kept going.

"I just never knew it could be like this. Sharp, flavorful, refreshing, and complex."

I was feeling warm and comfortable. I could sit here all night and talk about beer with this smart, pretty woman. I had spent the day trying to focus and avoid the many charms of Cecelia Leary, but hearing her wax poetic about beer, and specifically my beer, made my heart soar. I found myself grinning like an idiot and wanting to make her try everything I've ever brewed just so I could hear her describe my creations.

"So," she continued, pleasantly unaware of my perviness, "you didn't tell me what your brothers are up to? I haven't seen them in years. I bet Callum is probably married with four kids by now."

"Actually, no. Both my brothers are currently single and childless, much to the great disappointment of my mother. Callum was married for a bit, but he and his wife divorced about two years ago. He and Declan both live in town actually."

"That's awesome that you all live here."

"Sometimes it is and sometimes it isn't. Callum is a financial advisor. He has an office in Boston and goes back and forth. Declan took over my father's fishing business after he got out of the navy." The fleet was decent sized and he spent most of his time on the business aspects of things. Processing, shipping, and delivery to all the local restaurants and stores. He didn't get out on the water much anymore, which was his true love. "He is basically the same antisocial grump he was in high school."

"That sounds about right. He was older than me but I heard he was not a social butterfly. I think he may have graduated with my sister Maggie. I can't believe the Captain retired. Wow."

"Yeah my mom basically forced him. And she is the only person on earth who outranks him."

We sipped our samples, and I walked her through the different beers in the tasting flight. Cece was surprisingly easy to talk to.

"So now that we are drinking buddies and colleagues, tell me the real reason you came back to Havenport."

She looked slightly uncomfortable. "What do you mean? I needed a break from my old life and wanted to be here with my family for a bit."

"Okay, I respect that. But you were a few hours away, so you could visit to connect with your family whenever you wanted to. Why did you pack up, move here, and force me to employ you?"

I could see her visibly pale, and I instantly felt bad. I thought this was friendly banter. "Listen, you do not have to answer that. I shouldn't have pushed." I was such an asshole.

"No, it's fine." She pushed her curls behind her ears. "At the risk of sounding like a pathetic loser, I just didn't really have a place to go. And I reached this point with my job and my relationship where I was numbly going through the motions every day. And so when things blew up, it seemed like a good time to change things up. And I've just been burnt out for years."

I nodded, not sure what to say in response.

"I worked crazy hours in a high pressure situation. Marketing is brutal and I was good at it, but I have been on a wild roller coaster for years. But as soon as I got laid off, I was inundated with calls from recruiters. And every single job offer made me want to throw up. It's like I didn't realize I was sick until I got off the ride." She twisted her hair in her hand and looked up at me with those big brown eyes. "I'm so sorry I'm rambling. You probably think I'm insane."

"Not at all. I get it. I have been there as well. Just surviving and not thriving." Oh my God, I can't believe I said that out loud. My brothers would kick my ass. My mom said new age shit like that all the time, and I couldn't believe it slipped out of my mouth.

She cracked a genuine smile, and I felt like I was eight feet tall. "Thanks for trying to make me feel better." Reaching for her glass, her fingers grazed my hand and our eyes connected. She looked so pretty and vulnerable and sad, and I never knew this was a turn-on for me. But I had the sneaking suspicion that everything about Cecelia would be a turn-on for me.

If I was capable of having a relationship right now I would be in trouble. Someday when the brewery was thriving and I'd opened a second location, I would find the time to meet a nice girl and settle down. Good thing I was too busy working myself to the bone because looking at Cece all pretty and freckled and vulnerable was giving me all sorts of ideas.

I sat down across from her and tried to lighten things up. "So you mentioned your relationship. Boyfriend? Fiancé? Husband?" I was blatantly fishing, but the exhaustion, good beer, and pretty smile had made me dumb.

"Ex-boyfriend. We broke up right after I got laid off. We lived together and I couldn't afford the rent on my own, so another reason it seemed like such a good idea to head to Havenport."

"I'm sorry to hear that." I tried to suppress a smile. *Don't look happy, dumbass. Be sympathetic.*

She looked away and fiddled with her beer stein. "Yeah. Don't be too sorry. Now that I'm looking back at the last two years, it was a pretty crappy relationship. I'm just glad I randomly stumbled on his penchant for texting dick pics so I had an excuse to get out before I settled for a shitty lukewarm marriage."

I almost spit out my beer. "Sorry. Dick pics?"

She gave me a brief version of the story, and I'm sure she could see the horror on my face. "I'm just glad I woke up and got out."

I clink her glass. "I'll drink to that."

She looked relieved. "Thanks. I appreciate it. Even though I live with my mother and just took a job that involves mopping floors."

"Hey. This job involves a lot more than just mopping, kid. We also have to drain grain mash and blah, blah, blah."

She laughed and her eyes twinkled.

"At the risk of sounding like even more of a pathetic loser, thank you for hiring me. This is fun and challenging and random. And the weirdest day at work I've had in years."

"I choose to take that as a compliment."

"It was."

When I headed back to the bar to pour another round, she took out her bun and shook out her hair. I have never really considered hair to be a turn-on, but the wild waves and curls were so beautiful. Her hair was a sort of medium brown color with streaks of gold and copper, like a full-bodied imperial amber ale. It was mesmerizing.

I jumped back when I realized I over poured and spilled beer all over the bar. *Jesus, Quinn, get it together. She just shook out her hair—she didn't strip down naked and give you a lap dance.*

Of course my brain immediately went to that possibility, and suddenly my jeans were feeling tight. Thank God I was standing behind the bar.

It hadn't been that long since I'd been with a woman, had it? I felt like a teenager again, desperately trying to hide an inconvenient boner. I needed to get myself under control and act like a professional. I had to set appropriate boundaries and stick to them.

After recovering and sitting down I thought it best to be straightforward. "Listen, Cece, I'm really glad this worked out. I look forward to working with you."

She smiled. God, she had such a beautiful smile.

"But I just want to be clear that our relationship has to remain strictly professional."

Her smile quickly morphed into a grimace. "Sorry. What?"

"I just want to set appropriate expectations."

She stood up, clearly pissed. "Thanks, Liam, but just so we're clear, I am here for a job. I am not here for a date or for your pity."

I was flailing. This was clearly not going the way I had planned. "No, sorry. I misunderstood. I shouldn't have said anything."

She stood there, arms crossed, looking angry and very hot.

"My mom may have mentioned you were nursing a broken heart."

"What? You have got to be kidding me." She started pacing around, and I shrank into my seat. "I am hardly heartbroken. Embarrassed and pissed, yes. But not heartbroken. And let's get something straight, okay? I am not looking for a boyfriend. I want a job, a new challenge, something to keep me busy for a few months. That's all."

"Okay, okay. I didn't mean to offend you." I was officially drowning in my own awkwardness. I wanted to crawl under this table and pretend this conversation had never happened. What was I thinking? That I am so goddamn irresistible that she was going to jump me at the first opportunity?

"Let's be clear, Liam. You offered me a job, and I accepted. End of story. If we're done with my training, I'll head home."

I was officially the world's biggest jackass. "No, please.

Sit and enjoy your beer. This is my fault. I got the wrong idea from my mom, and instead of thinking it through like an adult, I just spoke without thinking. Of course you're not interested in me. And I'm glad to have you here in a professional capacity."

She was still standing, giving me a death glare, so I continued. "You know my mom. My brothers convinced me she sent you here as a matchmaking scheme. I am so sorry I fell for it. I am really fucking things up right now. Please sit and we can talk about the job." I knew I had to get this conversation back on track. The thought of her walking out of here embarrassed and hating me was unbearable. I had to change tracks.

"I am a bit of a mess right now. Things are going poorly, and I need to inject some fresh ideas into this place. I feel like I've been so careful not to overextend myself and build this business slowly and carefully, but it's just not where it's supposed to be yet."

She sat back down and gestured for me to continue.

"I've spent years convinced I could do it all on my own—but I can't. I am not good at PR or marketing or social media. I am not a hospitality manager, and I don't know shit about graphics. I can brew decent beer and I'm fucking great at drinking it, but other than that I need help badly."

She grabbed her pen and started jotting down some notes. I sat silently and drank my beer, praying she wasn't going to quit and walk out the door.

"Okay," she said, looking up from her notebook, brown eyes blazing. "I forgive you for thinking I was here to try and date you. Let's talk marketing strategy."

It was a good thing I was too focused on trying to save my business because in another life, Cecelia Leary could be *very* distracting.

## 9

CECELIA

AFTER TWO DAYS OF TRAINING, I HAD TO TAKE THE lead on bar for my first Saturday night. I was definitely not prepared for this. Without my usual work armor of suits and heels, I felt positively exposed. I know it was just pouring beer but I couldn't help but feel a little nervous. I wore my new jeans for luck and knotted my Binnacle brewing T-shirt at the waist. Unlike my usual New York style, my hair was in a high pony, messy curls escaping everywhere. Sneakers rounded out my work look with more than a little makeup to help hide my nerves.

Nora was pissed because I couldn't go to the fundraiser for the shelter with her. I told her to stay home and make a donation, but she insisted she had to "teach Lucas Kim a lesson," whatever that means. I swear, the only lesson she wants to teach him is with her vagina, but I know better than to say that out loud.

It was early, but things were going moderately well. I poured beers and answered a few questions and just generally smiled and kept busy.

At that very moment a guy about my age sat down at

the bar and got my attention. I grabbed a glass and headed over.

"Hey. How are you tonight? What can I get you?"

"Hm…I'm not sure." He gave me a blatant once-over and smiled. He was clean-shaven and had dirty blond, neatly trimmed hair. He was wearing a tight polo shirt and a large flashy watch. He looked like he worked out a lot. While handsome and definitely my type, I could not be less interested. I clearly need a nice long man break.

He gave me a smile. "What's good here?"

"Well, that depends on what you like. Our signature beer is the All Hops on Deck New England style IPA. It won the Golden Stein beer prize this year. If you don't like things too hoppy, I am a big fan of our Leeward Lager. It's smooth with some citrus notes."

He nodded, his eyes locked on my chest. "Okay, cutie. What else do you have?"

I was starting to get flustered. This guy was clearly flirting with me—albeit in a slightly pervy way—and I just wanted to sell him a damn beer and move on to the dozen or so other customers who needed service.

The old Cecelia would just mumble something and get out of this situation as quickly as possible. But new Cecelia was a ballsy bitch so instead I leaned over and propped my elbows up on the bar and made eye contact with him, giving him a smirk that said *"I know you were checking out my rack."*

"Well," I said flirtatiously, "if you want something a little more out of ordinary, our sour is fantastic. My personal favorite."

He gave me a slight head nod. "Okay."

I interrupted him. "Actually, on second thought. I think you need to try our Helmsman Double IPA. It is really intense—will put some hair on your chest." And I blatantly looked at his chest to see if he would get the memo.

"Okay, then. I guess I'll have to drink it and prove I'm man enough."

I poured his beer and handed it to him before giving him a wink and turning around, only to smack right into a wall of hot bearded man. I felt a jolt of electricity shoot up my spine. Liam put his hands on my hips to steady me, and I felt my entire body flush. He leaned in close so I could hear him in the noisy bar, and I was hit by a wall of his masculine scent. "Just came to bring you some clean glassware," he mumbled into my hair.

I took a step back knowing my entire face and neck were flushed. "Okay, great." I reached to grab the glass rack he had set on the counter, but he stopped me. "Here," he said, grabbing the rack of glasses from my hands, "let me get this for you."

He effortlessly picked it up and started filling the shelves under the bar while balancing the heavy rack in one hand. He looked so confident and capable and way too good for an overworked brewery owner on a busy Saturday night. He was wearing a Binnacle Brewing Company T-shirt that highlighted every toned muscle in his torso. His jeans were low slung and hugged all the right places. A hint of a tattoo peeked out of his left bicep and his ever present leather cuff bracelet hung on his wrist. I found myself mesmerized by his forearm muscles as he quickly packed the glasses.

*Damn, girl, you are being way too obvious. Better look away.*

A group of older ladies wandered up and ordered some tasting flights. I walked them through the different options from lightest to darkest and sent them on their way.

Liam was leaning against the back of the bar watching

me. His arms were crossed over his chest making his forearms look extra veiny.

He gave me a sly smirk. "Look at you. Showing off your beer knowledge."

I tried to hide my blush. "Thanks. I'm having fun."

"I can see that. You're doing a great job. Everyone's glasses are full, and you are answering questions and chatting about beer. I'd say you are crushing your first Saturday night on the job."

"Hey. It's only nine thirty. The night is still young. I need to stay focused. Also, the keg on the raspberry sour is tapped. Can you ask Trent to change it for me?"

"No problem. I'll do it right now. We have never sold this much of the sour."

"Well, it's my favorite and when people ask, I am pouring them samples."

"Attagirl. Okay, go back to selling beer and I'll make sure you have fresh kegs."

I went back to pouring beers, filling pretzel bowls, and chatting with customers. I snagged empties and put them in the bus bucket that Trent collected every half hour. Someone had put some eighties hits on the jukebox, and I found myself swaying to the music while I rushed around. It was the strangest feeling, I was busy—like, really busy—but I felt great.

I was chatting and laughing and smiling and everyone was pretty polite and positive because, hey—I was the lady with the beer—and the night just sort of flew by.

Before I knew it, it was eleven and we were loading the dishwasher and wiping down the bar.

"Who was that guy?" Liam asked as we worked.

"What guy?"

"That blond pretty boy who was flirting with you all night. Do you know him?"

"I don't know." I was starting to get sassy. "A customer

who wanted my thoughts on the double IPA?" Why was he interrogating me?

"Okay. I thought maybe he was a friend of yours."

"Nope. Total stranger. But if he was—am I not allowed to serve drinks to my friends?"

"Of course you are, as long as they're paying. I just wanted to check."

I was instantly annoyed by his cranky attitude. "Did I do something wrong? Did I not pour the beer fast enough? Was I rude or unhelpful?"

"No. Not at all. You were great. You are a natural. Friendly and approachable and knowledgeable. You are probably the best bartender we've had. I am always too busy worrying about other stuff to really pay attention to the customers, and Trent lacks your social finesse." He pauses, wiping down the already clean counter. "It also doesn't hurt to have a cute girl working the bar."

And my hackles were up. He does not get to call me cute after telling me he would never dream of dating me. "Cute girl?"

"Sorry. A lovely and accomplished grown woman." He shot me a cocky grin, and I couldn't decide if I wanted to smack him or kiss him. I needed to get home and get my shit together. I was on a high of a fun night and great tips. So what if he thought I was cute? I supposed that being cute wasn't the worst thing in the world.

Sensing that I needed to get out of there, I got his attention. "Liam, what else do I have to do to close down the bar?"

"We're pretty much done. Do you need to be somewhere?"

"No. Just want to go home, put my feet up, and relax."

"Can I tempt you with a beer? I want to talk to you about Oktoberfest and get your thoughts."

"Okay, fine. But only if I can sit in the comfy chairs," I

say, gesturing to the large leather club chairs clustered in the corner of the taproom.

"Of course. Those are my favorite. Take a load off. You've earned it. We had a great night." And just like that he was back to being sweet, friendly Liam, not broody weird Liam. This guy was going to give me whiplash.

## 10

LIAM

I don't know why I was keeping her here. She deserved to go home. But I wanted more time with her. And I didn't want to snap at her like I did earlier. I needed to make amends for last night. How could I assume she wanted to date me? I wasn't that guy. I wasn't a cocky asshole who assumed all women wanted a piece of me. My mother got in my head and I said something boneheaded. She seemed like she had forgiven me tonight, but I wanted to make sure.

Cece slumped into the chair and undid her ponytail. I was mesmerized as her wild curls cascaded over her back. I tried to hide my smile. "What can I pour you?"

"The raspberry sour, please. I love it."

"I could tell. You sold the shit out of this beer tonight."

"It's just like nothing I've ever tasted before."

"Well, thank you for that compliment." I winked at her, biting my tongue to keep the "that's what she said" from flying out of my mouth like a total perv.

"I'm serious. It's complex and interesting and tart and fun and it's a pleasant surprise, that's all." She smiled and my heart soared. I liked making people happy. It probably sounds silly—maybe it's a youngest child thing.

"Well, enjoy it. We only brewed it for the summer." Sours were popular in the summertime. They could be hard to brew and get right. I wasn't brewing juice, so it had to be perfect. We had spent months figuring out this raspberry, and Cece was right—it really was something special.

She seemed upset. "You aren't going to make any more?"

"Not until next summer. We have a few kegs left and then it's done until next year."

"What about a fall sour?"

"Our fall seasonal is a pumpkin IPA."

"Doesn't everyone do pumpkin beer in fall?"

"Yes. Because it sells really well." I was getting annoyed. I was the beer expert here.

She pushed her hair behind her ears. "Pumpkin is pretty basic right now. Maybe something unexpected. Something fruity and crisp, yet seasonal too."

Normally, I would get furious with anyone who tried to tell me how to run my business. But Cece was genuinely brainstorming and I liked it. Her mind was whirring around and I could see her thinking critically about beer and the marketplace and our business. Although I hated being told what to do, I was at least marginally interested in what she had to say.

"Okay. So I'm sure your pumpkin beer is great. But maybe something else, like a super limited edition that we can promote on Instagram or at a local festival. Something small batch and really unique." She got up and started pacing around, sipping her beer and thinking.

I liked this idea. She was right. From a marketing perspective, it would be great to have something exclusive and special that we could promote. She was already thinking like a marketer and I respected her for it.

"What about cranberry?" I suggested.

"Could you do a cranberry sour?"

The wheels in my brain were turning, and I could already taste this hypothetical beer. Something about her brought out my creativity as well. "Something cloudy and tart with maybe hints of some kind of fall spice, like nutmeg? So you get the fall seasonal but as a sour—which there are far fewer of on the market."

"Yes." She pumped her fist. "I am envisioning a rollout campaign—we can blast social media, have an unveiling event here at the brewery when we tap the first keg, really get all the beer snobs excited." She continued to pace, and I could see the excitement in her eyes.

I had to stop my jaw from hitting the ground. This woman was forty-eight hours into the job and already figuring out how to brew, promote, and sell specialty beers? I couldn't decide if I was angry or enamored with her. On one hand, it was actually an awesome idea. On the other, I had devoted my entire adult life to brewing beer. I was the expert here, but she was really onto something.

I took out my phone and started jotting down notes in my app. She was bouncing around, so excited about this idea that I couldn't muster up the energy to shoot her down. "Okay. It's a good idea. Let's take it to the team during Monday's meeting. It might not be possible. I have to talk to Karl and then try to source cranberries." The more I thought about this, the more fun it sounded. A special, limited edition beer? Maybe for Thanksgiving? We could brew a small amount and then hype it up. I jotted down some more notes in my phone. We could divert some bandwidth to this as a special project to see if the concept could work.

As difficult as it was for me to admit, she certainly brought new energy to this place. "You may be onto something, Cece."

She beamed at me. "I'll drink to that."

I held up my glass. "To a really busy and successful Saturday night and new ideas for the future." We toasted and sipped our beers. It was nice, sitting here with her.

"So," she said after a few minutes of silence. "If it was such a great night, why do you look like you're going to vomit?"

"I'm just a bit stressed."

"Care to elaborate?"

I hesitated for a moment. I never talked about this stuff. Not even with Callum, who knows the full extent of my financial situation. I wasn't one to open up and talk about my feelings, but there was something about Cece that made me feel like trying. "This place is doing great, but not great enough. The overhead for a brewery is so high, and I'm struggling to pay back some of the loans I took out to open the place. It's not enough to brew amazing beer. We need gimmicks, and additional revenue streams, and all kinds of shit to make money." I took a big gulp of my beer to stop from saying more. Why was I pouring my heart out to this girl? I needed to get it together. "Sorry. I don't want to dump this all on you."

She looked at me curiously. "I get it. It must be a ton of pressure to do this. Lots of people depend on you and you are out here living your dream every day, but you have to live with the constant stress."

"Yeah."

"I would be terrified. But I think you're really brave."

"Ha! Brave? Not exactly."

"No, I mean it." She leaned forward, and her face was illuminated by the firelight. She looked so beautiful. "You are only what, thirty-two?"

"Yeah."

"And you had a dream and you worked for it and made it happen. I don't even know what my dreams are, and I certainly could never just start from scratch and build something like this."

"I appreciate that. But dreams can be terrifying. Because if it doesn't work out, then what? If I pour all my passion and my soul into something and then it goes nowhere, what does that make me?"

"It makes you brave. And it makes you human."

I was emotionally vomiting all over her and I knew I would live to regret it. "Most days I am terrified that I am screwing everything up and that I am in over my head."

"You are not. You are crushing it. Look at this place." She gestured around.

"Thanks. But things are not as great as they look. I need to pick things up, get more revenue, and take this place to the next level if it's going to last. I just need some fresh ideas. Frankly, that's why I hired you. Because I work so much and I live in survival mode, I can't get creative about things. I can't see the forest through the trees. As much as I can't really afford to pay you what you are worth, I need someone to take some of my workload so I can actually think and figure out this mess I've got myself and my business into."

She leaned forward in her chair and covered my hand with hers. Her hand was warm and soft and looked so small in my calloused bear paw. But it felt nice. "Take a breath, Liam. I can help." She was so kind and disarming, and I just needed someone to talk to. I walked around like a volcano ready to explode with anxiety most days. It felt nice to share it with someone and have them believe in me.

"I may have sold drugs, but I was damn good at it. And your beer is amazing and this space has a ton of potential. Right now I have like five hundred ideas of how we can get more people in the taproom. You have a whole commercial kitchen you don't use. And that patio area? We can dress that up and make it an amazing place to hang out."

"I know, this place is awesome. But we don't have the staff to run it and do all this extra stuff."

"You don't need extra staff, kid, you have me now." She looked at me with those soft brown eyes, and I really started to feel a bit better, like I may actually have a chance.

"So you want to stay and help me figure this out?" I didn't know what I was asking her, but I felt like I couldn't do it without her. I didn't want to face the future without this creative, spunky woman by my side.

"I have to be back in New York in January when my subletter moves out. But I'm here until then. The past couple of days have been the most fun I've had at work in years. And I get to wear sneakers. Do you have any idea how much heels suck?" She laughed and I felt warm all over. I didn't know from experience, but I was willing to bet that yes, heels did in fact suck. "I can stay here with you until the end of the year. So we have four months to sell the shit out of your beer and your brewery and your vision."

I couldn't believe I had just spilled all that to her. I didn't even tell my family about this stuff. I was a one-man show, and I took care of my own problems. But sitting here, talking to Cece and brainstorming about my business, my passion, I felt more relaxed and content than I had in years. I barely knew her, but somewhere deep inside I felt like she just might be the thing this place needed. She might just be the thing I needed.

# 11

CECELIA

LIAM QUINN WAS FASCINATING. IT HAD ONLY BEEN A week, but I was learning so much about him every day. He took responsibility for everything. No problem was too small for his attention. He pored over quality reports with Karl, analyzed sales with Shane, designed cans with Mark, and even mopped the floors when necessary.

He was positive without being insincere and treated everyone the same. He helped and encouraged and smiled at everyone. It became very clear after a few days that I was not special. He made everyone feel appreciated and valued. He remembered every detail about people, asking Karl about his granddaughter's dance recital and Kyle about the new Marvel movie that just came out. He would top off people's coffee, order pizzas when the team worked late, and call Ubers if someone had a few too many in the taproom.

Initially, I had been attracted to his overwhelming hotness. But as I got to know him more, I found myself attracted to his inherent goodness. My attraction to him was so distracting, I started avoiding his office and working on my laptop in the taproom instead.

When I had agreed to assume responsibility for the annual Oktoberfest event, I assumed it was actually in October. Apparently, Oktoberfest technically starts in September, which meant I had even less time than I thought to pull this off. I got right to work, nailing down the details - vendors, music, working through the menu with the caterers, and ordering decorations and other necessities. I had no background in event planning, but as a naturally organized person I was finding it to be an exciting challenge. Liam rolled his eyes at my color-coded binder, but I knew deep down he was impressed.

I had also developed a really annoying radar for when he was around. It was like my body felt his presence before my eyes saw him enter a room. I chalked it up to my deep-seated need to people please. I always wanted to make sure the boss saw me being productive. Did I mention I was great at lying to myself?

Anyway, I was clicking away when I felt his warm, masculine presence. I looked up to see him exiting the men's room, sweaty, dirty and wearing rubber gloves. He carried a bucket of cleaning supplies and my heart stopped. It was not uncommon to see Liam cleaning or sanitizing or mopping floors. There was so much to be done every day. But he was the owner of this place, and he was not above scrubbing toilets. He had several people he could order to do it, but he didn't. He took the shit work himself, pun intended.

Despite the fact that he had most definitely just been scrubbing toilets, he looked so hot I could feel my panties catch fire. His T-shirt clung to every muscle in his back and his hair was a mess. His beard needed a trim and his blue eyes shone. He was in jeans, but they sat so low that when he reached up, I could see a sliver of his abs and a very happy trail, leading down to what I imagined was an impressive package.

Truly, the godlike face and hot bod didn't hurt, but a man who willingly cleaned bathrooms? A unicorn. A bearded, blue-eyed unicorn and I wanted him so badly I ached. My LELO was going to be working overtime tonight. And as much as I wanted the real thing, my battery-operated friend would have to do.

Because nothing could ever happen between us. He was not the type of guy for a quick roll in the hay. I knew it would probably be a fantastic roll, but he did not seem like the love 'em and leave 'em type. Neither was I, actually, despite Nora's protestations. And I couldn't risk getting attached and getting my heart broken. I was here for a reason—to learn more about myself and what I want. To become New Cecelia and find my purpose. I couldn't afford to be distracted by my hot boss.

"How's it going, Cece?"

I gave him my best *I wasn't just eye fucking you* smile. "Great. Just working through the event details."

"Excellent. Can we walk through some things in like thirty minutes? I have some stuff to do but should be free after three o'clock. Does that work?"

*You can have me anytime anywhere. Stop it.* "Yes. No problem."

"Great. Meet me in my office then."

I nodded and pretended to get back to my laptop while I discreetly watched him walk down the corridor to the brewing area. I couldn't decide if I enjoyed watching his back muscles or his butt muscles walk away more, but it was a close call.

I was getting comfortable here. I was learning the ropes and finding my footing. We had some big plans for the next few weeks, and I was anxious to get started. I had my work cut out for me. The brewery website needed updating, the social media accounts were positively anemic, and all the event planning had to start from scratch. It would take all of my marketing experience and a lot of luck to put this place on the map, but I was getting a bit more confident every day.

When I accepted this job, I saw it as a way to fill some time between "real" jobs. But now, I was seeing more and more how this place was stretching and growing me professionally. I was learning things, getting out of my comfort zone, and taking on more and more responsibility every day.

I wanted to help Liam and all the new friends I had made here. I wanted this for him and for Havenport. He cared so deeply about everyone and what they were doing. He took responsibility for everything and never cast blame. He remained positive and upbeat, despite the crushing pressure of sustaining this business. Unlike me, who couldn't conceal my hot mess if my life depended on it, Liam exuded calm confidence at all times.

He did not share his stress or anxieties with anyone, instead he just worked even harder. It made me feel special that he had opened up to me, told me the truth, and unburdened himself. It was like we shared an intimate secret and he trusted me to keep it for him.

# 12

CECELIA

Most days I couldn't believe what I had gotten myself into. Marketing this place was going to be a massive undertaking. I promised Liam I would stay in Havenport and help out at the brewery for the next four months and I intended to see it through. But I was feeling overwhelmed and nervous that I had bitten off more than I could chew.

So I squared my shoulders, ignored the nagging thoughts about sleeping in my high school bedroom at thirty-one years old, and got to work. I had grown attached to the brewery and loved this ragtag team and wanted them to succeed.

Two weeks into the job, I was seeing more and more potential every day. At first, these Monday team meetings were intimidating, but I was slowly getting more comfortable. The atmosphere was jovial and fun. Everyone was laughing and trading stories and trying beers. This was a team, a family. In addition to the brewing staff, the team included Mark, their graphic designer and packaging guru, and Shane, the account manager. Like myself, these guys worked here part time to chase their beer dreams while holding down other gigs as well. I hadn't been here that long, but I really liked the beer. And I really liked Liam.

But sitting here around the table while Trent filled glasses for everyone, I was beginning to feel like I finally belonged. And there was a part of me that knew that I could help this place grow and thrive. That I could help Liam achieve his dreams.

And I was starting to think my mom and Nora might be onto something. Maybe I had been too cautious and careful. Maybe I hadn't been true to myself and what I really wanted. I looked at Liam, going over graphs and data related to brewing schedules, and smiled. He was so handsome and confident. He was good at this and he knew it. It made the vulnerability he'd shown me even more precious. We'd become friends, and he had really opened up to me about his struggles and anxieties about this place. All of it made me more resolute to help him as much as I could.

The more time I spent at the brewery, the more ideas started flying around my brain. I felt a shiver of possibility run down my spine and creativity flow through my veins every time I walked through the door. I discovered my old camera in the attic and had started taking photos for social media as well. I found so much of the work here really inspiring. Today I was making my first presentation to the team and I was nervous. What if they didn't like my ideas? What if I spent all weekend doing research for nothing? In my previous life I had made presentations to executives and shareholders and never felt this nervous. I was a good presenter and I came prepared.

After about an hour of technical talk, Liam finally turned to me. "And now I'm going to turn it over to Cecelia."

I took a minute to compose myself and sync my laptop to the projector.

Mark piped up. "Sorry, I missed last week's meeting. Are you a new brewer?"

Kyle jabbed him. "Dude, she's clearly not a brewer."

"What is that supposed to mean?" said Trent. "Women can be brewers."

"Of course they can. But we already have plenty of brewers, and if she were a brewer she would probably work someplace nicer than here." Kyle gave me a dazzling smile. He was in his early twenties, boyishly handsome, and knew it.

Liam jumped in, trying to control the conversation. "Guys, settle down. Cecelia is spearheading the new marketing initiatives and running point on upcoming events. She'll be doing a bit of everything. Think of her as my Girl Friday."

"Isn't that regressive and sexist?" A few people chuckled.

"Thanks, Karl. I didn't mean it in a regressive way. Just that she's going to be helping out and doing a bit of everything."

"Hey. My wife and I watch the Daily Show every night. I'm woke now." There was a collective eye roll at Karl.

I gave him a kind smile. "Thanks, Karl."

"Anyway. She has been brainstorming ways for us to increase revenue and exposure and help build our brand. Please be quiet and let her speak."

Everyone quieted down and I walked them through my PowerPoint.

"I think increasing the use of the taproom for special events and broader weekend hours is an easy way to get more people through the door, especially in the fall."

"I also think we can do some outreach to specific

demographics. For example, I think we should have afternoon hours on Saturdays and Sundays and have kid-friendly activities and menu items. Have you guys ever brewed root beer or ginger ale?"

"Yes, I can brew fantastic root beer," Karl said.

Liam seemed dubious. "But do families want to come to a brewery?"

I shot him a look. "Have you been to any of your competitors lately? Go to Cambridge or Somerville or Portsmouth right now. Breweries are packed with families on weekends."

"That's a good point. People with small kids need all the alcohol they can get." I didn't know whether Shane had kids, but he had a general air of exhaustion that made me suspect he might.

"Exactly," I said excitedly.

"But won't we have to serve food and other stuff too?"

"Yes. Thank you, Trent. I have a plan for that. Havenport and the surrounding area has a robust food truck scene. We can coordinate with some food trucks to park in the parking lot on weekends. We can negotiate a percentage of their sales and then people will stick around longer and order more drinks if there is also food available."

"Okay, but are the food trucks willing to do that?"

I flipped to the next slide of my PowerPoint. "Here is a list of the fifteen most popular food trucks in the greater Havenport region and their contact info. If you guys are on board, I plan on reaching out ASAP to start scheduling them for weekend shifts. We will promote them on our social platforms and they will agree to do the same. Given the market research I did, I think we can ask for fifteen percent of their sales in exchange for parking in our lot and promotion. I am going to make some calls and see what I can negotiate."

I walked them through my other ideas—upgrading the patio seating, a dog friendly area, senior night, and pursuing more events like weddings. Everyone got excited about my ideas and pretty soon everyone was brainstorming ideas around the table.

The only person not contributing was Liam. If anything, he looked angry. My research was sound and my ideas were good. I knew that. What was his problem?

He waited for everyone to quiet down before speaking up. "This is great, Cece, but most of what you are proposing sounds expensive. I would love to upgrade the outdoor area to accommodate more seating and be a fun space, but that is going to cost a ton. And weddings? You need some really jaw-dropping visuals to get wedding business."

"I don't disagree, but I also think many small changes can be inexpensive and still yield big results." I flipped to the next slide where I laid out some ideas for upgrades and cost ranges. The brewery was an incredible space, and my suggestions were just a few small things to create more opportunities for people to love it.

"Yeah," Mark piped up. He seemed like a thoughtful, quiet type. In his late forties with close-cropped salt and pepper hair, he gave off a very mellow dad energy. "My wife is an interior designer. She is able to get all kinds of things wholesale. She would love to get her hands on this place."

"Awesome." I leaned over and high-fived Mark, who looked sheepish. "I think we could do a lot of this cheaply and really spruce the place up."

Kyle jumped in. "My aunt Gail owns the garden center."

"Gail who is married to Mayor Liza?"

"Yup. They are my aunts. They are super invested in

the town. I bet we could get trees and shrubs and stuff from her at a discount."

"Kyle, that is amazing." I was beaming and feeling so elated. I really was part of the team. They were embracing me and my ideas. Liam was going to be harder to win over, but for the first time in a long time, I felt up for the challenge.

# 13

LIAM

ALLOWING HURRICANE CECELIA INTO MY LIFE AND MY business was proving to be quite disruptive.

The Cecelia standing before me with a tape measure and a clipboard was nothing like the defeated woman who came here and begged me for a job three weeks ago. Clad in jean shorts—oh my God, those shapely thighs—and a Binnacle Brewing T-shirt, she was directing people around and taking measurements. Part of me was terrified. I had never given up control like this before. But I had never had a marketing dynamo come in and whip my ass into shape either.

The guys were more energized than they had been in months. Karl was brewing up test batches of root beer for our kids' events and Mark was at work on updating our logos for new T-shirts and merchandise to sell at Oktoberfest. We were brewing our assess off, working on our seasonal beers and upping production to hopefully cover for the expanded taproom hours. Cece had convinced me to expand the hours starting this weekend, giving us only a few days to make a ton of upgrades to accommodate the extra customers, not to mention the specific areas for kids and dogs that she insisted were necessary to the survival of my business.

Speaking of the devil herself, she was currently doing a walk-through with Ellie, Mark's interior designer wife. A tall, icy blonde with a large designer handbag, she was a bit intimidating and nothing like I expected for artsy, tech nerd Mark. But she seemed really smart and was very excited to help us out.

"You guys are doing me a favor," she insisted. "I am trying to branch out from homes to more commercial spaces. This is going to be an awesome project for my portfolio. I think you have a great space here and only need a few tweaks. The big issue is lighting. We need to highlight the industrial nature of the interior space and soften the transition from the taproom to the brewing floor. I think some lighting tweaks and a few other flourishes can make things work. I am going to swing by my lighting supplier later and see what I can get you at wholesale."

Cece grabbed my arm excitedly. "Liam, this is going to be so great!" I tried to ignore the zing I felt when she touched me. It happened every damn time. And sometimes I would catch a whiff of her lavender shampoo and spend the next hour trying to get another hit. All in all, "Operation Ignore Cecelia" was not going well so far. My brain respected and trusted her, but I could not stop my body from wanting her.

"Come see how things are going outside."

She steered me toward the back patio where Trent was unloading one of our trucks with Kyle. The truck was stuffed with what looked like fancy picnic tables and Adirondack chairs. She gestured with her free hand while her other rested comfortably on my bicep. "We are setting up a few designated seating areas over here," she said, gesturing to part of the yard that had previously been dead grass and leaves. "And tomorrow we are installing the string lights and some path lights back up to the building for safety in the dark."

"You really think this will work? People will want to hang out here all night?" I looked at her, only a few inches from my face, her hand still gripping my bicep. I had to resist the urge to flex. "Oh, Liam. You have no faith in me. I will have this place filled. Just you wait."

She whipped around me, letting go of my arm, and I instantly missed the warmth of her strong grip. I wanted her hands on me, anytime and anywhere. It was weird to admit, but also true. I ran my hands through my messy hair. As exciting as these changes were, my inner control freak was screaming out in pain. I wanted to trust Cece, and so far she had not given me any reason not to, but this brewery was my baby. I had been burned before and I was determined to do this on my own. Succeed on my own and, if necessary, fail on my own.

I knew I had to make some big changes before the end of the year. If we could eke out some more revenue and expand our events, I would be able to keep up with the loan payments and float us into next year. This was doable. I just had to keep my head in the game.

Lost in my thoughts, I didn't even see her sneak up next to me. "Here, take a selfie with me," she said, wrapping an arm around my waist.

I was momentarily stunned as I felt her ample chest crush into my ribs. I cleared my throat. "Why?"

"For our Instagram page. I am documenting the upgrades and promoting the new expanded weekend hours." She stood on her tiptoes and put her other arm around my neck, drawing me into her. Her hair smelled like lavender and I loved it. I found my hand snaking around her waist and resting on her hip. It felt good. My hand fit there perfectly on the flare of her hip, and all I could think about was moving it slightly and copping a feel of her generous ass. Before I could hate myself for being such a perv, she aimed her phone and got a photo of us smiling with the new furniture and layout in the background.

I had never felt so out of control. My brewery, my passion, my business was changing right in front of my eyes and I was both hopeful and terrified. And, for better or worse, it was all because this smart, wild, and creative woman swept into my life.

———

On day later, I stood on the deck, surveying what was once a sad patch of grass with some decent water views. I felt a lump form in my throat. The entire spaced had been transformed in less than 24 hours. The community, my community, was here pitching in and helping. All these people took time out of their busy lives to come here and help me improve my business.

Callum was planting trees and shrubs and flirting with the old ladies from the horticultural society who came out to landscape. Declan was busy building outdoor furniture with Kyle, and Karl and his wife were power washing the cement patio and stairs. My dad was installing a new railing around the deck area while my mom supervised and tut-tutted.

Ellie was working with Tim, the electrician, who was rigging up all kinds of lighting while Mark chased their three kids around the lawn.

Trent sidled up to me and handed me a beer. "This is incredible, boss." I nodded at Trent. He was a good friend and great employee. We grew up together here in Havenport under very different circumstances. Where I had loving supportive parents who modeled tough love and hard work for me, Trent was raised in and out of foster care. Some learning disabilities made school painful for him, and he had no family to support him. As early as second or third grade, I knew just how lucky I was. My mom always packed an extra sandwich for Trent and sometimes accidentally bought an extra pair of sneakers for him at TJ Maxx. When I was away at college, she invited him over for Sunday dinner and my dad helped him get set up with classes at the local technical college where he was able to study mechanics. As soon as I opened the brewery, I knew I would hire him and I did. The thought of losing this place and not coming to work with him every day filled me with fear.

He leaned over and clinked my can with his. "I can't believe what we've accomplished in three days. Oktoberfest is going to be amazing."

I couldn't believe it either. Seeing the community come together was both warming my heart and messing with my head.

"Are you okay, boss?"

"Is it dusty in here?" I turned around to compose myself. "Hey, Trent, do me a favor. Can you call Havenport Pizza and order dinner for everyone?"

"No problem."

I sat and surveyed and sipped my beer. My heart had never felt so full. But I was also terrified that I was going to fail everyone. That despite not only my best efforts, but the efforts of a lot of people I respected and cared about, I was going to fail. I wasn't going to be enough.

It was one thing to fail myself. But to fail my town, to fail the people I cared about deeply? It was unconscionable.

Shane sidled up to me. He looked so different in a T-shirt and work boots. He was such a smooth salesman, I don't think I'd ever see him without a collared shirt. He was in his late thirties, divorced, and a bit of a man whore. Not that I would say that to his face. He was a good guy, and despite his day job as a realtor, he gave everything he had to selling our beer and keeping our accounts happy.

He clapped my shoulder. "Liam, my man. This is amazing."

"I know."

"*She* is amazing. I can't believe how much she's accomplished in a few days. I also can't believe that you gave up control long enough to let her."

I was feeling defensive. "What does that mean?"

"I mean no offense, man. It's just you are a bit of a control freak who wants to do everything himself."

He had a point. We had worked together for four years, and at this point my control freak tendencies were a well-known fact. "Yeah, yeah, none taken."

"So, speaking of hurricane Cece," he said, rocking back on his heels. "Is she single?"

I instantly got very annoyed with Shane. "I don't know. She is our colleague so it would probably be inappropriate to ask." He better not try anything with her. That was the last thing I needed right now. Cecelia was way too good for him anyway.

"The word on the street is that she is single. I overheard your mom talking to her mom. I think I'm going to ask her out. She's not my usual type, but she is hot in that natural sort of way." He took another sip, and I hoped he choked on it. "And damn, I'm glad it's tank top weather because she's been hiding those spectacular tits."

I instantly saw red and wanted to punch his smug face. I was a lot bigger than him, so it wouldn't even be a fair fight. Trying to gain some control, I instead grabbed him by the shoulder and pushed him up against the back wall of the building. "Don't you fucking talk about her like that. She is not a piece of meat, you sexist asshole." I was inches from his face. I could feel my blood boiling in my veins. How dare he speak about Cecelia like that?

He pushed me back. "Sorry. Didn't mean to offend."

"Don't you have two daughters? You're a fucking pig. I don't care how long we've been friends. Don't you dare ever speak about one of my employees like that, or any woman on earth, for that matter."

"I said sorry. Why are you overreacting, Liam?" He took another step back to put some distance between us. "What? Do you have a thing for her?"

"No, I don't have a thing for her. What a ridiculous thing to say."

Trent, ever the peacemaker, clearly sensed the tension and hurried over to the deck where we were standing. "Everything okay, guys?" he asked nervously.

"No. Liam just went psycho because I said I was thinking about asking Cece out."

Trent punched Shane in the shoulder. "What is wrong with you, dude? You can't ask her out. Liam obviously has a thing for her."

"You guys are insane. I do not."

Trent, my oldest and closet friend, rolled his eyes at me. He turned to Shane. "Yeah, boss man definitely has a crush on her. I don't blame him, she is pretty awesome. And she calls him out on his shit." I hated Trent in that moment. The problem with him knowing me since grade school was that he could apparently read me like a book. But hearing him say those words out loud made my eye twitch.

I shoved him. "Lower your voice, dumbass. Cecelia is my employee, and a very good one that I would like to retain. She is smarter and more resourceful than both of you idiots combined. I admire her professionally, and that is all." I took a long sip of my beer, willing my heart rate to slow down. "This is a business. Both of you need to act professionally."

Trent gave me a look that said *"dude, I'm your best friend so stop* lying *to yourself."* Thankfully he didn't share those sentiments out loud.

"Sorry. I didn't realize you had called dibs. I didn't mean to offend you." Shane smirked at Trent who tried to look innocent. Trent clinked his glass. "I totally called this after our staff meeting last week."

Shane looked at him incredulously. "Bullshit. No, you didn't."

"I so did. I could see the sparks fly. I'll bet you a hundred bucks they get married."

"Done. I'll take that bet." Behind me, Shane and Trent shook hands and I couldn't even muster up the energy to object. Because I was too busy watching Cecelia. She was helping Kyle move one of the tables that Declan had finished building. She was laughing and smiling in the late summer sunlight and she looked so capable and beautiful it took my breath away. She was wearing cutoffs and a tank top, her wild hair in a knot on top of her head. She didn't have a scrap of makeup or jewelry on, but she was breathtaking. Her intellect and confidence were as much of a turn-on as her spectacular curves. She had ideas and enthusiasm and passion. I was awestruck watching her in her element with the community, directing everyone to get the job done. And it was so hot. I had to look away and find something productive to do before I found myself agreeing with Trent and setting a wedding date.

I turned around to see both guys staring at me. They had clearly seen me lusting after Cece. I needed to put a stop to all this bullshit and get my head on straight.

"Okay, guys. I'm going to go pick up pizza. Get your asses back to work."

## 14

CECELIA

"I can't believe I let you talk me into this." Liam was sweeping the patio area which was covered in dirt from our plantings. His head was down so I couldn't see his face in the dark, but his tone was clipped.

It was one of those sticky early September nights and we were both sweaty and exhausted from a long day of work. Everyone else had headed home and it was just the two of us, finishing up outside. On Saturday afternoon, the taproom would open for the first weekend since our upgrades. I had been promoting the hell out of it on social media, and I had food trucks lined up for the entire weekend. I was praying these efforts got more customers in the door and introduced more people to Liam's amazing beer. Even the weather looked like it would cooperate.

I stopped watering the new shrubs and put my hand on my hip. "Oh, please. Look at what we accomplished in two days. This place is transformed. I have been Instagramming photos all day and promoting our new weekend hours. We have thousands of likes already." I held up my phone and shook it at him.

He shrugged at me and went back to sweeping. Goddamn, he was infuriating.

"You should schedule some extra help for this weekend. We are going to be really, really busy. Especially if the weather stays this nice." I turned around and resumed watering.

"I'll believe it when I see it," he replied sarcastically.

I whipped around with the hose. "Excuse me? I know your tiny man brain does not allow you to express gratitude, but a simple thank you should suffice."

"Thank you for what? Planting a botanical garden? Taking my staff away from brewing for the last two days? Or for spending money I don't have?" He was walking toward me, fists clenched, and I could tell he was itching for an argument.

"Liam, get your head out of your ass. Your community came together today to help you and your business. Busy people took time out of their lives because they want to support you. Not the brewery, not the beer—you."

He stopped a few feet away from me and ran his hands through his hair. His shoulders slumped, and he looked almost defeated.

"I know." His response caught me off guard.

"So what's with the attitude?"

He shoved his hands in his pockets and looked down at his feet. "I am just worried. What if this isn't enough? It's one thing to fail myself or fail my employees. But my family? The entire town? Everyone came here today because they believe in me and believe in Binnacle Brewing. What if I let them down?"

He looked up at me with the most soulful expression. Under the soft glow of the new outdoor lights his handsome face was illuminated, and I could see every worry stretched across his forehead. I wanted to throw my arms around him and hug him. Honestly I wanted to do a lot more than hug him. Vulnerability was my romantic weakness. I wanted to comfort him and then jump his sexy moody bones. But my feet felt rooted to the ground.

I held his gaze. "Liam, you aren't going to fail. And even if you did, you aren't letting anyone down. You've done a pretty incredible job on your own so far. And with all this extra help, not to mention my superior business acumen"—I tapped my head and winked at him—"you will not fail. This place is going to be packed this weekend and then we are going to blow Oktoberfest out of the water and you won't even remember these doubts."

He smiled, a big genuine smile, and those gorgeous blue eyes crinkled. I swear I could feel my ovaries tingle. We stood there for a few minutes staring at each other. Needing to break the crazy tension, I tried to pivot. "Okay, that's settled. Get back to work," I barked at him.

"Okay, boss lady. Make me." His grin turned mischievous.

"Oh, I'll make you." I turned the hose and sprayed him in the chest. He was caught totally by surprise and turned and ran from me. I took off, spraying him continuously while he weaved around the new tables. Just as I thought I could get his face, he ducked and ran straight at me, wrestling the hose from my hands.

"Ha," he said, panting. "I got you now."

I held my hands up in surrender. "Do your worst, Quinn." I thought he would spare me. I thought wrong. He shot the hose of freezing cold water straight into my stomach. I doubled over and tried to run but he was faster. I ducked behind the closest table and tried to head inside where I would be safe. I turned around the concrete stairs that led up to the deck area but he cut me off and was able to corner me.

"Nice try." He held the hose up at me and smirked.

I was out of breath and my chest was heaving. Despite the freezing cold water, my entire body felt hot.

He stood there for a minute staring at me with an almost feral expression. His Binnacle Brewing T-shirt clung to the muscles in his chest and his damp hair fell across his forehead. He looked muscular and intimidating and oh so hot. In other circumstances I would be scared by the giant wall of sexy man looking at me like I was his next meal. But my entire body was on high alert. I was hot, sweaty, and turned on. I could feel my nipples standing at attention and I had to squeeze my thighs together to stop the full body shiver running through my core. We stood there, staring, chests heaving, for what felt like an hour but was probably more like two minutes.

He dropped the hose on the ground. Next thing I knew he stalked over to me, grabbed me by the waist, and pulled me into his hard, wet chest. His mouth descended on mine, and I was completely lost to the sensation of his full, tender lips. It was messy and frantic and I held onto him for dear life. He smelled like hops and pine trees. Our hands were everywhere. He was gripping my ass as I ran my fingers through his hair. Our mouths and tongues danced desperately as if we had waited years for this moment.

This was more than a kiss. This was an epic sensory experience. His lips, his hands, his hard muscular chest. Oh my God, his intoxicating manly smell. I had never been kissed like this in my life, and it was melting my brain. His hands found my hips and picked me up as if I weighed nothing. I instinctively wrapped my legs around his waist without breaking the kiss. Suddenly I was aware of something very large and hard nudging at my core. Instead of breaking away, it made me want more.

My entire body throbbed for him. I wanted to take him home and lick every inch of his body, including what felt like a very impressive erection. I moaned into his mouth as his hand found my breast. He curled a fist into my hair and tugged my hair back, exposing my neck to his frenzied lust. I moaned when he found my sweet spot and I longed for friction, for nudity, for more. Under normal circumstances I would be freaking out that I was doing something wrong or wondering if this guy actually liked me. But somehow I didn't want to stop or analyze. In that moment, I was overwhelmed by Liam Quinn.

I was backed up against a wall with my legs wrapped around him as we devoured each other. This was passion. This was intensity. This was adrenaline-fueled lust. This was what had been missing in my life.

And just like that, it was over. He gently placed me on the ground and took a step back. His face was flushed and his eyes were glazed. At least I wasn't the only one who couldn't form a coherent thought at that moment. He scratched the back of his neck nervously and looked at me intensely. I was frozen to the spot. I needed to say something, but my mouth couldn't formulate words. I just stood there and stared at him like an idiot.

"Ah. I'm sorry. I shouldn't. No. Sorry," he stammered. He took off his hat and ran his hands through his hair.

He took another big step back, widening the gulf between us. "Thank you, Cece. This place looks great. Now go home and get some sleep. It's going to be a busy weekend."

And with that he turned around, walked back to where he had dropped his broom, and got back to work.

And I stood there, staring at him while he swept the patio, trying to regain my powers of speech after experiencing the hottest make-out session of my life.

# 15

"ARE YOU FUCKING KIDDING ME?"

Nora was flopped on my bed, clutching my Cabbage Patch dolls with her feet in the air. I had a weird déjà vu back to high school where we spent tons of time lying on my bed listening to Justin Timberlake and talking about boys. It was Friday night and the taproom was reopening tomorrow. The brewing staff spent the day bottling and so I had an unexpected evening off to spend with my bestie.

"Nope. Not kidding," I said as I held my hand out. She handed me another Red Vine and paused.

"So...he grabbed you and kissed you senseless, thrust his giant cock at you, and then just up and ran away?" Nora sat up quickly, sending a tidal wave of dark hair into my face. I pushed her back on the pillows.

"Pretty much," I confirmed, chewing on my Red Vine.

"That is some fuckboy shit." She paused and took another bite. "What a prick."

"Don't be like that, Nora. It was a weird night." I still hadn't figured out how I felt about it. It was the hottest kiss of my life. But he was my boss. And he walked away from me without saying another word. Was it bad for him? I had been under the impression for a number of years now that I was competent in the kissing department. It was a blow to my ego.

Nora vigorously shook her head. "Nope. He had the once-in-a-lifetime opportunity to make out with Cecelia Goddamn Leary. And he ran away and hasn't said a word since." She shook her Red Vine in my face. "Fuckboy."

"It's fine."

"It's really not. But I admire your positive attitude. We shouldn't have expected better. He's a Quinn. Those Quinn brothers are hot as sin but terrible at relationships."

"Regardless, it is def not happening again." I downed the last of my wine from the Havenport Annual Summer Festival 2003 mug I was drinking out of. My mother owned plenty of wine glasses, but Nora and I used to sneak white wine and drink it out of coffee mugs in high school, so even as adults, we insisted on continuing our tradition.

Nora leaned over to my nightstand and grabbed the bottle to refill me. "Do you want it to happen again?"

"No. I mean yes. No, really no."

"Wow, you are really selling this, kid."

I took a big sip of my wine. "Well, he's undeniably hot and smart and fun to hang out with. I like him as a person, and when he kissed me I felt things. Things I'm not sure I've felt before. It was unsettling."

"But also unbelievably hot?"

"Oh yeah. Crazy hot. Brain-meltingly hot. I was ready to rip off my panties right there. And you know I'm not that type of girl."

"Yes, dear. We know you are super vanilla and boring."

I rolled my eyes at her. "But anyway. He is clearly not into me."

Nora smiled at me and nodded into her wine mug like she was not buying anything I was selling right now. "You know," she said cautiously, "he doesn't have the best reputation. He has dated a few people that I know, friends of friends and that sort of thing."

"What do you mean?" It came out a bit harsher than I was intending, but I felt strangely protective of Liam.

"Nothing bad. Just that he's not a relationship type of guy. Really focused on work, doesn't make much time for other stuff. I've never heard anyone say anything bad about him, but just that he's not settling down material."

"Well, that's good news for me. Because I have no intention of settling down, and at least I know he won't get the wrong idea."

"Okay, if you're sure. I just don't want you to get hurt. You aren't exactly the "hit it and quit it" type, Cece."

I sighed. "I appreciate your concern, Nora, but I don't know what 'type' I am anymore. I came here to work some stuff out and get out of New York. I am not interested in dating. I am off men. I need to focus on myself. And that's fine. I like this job. I have a mission to complete. I am going to market the shit out of this brewery for the next few months and then move onto something else."

It was the truth. I was learning a lot and having a blast. "I like a challenge. It's nice not working nine to five behind a desk every damn day."

"A-women, sister. I hear you on that front." She raised her mug. "And I respect the hell out of what you are doing. And clearly Liam does too. Which is probably why he doesn't want to make a move and compromise that."

"Maybe. But the reasons don't really matter, do they? Nothing can happen. I don't want to be in a relationship. And I don't want to compromise my new job by hooking up with the boss."

"True."

"And I'm going to leave town anyway. I have to go

back to New York in January and restart my life. There is no way my next chapter is starting in Havenport."

"You say that. But maybe the next chapter has already started?"

Her comment unsettled me. I decided to push the feeling away and deal with it later. "Oh, stop philosophizing and focus on Channing Tatum." I grabbed the remote and clicked play on the tiny twenty-year-old TV.

We were rewatching one of our high school favorites, *She's the Man*, which was the genesis of our Channing Tatum obsession.

After about twenty minutes of drinking and enjoying Channing playing soccer shirtless, Nora turned to me.

"So tell me about his dick."

I playfully hit her shoulder. "Gross, Nora. No!"

"So it was gross? Such a shame."

"No." I was exasperated and did not want to continue this conversation. "I didn't see it or anything. I just briefly felt it and it felt good."

"Like long and strong good?" She wiggled her eyebrows.

I laughed. "Yeah. Really long and really strong if you know what I mean."

"I'll toast to that." And we clinked mugs.

"So that's it. You are really going to do nothing about this?"

"Yup. I am going to stay focused and not get hung up on this. I am new Cecelia." And it was true. For once, I was not obsessing or planning or trying to find the safest option. I had decided to enjoy my life day by day and try new things. Making out with my hot boss was a new adventure and I wasn't going to dwell on it or feel bad about it.

"Well, I like the new Cece."

"Thank you. So what's happening with you?" I said, trying to pivot the conversation in another direction.

"Not much. Work, work, work. I am building up the Jeanious Bar website and trying to diversify." One of my favorite things about Nora is how fired up she gets about her business and helping women feel good. I sometimes feel a bit jealous about how passionate she is about her career. "I get messages on Insta all the time from women who want the JB experience, but are all over the country and the world. I have a website, but it's not set up for this kind of e-commerce."

"But the magic of your store is you, Nora. How do you replicate that online?"

"Well, thanks, darling. But part of the magic is the diversity of styles, sizes, and prices, and that can be done online. But to actually make it work, we need to find a way to build in some kind of system that helps the buyer navigate all the sizes and styles and cuts to find what is uniquely right for them. So I am looking to hire some tech people to help me out. But their help does not come cheaply, so I've been holding back a bit."

"I think you should go for it. If there is some tech genius out there who can create a robot Nora to find people their best jeans just by looking at them, then that is something the world needs."

Nora shrieked. "That would be amazing! Robot Nora would be super helpful for many things." She sighed. "But anyway, it's hard for a brick and mortar store to survive. I've got to diversify and find new ways of promoting and marketing."

"I get that. But I think what makes JB so unique is you. Your social media feed markets the store and your products, but shouldn't you be marketing yourself and your expertise?"

"That sounds great, but how do I practically do that?"

"Well, I've been telling you for years that you need to post more social media content about yourself."

Nora rolled her eyes. "I know, I know."

"Seriously. You want people to trust you to help them find the best clothes for their bodies? If you show them how totally gorgeous you look every day, that will build your credibility."

"Wow. I never thought about it that way."

"And, in addition to showcasing stuff like that, you could also explain why different fits, cuts, and fabrics can help or hurt certain body types. Use yourself as a guinea pig for new styles and people will respect the authenticity."

"Yes! You are a marketing genius. The thought of posting photos of my fat ass on the Internet scares me, but everything else you've said is amazing."

I smiled. It was fun helping Nora. It was the least I could do given how many free pairs of jeans she had given me over the years.

"Do you want a new client?" she asked with a grin. "I would love to hire you to help with the transition to the web and figuring out how to bring JB to more people."

She looked so excited I didn't want to let her down. "Thank you. But that's not really what I do."

"But it could be what you do? I see what you are trying to do with the brewery and it's great. You are a marketing guru, sweetie. Give yourself some more credit."

Nora was so kind and enthusiastic. My head was spinning with ideas for her. What Nora did, making women feel confident and beautiful, was the opposite of what most clothing stores did. Her brand of inclusiveness and diversity with a playful attitude would kill online if properly marketed. Part of me wanted to say yes and help her, but the other part knew that I wasn't qualified. And more importantly, that's not the kind of future I'm looking for. I don't want to freelance or build my own practice, I just want a stable, secure career. And as exciting as taking on these types of opportunities felt, it wasn't a solid long-term plan.

I smiled at my friend. "I'm just helping out at the brewery, and you don't want me. I'm sure we can find you a professional brand consultant or marketer who will do a way better job."

Nora's face fell. "For the record, I think you're full of shit. But I am not going to push you."

"Thanks."

"But I think you should also just be honest with me and admit you only do marketing favors for hot guys with big dicks." She swung a pillow at me and hit me in the side of the head.

"Shut up," I yelled back and scrambled to find another throw pillow.

# 16

LIAM

I DIDN'T DESERVE CECELIA LEARY. IN ADDITION TO being my most energetic and engaged employee, she also gracefully ignored my animalistic advances from Thursday night, sparing me the shame and awkwardness of my actions. I was not proud of myself. I mauled her like a starving tiger. What was I thinking? I couldn't go around attacking women with my tongue. Yes it was amazing. Yes, she felt better in my arms than any woman I have ever met. But that's not a reason to throw out all the rules and let my cock take the wheel.

Not to toot my own horn or anything, but it seemed like she was really into it. And it was an incredible kiss. I thought I felt a fire for her before I kissed her, but as we kissed, it only burned brighter and hotter than I could have imagined. Her body fit so perfectly with mine, and I will never forget the way her legs wrapped around my waist when she ground up against my cock. And so I panicked. I ran away like a coward because even I know it was more than kissing. And I couldn't go there right now. I couldn't get distracted. So instead of apologizing, instead of promising never to let that happen again, what did I do? I fucking ran away like a coward, leaving her shell-shocked and confused.

I couldn't get into a relationship right now, and face it, Cecelia was a relationship kind of girl. She deserved a guy who could give her everything. I had way too much on my plate, and she was an essential part of saving the brewery. I couldn't afford to screw this up. I just needed to keep my focus on the brewery and my cock in my pants. Easier said than done since I couldn't erase the feel of her in my arms, the sweet taste of her mouth, and the sound of her sexy moan when she felt my cock for the first time. She seemed like such a good girl, but the way she bit my lower lip, I couldn't even imagine what she's like in bed. Actually, that was a lie. I had spent a lot of time imagining what she was like in bed and I had many working hypotheses.

But it was a mistake. I had to keep telling myself that. Cecelia was more than an employee, she was my friend. She was on the rebound. I know her douchebag ex hurt her deeply and I wouldn't want to make things worse than I already had. So now I just had to pray that she didn't quit and/or file a sexual harassment lawsuit against me. Both possibilities were equally horrifying. I wanted to say something. I *should* have said something. But I didn't know how without making things worse. I was a total coward. Luckily, we were so busy with the brewery that we didn't even have a minute to speak to one another, let alone have the extremely awkward "sorry I stuck my tongue down your throat even though you are my employee" talk.

But she hasn't seemed to hold it against me. In fact, she was clearly the professional in this situation. She has been working and hustling like everything is fine. Allowing me to stew in my shame. Luckily, the taproom was packed for our grand re-opening. Cece and Trent were bartending while Kyle and I bussed tables and barbacked.

We had been booming since we opened at noon. The
entire town had come out for our unofficial reopening
weekend.

Usually, my bar was filled with beer snobs and
hipsters. This was the most diverse crowd I had ever seen.
My dad, the Captain, was holding court at one of the
outdoor tables with his posse of old man friends, probably
telling some wild navy story. Parents were clustered
together while their kids ran on the lawn and played with
the giant Connect Four game Cece insisted I order from
Amazon. Mayor Liza and Gail were at the bar, greeting
everyone and ordering round after round for friends and
neighbors. Gail made sure to compliment the new
plantings and suggested I run a drip irrigation system to
the flower beds. Even my brothers turned out, which was
rare for a weekend. Callum was working the room like he
was running for office and Declan was, predictably, sitting
in the back emitting a strong "don't fuck with me" vibe.

But no matter how crowded and busy it was, my body
instinctively knew where Cecelia was at all times. My
senses were always on high alert when she was around.
Every time we brushed by each other behind the bar I
made sure to inhale a whiff of her shampoo, hoping she
didn't notice. I clearly needed some kind of exorcism
because I was beginning to scare myself. I knew I couldn't
have her, but my stupid body didn't want to listen. I
needed to get my head on straight. This was the busiest
weekend since we opened four years ago and I needed to
be busting my ass to make sure every single one of these
customers wanted to come back again.

I accepted congratulations from friends and neighbors
and my family. It was nice, seeing the whole community
here on a beautiful sunny day, enjoying my beer. Made me
feel even more sure that Havenport was the best place to
open my brewery. Callum came and stood beside me,

clapping me on the shoulder. "Well done, little bro. This outdoor area is genius."

"Thanks. I can't take credit for it. It was Cecelia's idea."

"Well, good job hiring her then."

We stood in silence for a few minutes before I realized I had to get back to work. "Hey Cal, have you seen Declan? He was here for a while but I wanted to thank him for coming out."

"He disappeared."

"Figures." Declan was the master of the Irish goodbye. He had been sneaking out of events and parties for years unnoticed. He would probably Irish goodbye his own wedding, if he could find a woman willing to marry him.

"Marcus Flint is here."

I nodded. That explained it. Marcus Flint had been Declan's mortal enemy since elementary school. He bullied Declan for years because of his stutter and anything else he could think of. Those two got in more fights than I can even count, many of which Cal and I joined.

Don't get me wrong, Marcus Flint was a dick and I hated him. But he was a cop in town now, so we had to make nice. As much as I would love to break his nose for all the shit he did to my brother, I am an adult and a business owner, so I have to choose the high road. But that definitely explained why Declan hightailed it out of here after one beer.

Callum nudged me. "Get back to work. This place isn't going to run itself."

———

I was so busy admiring the packed house that I didn't notice the small woman tapping me on the shoulder.

"Um, Liam?"

"Yes." I turned around and was faced with a tiny, intense-looking woman. She wore a tight tank top, jean shorts and Timberland boots. Her hair was slicked back in a high ponytail, and enormous hoop earrings hung from her ears. She was cute in a slightly scary sort of way.

She gave me a kind smile that softened her intense features. "Sorry to startle you. I'm Maya." She stuck her hand out and gave me a firm shake. "I own the taco truck outside. We were just wrapping up our shift and I wanted to come and say thank you. We sold out of almost everything, and I would love to continue partnering with you in the future."

"Um...sure," I stumbled. "Cece handles the scheduling, but we would love to have you back. I didn't get a chance to try anything, but the smells have been making my mouth water."

"Ah." She smiled. "Then it's a good thing I brought you the house special as a thank you. Tacos al pastor." She handed me a to-go box that smelled like heaven.

"These smell incredible and I'm starving. Thanks so much."

"Anytime, cutie" She reached out and touched my bicep and I noticed she was standing even closer to me. "Can I get your number?" She shifted even closer. "So we can discuss scheduling in the future." Her eyes twinkled and I didn't know what to say. I knew she was flirting with me, but I didn't know how to extricate myself from this conversation.

"Sure," I said tentatively. While she punched my number into her phone I looked up across the taproom and saw Cece glaring at us. I caught her eye and then she turned and stormed into the kitchen.

I excused myself after thanking Maya for the tacos.

I headed in after Cece.

"What's up?"

She was gripping the countertop with her eyes closed. It looked like she was either having a stroke or doing some kind of new age breathing exercises.

"Cece, are you okay?"

She looked up at me. "Yes, I'm fine." She plastered on a fake smile.

"Is everything okay out there? We are really busy."

"No, everything is totally fine. Trent and I have the bar under control, and Kyle is changing kegs right now. I think we're in good shape."

"Okay," I stumbled. "Do you want a taco? They smell amazing."

"Did Maya give you those?"

"Yes. She wanted to say thank you."

"I'm sure she did." She rolled her eyes.

"I don't follow."

"Don't pull the dumb guy routine with me. She was blatantly flirting with you."

"Okay, but I really don't think so."

"Yes, she was. She probably couldn't help herself since you are so stupid hot." She kicked the metal prep table with her sneaker and it was really cute.

My mind was spinning. What the hell was happening? "You think I'm hot?"

"Oh, please." She started pacing around and ignored my question. "I am the one that found her and invited her to come here and helped her make money, but I don't rate free tacos."

"Well, I think you do. Please have one." My mind was at war. On the one hand, her jealousy was adorable, on the other, we had a packed house out there and needed to keep our heads in the game.

I gestured at her with an amazing-looking taco. She took a bite.

"Oh, wow." Her contented groan shot straight to my

dick. "Of course they are delicious. They are farm-to-table too. She's a goddamn culinary genius." She took the taco out of my hand and took another bite. "You should ask her out. She is very pretty."

Angry, jealous Cece pacing around my kitchen was irresistible. I had to fight the urge to grab her and kiss some sense into her. Watching her freak out was so endearing I couldn't help myself. I grabbed her by the arm, and she looked up at me, her eyes full of confusion.

I took a deep breath. "I think we need to talk about Thursday night."

She looked up and held my eye contact. "Yes. We. Do." She pushed me away from her. "You kissed the hell out of me."

"Yes, I did," I said, puffing my chest out with pride

"And then you ran away."

"Yes, I did," I agreed, feeling deflated.

"What the hell, Liam?" She was mad and she had every right to be. This was just another example of me fucking up. I didn't want to hurt her. She was my friend and my employee. I had to keep my traitorous dick under control.

"I'm sorry. I have felt like shit for the past two days about it."

"Are you sorry for kissing me or running away?"

I panicked. This felt like a cross-examination. "Both. I think."

She took a big step back from me, looking hurt.

*What are you doing, idiot? Talk to her. Don't hurt her more than you already have. Put on your big boy pants.* "Listen, Cecelia. I don't regret kissing you. It was great. But it can't happen again. You work for me. And you are my most valuable employee at the moment. I don't want to jeopardize that."

"I understand. I really like working here. And I'm

committed to seeing things through to the end of the year."

"Exactly. We have a ton of work to do together."

"Yes, so much work."

We both stood there nodding at each other like idiots. She took pity on me and broke the silence first. "And I just got out of a long-term relationship. And I'm not staying in Havenport. So there's no point in exploring this further anyway."

"Yes. Of course. And I need to be focused on saving my business right now."

"Of course you do."

This was good. We were acting like mature, responsible adults. We were going to crush it at work and ignore whatever this was between us. I could control my lust and be a good boss and friend. No problem. Crisis averted.

Cece took another huge bite of her taco. "Oh my God, this is delicious. She is cute and can cook. You should marry her and have lots of babies."

"I can't do that. I am not into her." I paused, willing the words to stay in my mouth, but they escaped. "I'm into someone else." *Shit. Stop. Wrong thing to say. Walk it back. Shut it down. Stop flirting and get your head on straight. We just established that we can't do this. Stop fucking it up.*

I needed to pivot out of this conversation. "And I can't date her, or I'd weigh four hundred pounds."

"Oh, please." She dramatically gestured to my torso. "This is natural-born hotness. A few tacos won't make a difference."

I laughed. "You know how much beer I drink. This," I said, mimicking her gesture, "is hard to maintain."

At least we were both laughing. I guess the sexual tension had been diffused. I finished my taco and looked at her. She was just so damn pretty and funny. The next few months were going to be torture.

"Well," she said, wiping her hands on a napkin. "We'd better get back to work."

I looked at her face. There was a bit of salsa verde on her bottom lip.

"Here," I said, taking a step toward her. "You have something on your lip."

I reached out with the pad of my thumb and gently wiped the salsa from her plump pink lip. Pure fire shot through my veins. I stood there, unsure what to do next. She met my eyes, and I saw undiluted lust mixed with defiance. It was unbearably hot. Before I knew what was happening, she opened her mouth and gently sucked my thumb, releasing it with a pop. My body froze, and for a second all I could feel was her wet tongue and her plump lips. Every ounce of blood in my body rushed south while my vision began to blur.

"Thanks," she said, licking her lips. And then she turned and sauntered out of the kitchen, hips and ponytail swinging.

This woman was going to kill me. And I was going to enjoy every fucking second of it.

## 17

LIAM

IT HAD BEEN ANOTHER LONG, BUT PRODUCTIVE DAY at the brewery. Things had really picked up in the last couple of weeks with the expanded weekend hours, which left me behind on a lot of maintenance projects. We had cleaned and sanitized all the lines in the keg room, and I was inspecting everything when I heard a scraping sound in the taproom. I peered around the corner and saw Cece, sitting at the bar with her laptop, looking super focused. She looked at home at my bar, at peace. She was clearly engrossed in what she was doing, but she also seemed serene and less jumpy than when she had first started. It was late, after seven, and I couldn't help but notice how the low light made her look like an angel. Her curly hair was wild in a halo around her face, and I could see her long, dark lashes casting shadows on her freckled cheeks. She really was beautiful, and I was hoping that one of these days I would stop noticing. I could not afford to be distracted.

"Whatcha working on?"

She looked flustered. "Oh, sorry. I didn't realize you were still here."

"Don't worry about it. I'm always here. I don't want to disturb you."

"Just finishing up some things. I'm editing some of the photos I took on my laptop and I didn't feel like driving home yet. I can get going."

That was the last thing I wanted. The pull to keep her here with me was so strong. "No, stay. It's nice to have company. I'm just cleaning and dealing with some paperwork."

I walked around to where she was sitting. "Show me what you're working on."

She blushed and broke eye contact. "Just some shots I took last week."

I stepped behind her and leaned over her shoulder, placing both my hands on the bar around her. From this angle, I was hit with the lavender smell of her hair and the warmth of her body heat.

I instantly fell silent when I saw what she was editing. It was a photo of me, standing on a platform next to one of the large fermentation tanks, taking a test batch. My ever-present hat was on backwards, and I was wearing my standard uniform of old T-shirt and jeans under my brewer's apron. But the photo was really something else. I was in profile, my face a mask of concentration, and my body was bathed in the diffused light coming through the large warehouse windows and then reflecting off the copper tanks. It was a really good photo. And also kind of embarrassing.

"You took this? With your old camera?"

"Yeah."

I took a big step back, instantly missing her heat and floral smell, but it seemed appropriate to put some space between us. "It's really good. You are talented." Not to be vain about it, but it was a good photo of me. I looked capable and strong. Was this how she saw me?

"Thanks," she replied sheepishly. "I was just editing this shot to post to our social media. I've found posts that talk about the art and science of brewing get a lot of engagement from our followers."

I admired how hard she was working. "I have no idea what you're talking about, but I don't think people want to see me testing a batch."

She rolled her eyes at me, and suddenly, sassy Cece was back. "Oh, bless your big dumb heart." She patted my hand like I was a child. "Um, yes they do. Photos of you get more likes than any others I post."

This made my head spin. Me? Who wanted to see photos of me? "How many people see these photos?"

"Well, it depends. When I started here, your Instagram account had six hundred forty-three followers. Since then I have grown the account to over four thousand."

"What, you grew it that much in the last month?"

"Yes. Beer and brewing are really popular on social media. I connected with some others in the space, started churning out content, and found some great hashtags."

While I had no idea what she was talking about, I was really impressed. She seemed engaged and passionate about what she was doing.

Since arriving here Cece was becoming more and more comfortable. She was outspoken with the guys and engaged in our meetings. Her ideas were great and it was like she was finally realizing that she had a lot to offer. Gone was the timid woman I interviewed. In her place was a self-confident marketing whiz. She had learned more and more about brewing and beer and seemed to be really enjoying herself.

"So wait. Does that mean four thousand people will see that photo?" Why on earth would that many people want to see my ugly mug?

"Well, actually more," she replied, typing away on her laptop. "If I use the right hashtags, hopefully a lot more will see and be interested in our content and potentially follow us."

"I have no idea what kind of magic you are working, but wow. So…do likes translate into selling more beer?"

She stopped typing and looked at me like I was an idiot, which I absolutely was. "Yes. Both directly and indirectly. My goal is to raise the profile of the brewery and highlight the work we are doing here as well as the incredible events." She stopped talking to save something and then continued. "We want visitors, and we want people to go seek out the product at their local stores. We also want to be influential in this space online so we can potentially develop and sell merchandise or form partnerships with relevant brands."

I've been brewing beer for a long time and I wasn't bad at it. But this? Social media marketing and engagement? I had been maintaining the brewery accounts for years, and clearly I had no idea what I was doing. "Okay, that all sounds awesome. How do we get more likes?"

She laughed. "The only way I could get more likes was if you were shirtless in this photo."

That caught me off guard. "What?" I sputtered. "That would be unsanitary!"

I moved behind the bar to get myself a beer. I needed something to get me through this conversation which had started out professional but had veered hard into awkward territory.

"Of course it would. But I don't think the Internet cares about the sanitation standards of this brewery—they just like hot, bearded dudes." She gave me one of her saucy smiles, and I almost dropped the glass I was holding.

Now I was the one blushing. I put my head down as I

poured from the tap. "You think I'm hot, Leary?" I raised my eyes to meet her gaze and threw her a wink.

Her face instantly flushed, and I could tell I wasn't the only person feeling embarrassed.

"You know what I mean."

I was feeling bold. Cece challenged me and excited me, and it was hard to deny the feelings she was creating inside me. "I *don't* know what you mean, actually." I walked back around and leaned on the side of the bar next to her. She tilted her head up to look at me, and her brown eyes were blazing.

I could see she was breathing heavily. It felt good to see that she was just as worked up as I was. It wasn't in my head—this connection between us was real, and she could feel it too.

I smirked and caged her in with my arms. "It's nothing to be ashamed of, Leary. Lots of women are powerless to my charms."

My bluster broke the spell because she pushed me hard. "Get over yourself," she said as she stood up from her barstool.

I grabbed her wrist and pulled her back toward me. She hit my chest hard, and I snaked my arm around her waist. "Maybe you can help me with that?"

Our faces were hovering inches away from one another. My entire body tingled with anticipation. I wanted to kiss her more than I have ever wanted to kiss a woman in my life. Her plump pink lips were there, just waiting for me. Her body was warm and soft, and I wanted to throw her over my shoulder like a caveman and have my way with her.

Just as I was working up the courage to kiss her, the door opened and in walked my brothers.

Declan whistled. The spell was broken, and we both scrambled to opposite sides of the bar. What was I thinking? I needed to get my hormones in check if I was going to make this work. I was a professional, not a hormonal teenager.

"What are you idiots doing here?" I shouted, trying to hide my irritation.

"It's Tuesday," Declan grunted.

"We always come by on Tuesdays to check on you," said Callum.

Callum and Declan stared at us for a minute before walking over and making themselves at home in the taproom.

"By all means, help yourselves, assholes," I replied with a sweeping gesture.

"Shut up, little brother. Your beer is the only thing about you that we like," said Declan, giving me a hard shove.

I rubbed my arm. "Awww, thanks Declan. I love it when you get mushy."

Cece was standing there looking shell-shocked. Perhaps I was not the only one pissed about the interruption. I looked down to see Ginger standing behind Declan. The dog, who was not on a leash, sauntered over to Cecelia and looked down her nose at her as if to say "who is this bitch?" and then slowly walked to the corner of the bar, where Callum was pulling out a plush dog bed from the storage closet. She settled down on her bed, watching and judging everyone.

"Cecelia," Callum asked, breaking the silence, "can I get you a drink? My brothers were obviously raised by wolves and have no manners."

She shook her head and smiled.

"You guys on a date or something?" growled Declan.

"No, dumbass. She works here, remember? Mom forced Liam to hire her, I think." Callum shoved Declan hard and Declan punched him in the arm in retaliation.

"Not quite," she replied, finally finding her voice. "And I was just packing up for the night." She grabbed her laptop and shoved it into her bag.

"Aww, Dec," Callum mused, "you scared her off. It's probably because you smell like a goat."

Declan shot Callum a side-eye and growled at him. "Billy called in sick and I had to make deliveries today."

"Sure, sure, most of the time you just look like a goat. Today, you smell like one too." Callum took a large gulp of beer, apparently pretty proud of himself.

"Fuck off, pretty boy, some of us have real jobs."

I chimed in, "Seriously, you smell pretty rank. You could at least shower before you go out in public smelling like fish guts."

"Sorry, your majesty, I didn't want to keep you waiting in case you needed to talk about your feelings again."

Cece shot me a look, and I tried to act cool. She didn't need to know that I occasionally spilled my guts to these idiots.

"Speaking of shit, Liam, you are not exactly looking your best these days."

I gave Declan a dirty look. "I'm stressed."

"Well, you could at least make an effort. You have ladies working here now," Callum piped in.

Cece stopped packing up her bag and turned around. She looked angry, and I was a bit worried about what she would do next. Usually she was pretty laid back, but right now she looked furious.

She slowly turned around and pinned Declan with an icy stare. "You know, you should be a lot nicer to your little brother, since he gives you all this free beer."

Declan paled. He was not used to being called out.

"And," she continued, walking closer to where they were sitting, "while I'm sure you work very hard, Liam works seven days a week to make this place a success." She played with her hair for a minute and then innocently asked, "Didn't you inherit your business from your daddy?" She threw him a smile and batted her eyelashes.

I almost spit out my beer. Callum was hysterically laughing. "Oh shit," he said to Declan. "Do you need some lotion for that burn?"

Cecelia looked at me intensely. Something silent and powerful passed between us. It was as if she was showing me she had my back. Declan glowered into his beer. He really did know when to shut up—it was one of his best qualities.

"You know," she continued, walking over to where I was standing, "Liam and I have some ambitious plans for this place. What are you doing next week?"

Declan looked panicked. He hated being dragged into things. "Not sure, I have a lot to do."

"Good, well, why don't you check your calendar and let me know if Wednesday or Thursday works best for you." She gave him a dazzling smile. "I'll wait while you look."

Callum and I exchanged looks. This was incredible to watch. Declan could barely lift his eyes from his beer. She had him by the balls and he knew it. I never knew quiet, timid Cecelia had this fire inside her.

Declan begrudgingly pulled out his phone and scrolled through. "I can make myself available on Wednesday."

"Excellent." She clapped him on the shoulder. "We're finishing the patio renovations next week and could really use your help. Since you're a real man with a real job and all, you could probably show us a thing or two." She batted her eyelashes at him, and I swear she was the most incredible woman in the world at that moment.

Declan took a swig of beer. "Okay. I'll help."

"Great! You are a gem. I'll need you here at 7am sharp."

"And Callum," she said, narrowing her eyes as he stared into his beer. "We're going to need you on Thursday." It was not a request. It was a demand.

"Um," he sputtered, clearly trying to come up with an excuse. She completely ignored him and kept going.

"And while I have you both here,"—she whipped out her phone and starting swiping around—"I am volunteering you both for Oktoberfest. We're really going to need all hands on deck because this is going to be the biggest event this brewery has ever seen." She made a few notes in her phone in a very businesslike manner. "I'll assign you both jobs soon, but you will be working setup crew on Friday, all day Saturday during the festival, and then cleanup duty the day after. There will be no pay and no drinking on the job." Her voice was clipped, and her tone indicated that she was not taking no for an answer.

My brothers looked at me, helpless and dumbfounded. They had just been steamrolled by this beautiful wild woman and, like me, were powerless to say no to her.

Cece jumped up and down with excitement and smiled. "Thanks so much. You guys are the best."

She walked over to the barstools and gave each a quick peck on the cheek. I was suddenly irrationally jealous of my brothers. What I wouldn't give to have those gorgeous lips on any part of my body....

"Have a good evening, gentlemen," she called, as she slung her bag over her shoulder and sauntered out.

Both my brothers sat in shock as I stared at the closed door, my erection straining my zipper. Cecelia Leary was one hell of a woman, and I was clearly in way over my head.

"Dude, you look like the heart eyes emoji right now," Declan said, recovering his snark after the door had shut.

"Shut up," I replied, still daydreaming about that goddess with the curly hair.

"That was scary," said Declan.

"And really fucking hot," said Callum.

"Are you in love with her yet?"

I shook my head, not liking where this conversation was going.

"Drink your beers, assholes."

Oh my God, she totally stood up to my brothers and threw their shit right back at them. I suspected she was a sexy badass, but having it confirmed had made me lightheaded. Fuck, that was hot. She not only defended me and put them in their place, but she wrangled some much needed free labor out of them too. My brain was cloudy with exhaustion, beer, and arousal, but I needed to remember every detail of this day because it was the day I fell a little bit in love with Cecelia Leary.

# 18

## CECELIA

"WHO IS READY TO KICK SOME OKTOBERFEST ASS?"

Oktoberfest was shaping up to be the event of the year. Or at least in my mind it was. We had spent the past two weeks prepping, brewing, and cleaning. We had Oktoberfest themed decorations, an authentic German brass band, and a catering menu filled with pretzels, wurst, and schnitzel to soak up all the beer people were going to drink. Liam's brother Declan had even hooked us up with one of the guys on his fishing crew who DJ'd on weekends to do a set on Saturday night. The entire day would be one giant party filled with fun, laughter, and hopefully a lot of beer.

Mark had kicked our graphics up a notch, creating a custom Oktoberfest design incorporating the brewery logo. We had new T-shirts and beer steins for sale, and I had ordered hundreds of rubber duckies wearing lederhosen to hand out to the kids.

We were having an all-hands meeting in the back office. Or as I had recently dubbed it, "the war room." It was kind of amazing how far I had come in six short weeks. The entire room was covered in white boards detailing every single thing that was going to happen. Each team member and volunteer had a personalized printed schedule detailing every possible situation that could arise. I was a general leading my troops, and it felt amazing.

"Trent and Kyle, you guys need to do the tablecloths and bunting tonight. There won't be enough time tomorrow."

Trent leaned back in his folding chair. "Copy that, boss lady. We're on it." I assigned jobs to the rest of the assembled crew.

The brewery would be open from ten a.m. to eleven p.m. It was ambitious, and we had several contingency plans if we ran out of beer, food, or paper goods. The fire marshal had come out this week to double-check the new upgrades and kindly reminded us not to exceed our certificate of occupancy. The weather forecast was perfect, and the new outdoor space would hopefully be filled.

I felt good. I was prepared and ready to lead my team to victory. "Okay, guys, I think that's it."

"Wait. I actually have one more thing to discuss," Liam's voice filled the room.

I gave him a look. We had completed my carefully crafted agenda. I had typed it up and emailed it to him this morning. I forgot nothing. There was no way there was some detail I had left out.

"We need to discuss wardrobe." Liam smiled, like he had a secret.

"What do you mean? We just got the new Oktoberfest T-shirts delivered."

Liam scratched the scruff on his chin and smiled. "I thought we could do better. So I got a surprise for you all."

He opened the door to the meeting room and pulled in a massive clothing rack. It was filled with what appeared to be authentic German costumes. "At the real

Oktoberfest in Munich, the servers wear traditional German costumes. So I thought it would only be appropriate for Binnacle staff to also be traditionally attired."

"What the heck is that?" Kyle yelled, as Liam held up an elaborate costume.

"That, my uncultured friend, is lederhosen. You will wear this, with knee-high socks and this very jaunty hat, for the duration of the Oktoberfest celebration."

Trent covered his mouth and tried to contain his giggles. Liam turned to him and added, "You are not getting off either, bud. I've got one for you. The entire front of house team will wear these costumes. The support staff, the caterers, food runners, barbacks, and dishwashers will wear the Oktoberfest T-shirts and jeans."

I was both appalled and impressed. I had not even thought of renting costumes. But wait, if all the guys were wearing lederhosen, what was I expected to wear?

As if sensing my dread, Liam pulled out a poufy dress with a low-cut lace-up bodice and a tiny white apron. It looked less like a cultural costume and more like a sexy Halloween getup. Oh no, there was no way that thing was going to fit on my body. "This is for you, Cece. A dirndl dress. Authentic." His smile was a mile wide. I had done this to myself. I had pushed to make this event the best ever. I had harassed everyone until each detail was perfect. I had advertised far and wide to come have an Oktoberfest experience at the brewery. Little did I know that I would end up dressed as the St. Pauli Girl. "I hope you don't mind. I asked Nora what size to order." He seemed sheepish, but I still wanted to punch him. And Nora. Just wait until I got my hands on her.

As everyone giggled about the costumes, Liam continued. "This is our third year hosting this event, and our first attempting something of this magnitude. I am humbled and grateful for all of your hard work and so excited to see how it all comes together. This is a family. A weird, slightly dysfunctional one, but a family nonetheless. I love you guys. And you know it's hard for me to ask for help."

The assembled crowd laughed.

"But I have needed a lot of help lately. And all of you have stepped up and given me more support and encouragement than I deserve."

I proudly watched as he motivated his team. I started to feel a warm, fuzzy sensation in my chest. As much as I was dreading having to squeeze my ass into that ridiculous outfit he had ordered me, I was a little bit proud of him. I didn't even think to get authentic costumes. He really was learning and evolving his business. It was almost as if all the branding and marketing info I had been shoving down his throat for the past month was working. As I looked around the table at our ragtag team, I was overcome with emotion. Liam was right. We were a weird, slightly dysfunctional family. Every person was ready and willing to make this event a success. I thought about my old job. When had I experienced this feeling? Not ever. I could not remember one project or situation where everyone came together to chip in.

———

The band was incredible, playing all sorts of Oktoberfest songs, most of which involved drinking. I was running between tables with fresh pitchers while Trent bussed all the empty glasses. The deck and patio area were packed, and laughter and music filled the air. My dress was ridiculous but actually sort of comfortable. As embarrassed as I felt wearing a short skirt with my boobs hanging out, I felt festive, and it definitely added to the atmosphere and the fun. Never had I ever worn such a crazy outfit to work, so I was determined to chalk this one up to experience.

Nora being Nora insisted on doing my hair and makeup. She said I had to "go all out" and be "the hottest beer wench in history." So my hair was braided and twisted into some elaborate German style. I have to hand it to her, not many people can tame my hair, and she did it well. It was out of my face and not misbehaving for a change. At my request she hadn't gone too heavy on the makeup, but I was definitely rocking a smoky eye and some glossy lips. I felt good—tired, but good. At the very least, coming back to Havenport had helped me regain some of my old self-confidence. And today was evidence of what I was capable of. I knew this was just a one-day event at a small brewery in a small town, but it felt like the start of something bigger.

I couldn't help but look at Liam with some longing. As much as I pretended not to want a relationship, deep down I did want to meet my person. I did want beautiful, magical love. It was just that after thirty-one years, I had become a pragmatist about it.

Growing up, it always appeared to my child eyes that my parents were madly in love. They held hands in the movie theater when they thought we weren't looking and were always sneaking kisses and offering each other bites of their dinners at restaurants.

Unlike some of my friends whose parents fought all the time, mine rarely did. I remember being super grossed out when we would develop the photos from our family vacations—in those crazy days before we all had digital cameras—and there would be a random photo my dad took of my mom's butt. At the time we pretended to be traumatized, but now, as a woman, I would kill to have my husband of fifteen years sneak a photo of my butt in a bathing suit. Looking back, I saw how well suited they

were, how much love and trust and partnership went into
building our family.

I would be lying if I said I didn't want that. But first, it
was statistically unlikely to happen. Especially as my older
sister had met the love of her life at nineteen and had been
blissfully in love for the last fifteen years. What was the
likelihood that lightning would strike twice in our family?
Probably not very high. So I settled. I settled for okay guys
and so-so relationships and jobs that I hated. I paid my
bills and went through the motions. I thought this was a
good, safe, responsible plan. But I realized how much
damage I did to myself. Denying what and who I wanted
just chipped away at my self-esteem until there was
nothing left.

I picked up two more pitchers from the bar and
headed back to table eleven where my mom was seated
with Burt, my aunt Joyce, and some other ladies from her
various town organizations and charities. "Cecelia! You
look gorgeous," my mother exclaimed, jumping up and
giving me a kiss on the cheek. "This event is fantastic. I am
so proud of you."

I blushed. You could always count on my mom to
deliver the praise. "Thanks, Mom."

I spun around to rush to my next table, and my
mother grabbed my arm. "Sweetie," she whispered in my
ear, "you look happy."

I smiled. "I am, Mom. I am having a lot of fun."

"Good. And I'm not the only one who noticed. I have
been watching a very handsome man in lederhosen stare at
you all day." She gestured behind me and I turned around.
Liam was standing at the bar waiting for an order, and our
eyes met. I could feel the heat across the large warehouse
and my stomach dropped. His hotness was distracting on
a good day. But today? Even the ridiculous costume
couldn't dilute it. The shorts highlighted his muscular

thighs, and the suspenders made his shoulders look even broader. It was becoming harder and harder to hide my attraction to him. The night we kissed, things changed for me. I could no longer ignore my feelings. That kiss detonated a lust bomb inside my brain. All I could think about was his velvety soft tongue, his strong arms, and that cock. Dear God, it had felt incredible, even through a thick layer of denim.

The moment passed and he looked away. I chatted with Mom and her friends for another minute and then rushed back to the bar to fill the next order. We were working hard, but it was a lot of fun. Watching all my careful planning come together made all the hard work worth it. Seeing the happy people having fun and drinking and eating and dancing warmed my heart. I did this. I mean, the brewery was Liam's and it was his original idea. But I added the color and the life to this event. It had been such a long time since I had felt pride in what I did. Usually I would give everyone else credit, and frankly the team here had been amazing, so they definitely deserved credit. But I was done ignoring myself and my talents. I busted my ass and accomplished something difficult. And I was damn proud of myself.

I had spent my life to this point comparing myself to my sister. Diminishing my own accomplishments because I thought I would never measure up. But I was done with that. I was ready to shine in my own way. I couldn't let fear hold me back. I couldn't let my feelings of inadequacy hold me back. I needed to step into the light and shine like a motherfucker. I was not going to make myself small. I was going to grow and shine and create my own future. Who knows? Maybe that future would include an incredible partner who was worthy of me.

# 19

LIAM

I WAS SIMULTANEOUSLY PULLING TWO PINTS AND taking four more orders from the bar. Loud music from the German brass band filled the air, and I was both excited and terrified by the massive crowd at the brewery.

We were tapping new kegs every half hour and the kitchen door was a blur with food coming in and out. Normally I would be thrilled, but we were severely understaffed and it was only three o'clock. We had eight more hours to go, and I didn't know if we could hold on. On the bright side, everyone was having a great time. But I didn't know if we had enough beer, food, and staff to pull this off. We'd hosted Oktoberfest before, so it's not like we didn't know what we were doing. But this was easily ten times more people than we usually had. Thankfully Cecelia had prepared everything. She knew we were going to draw a big crowd. Once again, she was ten steps ahead of me and I had to catch up.

I had been pouring beers for hours. I was supposed to greet and mingle and oversee everything, but that went out the window the minute the place became standing room only. I would love a bathroom break or a drink of water, but those seem like faraway dreams at the moment. In my peripheral vision I can see Cece directing Trent and Kyle and hugging some customers who just came in. From the corner of my eye it looked like my parents. I made my way over to the other side of the bar.

"Liam," Cece exclaimed. "There you are! I called in some reinforcements." I had been internally high-fiving myself all day for renting the German costumes. Cecelia looked so unbelievably hot in that outfit, the image would be seared in my brain forever. She had done her hair in some fancy braid thing and was wearing red lipstick. When we got here this morning, the sight of her carrying beer steins in that outfit, with the short skirt and low top, gave me an erection so painful I had to go to my office and read sports scores on my phone until it went away. All I wanted was to flip that skirt up and…*focus idiot, this is the biggest day of your career and your mother is five feet away.*

"Sweetheart," my mom exclaimed, "this is incredible." She was already rolling up her sleeves, clearly ready to jump in. My mom was the best.

The Captain smiled at me. "Well done, son. This is quite the turnout. How can we help?" The military man was always ready and willing to take orders.

Cece swooped in with a charming smile. "Mrs. Quinn, could you take over host duties? We need to collect and wipe down the menus and get the tables turned over for those waiting. I have a feeling you'd do a great job."

My mother was tickled. "Of course, dear, I'll keep everyone moving."

"And Captain," she said, putting her arm around his shoulders, "could you man the front door? We need someone to greet, help people find tables, and keep an eye on our numbers. I have Declan outside setting up a waiting area because I think we are getting really close to capacity."

"Got it, sweetheart." And my dad winked at her. He winked. The man can barely hug us on our birthdays, but Cecelia Leary had him eating out of her hand. I wish I could say that I was not totally impressed by how easily she charmed my parents. Jesus, I was a goner for this girl.

Also, how was she keeping tabs on the numbers while running everything else and serving food and drinks? And Declan wasn't even supposed to be here until five. She must have texted him. And she knew to give him a Declan-friendly activity. She even found time to pop around with her camera, taking tons of photos and documenting the event. My mind, heart, and dick could not take the constant onslaught of her awesomeness. It was making me dizzy.

———

The day was a wild, happy blur. Beer, pretzels, smiling faces, and congratulations from friends and family. It was incredible.

Burt was sitting in the dog area with his yorkie. He was wearing a blue and white checked bowtie in honor of Oktoberfest. "Liam," he called over to me, "I usually like a carefully crafted cocktail or a glass of fine wine, but your beer is fantastic. This event is so wonderful. Bravo for you, son."

"Ooh yes," squealed Mayor Liza, who was sitting at the next table with her wife, Gail, and some of the ladies from the horticultural society. "Susan over here is retiring this spring." She gestured to a middle aged woman with a closely cropped afro. "We were just saying she should have her party here. How do we get on your event calendar?"

I gave Susan my card and told her to email me next week. I'd have to talk to Cecelia about parties. But that sounded like a great idea.

I bussed tables, said hello to various friends and acquaintances, and worked my ass off. At one point, I was running an order of soft pretzels to the lawn, where parents were sprawled out while their kids ran in the grass and played with the outdoor toys, when I felt a hand on my arm.

"Hey, Liam." It was Maggie Leary, Cece's older sister. She was sitting at a table with Mark's wife, Ellie, while their kids played. For sisters, they didn't look much alike. Maggie was tall, serious, and imposing. She was beautiful, for sure, but she didn't have the warmth and spark that Cecelia did. But then I guess I was just biased. I didn't know her very well, but her husband Josh was friends with Callum and sometimes played basketball with us on Sunday mornings. I didn't see him, but assumed he was around somewhere.

"I just wanted to say congrats. This event is fantastic."

"Thank you. I appreciate that."

"And thank you for taking a chance on my sister. She really needed a chance to spread her wings a bit."

"Don't thank me. I would be lost without her. She did all of this," I said, gesturing around me.

"Awesome. Well, I hope you appreciate how amazing she is."

Huh. That sounded coded and ominous. Was I missing something? "Oh, don't worry," I said awkwardly. "I know how lucky we are to have her."

"Good," she said, giving me an icy glare. "Don't forget it."

I excused myself and headed back into the bar. That was uncomfortable and weird. Before I could analyze it further, a twirl of a skirt caught my eye.

The eighty-year-old band leader had grabbed Cecelia and was dancing with her to the music. She followed his lead as they pranced around to this traditional German tune that I could not name if my life depended on it.

I was mesmerized. Cece was irresistible. The outfit, her hair, her dazzling smile. She looked so joyful and free. The old man was having the time of his life and so was she. People were clapping along to the beat, and others joined them dancing. I watched him expertly twirl her, and her full skirt splayed out, rising just a few inches to display a tantalizing glimpse of those gorgeous thighs. Her wild hair had begun to escape her braid, with curly tendrils framing her face. She was incredible, and the ache inside me grew. I wanted her so badly, but what could I do about it? I couldn't act on these feelings. I couldn't address the tension between us. I just had to keep my head down and hope it eventually went away.

# 20

LIAM

WE WERE HAPPY, TIPSY, AND A LITTLE MESSY. AFTER closing the bar at eleven thirty, most of the crew stayed to clean up. High on the success of the day, it turned into an impromptu party. Trent set up the Bluetooth speaker we use while brewing, and we were all drinking, dancing, and eating leftover soft pretzels.

Some significant others had come by, and by one a.m. I was having a pretty good time. What a day. Things had been crazy busy but so exciting. In addition to the entire town of Havenport, hundreds of new people had visited the brewery. The parking lot had cars with plates from several other states. The band was a hit, the food was amazing, and the weather was incredible. I was feeling damn happy.

Cece sat on a folding chair with her legs up, beer in hand. She still wore her dirndl dress, but the ornate braids were coming unpinned. Her wild curls were escaping in every direction creating a light brown halo around her pretty face. The skirt rode up those glorious creamy thighs and her feet were bare. I could tell she was exhausted but happy too. All day I had been tortured by the sight of her. I was a man obsessed. It was official. She was the sexiest thing I had ever seen in my life and I knew that—rules be damned—I was going to make a move tonight. I had to at least try. Today had been one of the best days of my life. I had to take a swing.

Since I was a bit tipsy and riding the high of my professional career, I decided I needed to hold her in my arms and immediately tell her how amazing she was. At this point I was running on a few hours of sleep, adrenaline, and beer, so my plan seemed rock solid in the moment.

So I did it. I grabbed her hand and pulled her up to dance. She wordlessly complied, resting her head on my chest. Dancing together, under the moonlight and the gorgeous Edison string lights she had carefully chosen, everything felt as it should. My business was growing and evolving, and I had a gorgeous woman in my arms who challenged me and made me better on every level. For this one incredible moment, everything was awesome and I could just stand still and enjoy myself.

She laughed, looking up at me, and her eyes twinkled. "This isn't exactly a slow dance song." I hadn't even noticed the music. It was a Taylor Swift song. Whatever. I didn't even care. I shrugged and kept on dancing with her in my arms. Her quizzical gaze turned into a beautiful smile. I felt a warm explosion inside my chest. I had so much affection for her. And being the recipient of her smile, I felt ten feet tall.

I gathered my courage. "You are incredible. I hope you know that."

She shrugged. "You're not so bad yourself."

"Don't do that. This was your idea. You took this event from zero to sixty in a few weeks, and I could never have imagined the success we had." In my wildest dreams for this place I never saw an event like this happening. We had hundreds of people, sold tons of beer and merchandise, and raised the profile of this brewery tenfold. And none of it would have been possible without her.

She didn't reply. Instead, she leaned in and rested her head back on my chest. Our bodies were flush. I leaned down and whispered in her ear. "I am in awe of you."

She stepped back and looked up at me with those big brown eyes. She looked so small and vulnerable. Like she had no idea what an epic badass she was. I suddenly could not control myself as I cupped her cheek and captured her mouth in a gentle kiss. She fisted the front of my shirt, kissing me back, tentatively at first. She tasted like beer and sunshine and every awesome thing on earth. Her other hand traveled down and rested on top of my belt buckle. With this one small gesture, every ounce of blood in my body rushed south. My vision tunneled and all I saw were her beautiful lips, wet from my kiss. My body pulsed with need. I wanted to devour her. I wanted to throw her over my shoulder and possess her in every possible way. Instead, I intensified the kiss, giving her everything I had and taking everything she had in return. My hands roved all over her body, and her soft warmth drove me crazy.

We were interrupted by hoots and hollers from the assembled crowd. We broke apart, disoriented by the sudden loss of contact. I looked up and saw Trent and Shane clapping and then Shane opening his wallet to give Trent some money. I saw Mark and his wife on the deck looking down at us with smug smiles, and some of the other guests and employees were clapping as well.

I pulled Cece into my arms again and she looked confused. My heart was pounding and nothing made sense. I met her eyes. "Come home with me tonight." I felt like an out of control caveman. I normally didn't give women commands. What the hell was I thinking?

Her chest heaved as she tried to catch her breath. Her eyes were glassy and her lips were swollen from our kiss. She stepped back and looked up at me with those gorgeous hazel eyes. "Yes please."

————

After the fastest cleanup in history and making everyone go home, we finally called an Uber and made it back to my place. We had both sobered up considerably, which made me worry she might have second thoughts.

Those worries disappeared the minute she walked through the door and threw herself at me. She clung to me while our mouths clashed in a desperate, hungry kiss. I should have been embarrassed by my lack of finesse, but this woman unlocked something positively feral inside me. Her eyes, her hair, that incredible body—my mind was swirling with lust. I didn't want to overwhelm her with the breadth of my desire for her, but I also didn't think I could hide it for another minute.

I kicked the door shut while picking her up and carrying her into my living room. "You are so incredibly hot in that outfit, I have been distracted all day. Your tits look good enough to eat. I want to kiss every inch of your gorgeous body." I had no idea where these words were coming from. I didn't normally talk like this. I couldn't blame the beer because I had stopped drinking a while ago to expedite the cleanup process and get her into my bed.

*Did I just ruin everything by opening my big mouth?* I stepped back and met her gaze. Her eyes were glassy with lust and her chest heaved. Her lips were kiss swollen and she met my gaze with steely determination. "If you're lucky I might let you."

I grabbed her and kissed her fiercely again. She broke away.

"Liam, wait."

Oh shit. She was having second thoughts.

"Before we do anything, I just want you to know I'm not looking for another relationship, okay?"

At this point I would have agreed to anything.

"Sure. Me neither."

"So this is just casual fun?"

I grabbed her ass. "Totally casual."

She resumed kissing me, then bit down hard on my lower lip. It was like this girl knew exactly what I needed. Gone was the nice guy from earlier and in his place was a wild beast. My desire for her was so overwhelming that I couldn't see straight. We pawed at each other while I led her to my couch. Laying her down gently, we continued to kiss and grope and grind up against each other urgently. I snaked my hand up under the full skirt of her dress and found a pair of cherry-red panties. There was a visible damp spot which made me crazy. This was my wildest fantasy come true, and we were just getting started.

My mind and body were at war. I wanted to strip her bare and fuck her through my mattress, but I also wanted to take my time, savor every moment, and fully explore her body. I slid my finger under the material of those cherry-red panties and I gently stroked her velvety pussy, finding her wet and ready. I carefully probed with one finger. I slipped in easily as I pumped in and out. I added a second and she started to groan and ride my hand.

"You are so ready for me. Your pussy feels amazing. I want to taste it before I fuck you."

"Yes. Yes. Please." Her voice was breathy and her breathing labored. If I could just control myself and slow down, I would have her screaming my name in no time.

I slowly pushed up the full skirt of her costume and

peeled the red panties down her legs. I wanted to worship her all night long. My aching cock protested, but I was a man on a mission. I was going to make Cecelia Leary scream my name and make her as crazy with lust as she made me. If I couldn't use words to tell her how much she meant to me, how much she had gotten under my skin this past month, then I would be using my mouth, my hands, and my cock to show her.

"Look at me," I growled from my perch between her creamy thighs. She opened her eyes and gave me a sultry stare. I slowly lowered my mouth down and inhaled her sweet feminine scent. I flicked my tongue gently against her slit and her tiny bundle of nerves. Her entire body shook with pleasure as I slowly teased her, gently circling her clit while my fingers stroked her. Her thighs quivered, and she cried out as I slowly sank two fingers into her wet heat.

I continued to suck and stroke and lick until she was shaking and screaming my name. I remained focused while her hips bucked off the couch. "Liam!" she screamed as she let go. She spasmed around my fingers and made my cock ache more. I felt her orgasm tear through her body and fought to keep going until the last tremor subsided. Watching her come apart was the sexiest moment of my life. My brain was racing with all the different things I could do to get her off. Once was not enough. I was determined to learn every detail about her body and how to drive her crazy.

I needed more. But I needed to be inside her. I needed to possess her completely. It wasn't rational—hell, it didn't even make sense. How could I want someone this much? How could I crave her body more even as I touched her?

Cece's eyes fluttered open. Her breathing was heavy and uneven. "That was incredible. Your...fingers! Your...mouth!"

"I'm just getting started."

I picked her up and carried her to my bedroom, secretly thanking Trent for working me so hard in the gym. I felt like a Greek god, carrying my woman to bed so I could ravage her. I threw her down on the bed, and she was a sight. Her hair was wild and spilling everywhere, her face was flushed, and her dress was bunched up around her hips, revealing a tease of her bare pussy. "Dress off," I commanded.

She met my gaze and gave me a shy smile. "Make me."

"Do I need to spank you?"

"I don't know. I have been pretty bad." This was definitely a side of Cece I had never seen before. And I wanted to see more of it.

"Fine. I'll just help myself." I threw the skirt of her dress up over her chest and grabbed her knees. I gave her a saucy grin as I pushed her legs open, lowering myself slowly. She wiggled beneath me and I kissed her neck while I reached behind to unzip her dress. I shucked my shirt, and she sat up and immediately started kissing my neck, shoulders, and chest. Her hands and mouth traveled down my torso to the top of my belt buckle. She looked up at me with wide eyes as she loosened my belt and unzipped my jeans.

The minute her hand touched my straining erection I saw stars. Competing impulses were scrambling my brain. I knew I wanted to take it slow and savor every moment with her. I'd been dreaming about this woman for weeks. But the other part of my brain, the caveman part, was screaming at me to fuck her hard, and my pulsing dick agreed.

Finally, we were both naked. I reached into my nightstand for a condom.

I looked at her, flushed and beautiful below me, and every cell in my body was on high alert. I wanted this woman in so many ways. "Are you okay?" I wanted her, but I wanted to make sure she truly wanted me.

"Yes." She writhed on the bed. "Liam...now."

That was all the encouragement I needed. I smiled, rolled the condom on, and pumped my cock a few times. "Are you sure this is okay?"

"Yes. Liam, I need you."

As I sank inside her I knew we were not just blowing off steam. I know we were not just a fling. That this was something real and something life-changing. We were joined together, and I paused, savoring the feel of her. She was hot and wet and tight and true perfection. It felt right.

She wrapped her legs around my waist as I started to move. Every thrust felt incredible, and I knew I was on a hair trigger. I needed to get ahold of myself and slow down, but this was an out-of-body experience. My mind had no control over my animal instincts. I stared into her eyes, willing myself not to glance down at her full tits, bouncing wildly with every thrust. She threw her head back, moaning loudly. "Oh yes. Yes. Liam."

"Is this what you needed, pretty girl."

"Oh yes. I need you, Liam, yes."

She wrapped her legs around me, and I adjusted my angle, going even deeper. Her nails dug into my back as she moaned. "Fuck, yes, Liam. That's the perfect spot. Just like that."

I drove into her harder, faster, and deeper as I willed myself to hold on. I wasn't ready to stop. I wanted this to last forever. I could feel her muscles tensing as her body climbed higher.

She was meeting my wild thrusts and moaning now. I kissed her neck and breasts and watched as she came apart underneath me. "Liam, just like that, oh yes. I think I'm going to..."

"Yes. Let go, Cece."

And just like that I felt her clamp down on me as her body soared. She writhed and screamed and shook as wave after wave crashed over her. I kept going, giving her everything I had and watching her body come undone. This was better than any fantasy I had ever had. Cecelia was real and sexy and screaming my name while her inner muscles squeezed me mercilessly. Suddenly, I couldn't hold on any longer. I felt my release as I pinned her to the bed and she throbbed around me.

I quickly got up to deal with the condom and collapsed on my bed. She was lying on her side staring at me dreamily. I spooned her naked body close, savoring the feel of her skin. "Do you want to stay over?"

She turned over her shoulder and gazed at me. "I think I'd like that."

## 21

CECELIA

WAKING UP NEXT TO SEXY-AS-HELL LIAM QUINN WAS my dream come true. I stared at his profile as he slept. His dark hair was mussed and his beard was in desperate need of a trim. *Oh my God, the things that beard did to me. I wonder if I have beard burn across my face...or between my thighs?*

His chest was broad and strong and peppered with chest hair. I never had opinions on the matter, but chest hair was so sexy on him. It made him look strong and masculine. And if last night was any indication, he was all man.

Just being in his proximity while he slept made me weak with desire. I debated waking him up for another round but decided to just enjoy the moment. I was buck naked in bed with a hot, kind man who effortlessly delivered multiple orgasms last night. I had never even slept naked before. I usually covered up immediately after sex, too self-conscious of my nakedness to relax. But here, in his big comfy bed, with his strong arms around me and his warm, muscular body curled up around me, I was happy and content.

*Should I leave? We had agreed this was a casual thing. If it's casual then I should go.* But I felt so good and so comfortable, I wasn't ready for this to be over yet. Plus, how often does the universe just throw a hot guy who is amazing in bed at you. Pretty much never. I owed it to myself to at least enjoy my amazing luck for a bit. Plus, the story of how I banged my hot boss would make a great anecdote to tell my friends in the nursing home someday.

I took a few moments to look around the bedroom. We were in such a rush to fall into bed last night I hadn't taken a very good look at the place. It was really nice with exposed brick walls, huge windows, and lots of light. The massive king-sized bed took up most of the floor space, and there was a nightstand with a coffee mug on it. No other furniture, rugs, or throw pillows, so basically the typical bachelor pad. I was debating whether to sneak off to the bathroom to deal with my morning breath when he opened his eyes.

His face was sleepy, but his eyes were sharp. His hair was a wild mess and he looked delectable. "Were you staring at me, Leary?" he asked playfully.

*How embarrassing. Stop being a weirdo.* Normally I would die of shame at this moment. However, this was a new day and I was New Cece. I did what I wanted and didn't apologize for it. I knew this wasn't going anywhere, and I knew that it was probably a bad idea to sleep with my boss. But I also knew that what we had was once-in-a-lifetime sexual chemistry. So instead of covering up, I decided to let him know just how much I wanted him. I sat up and let the sheet drop, exposing my bare breasts. I threw him my sauciest look. "I was definitely staring. What are you going to do about it?"

He pounced like a cat, pinning me to the mattress with his strong arms. I inhaled his masculine scent and luxuriated in the feel of his large body on top of mine. "I am going to make you scream, that's what I'm going to do about it." I was not in the habit of just whipping my tits out. But his reaction indicated that maybe I should rethink that strategy. I had never been one of those women who was comfortable naked. I was a grown-ass adult woman and had done a lot of inner work to be secure and confident in my body. But that was still a far cry from strutting-around-naked confident. But it didn't matter. Liam brought out something in me that was positively primal.

I moaned and wiggled under him, feeling his cock harden against my thigh. Who was this brazen hussy and where had she come from? New Cece was a wild sex goddess, and Liam knew just how to bring her out of me. "I knew it," I gasped between his kisses. "I knew you were a boob man."

Liam pulled back and looked down at me seriously. "Nope. I'm not. I'm a Cece man. Your elbows and toenails turn me on, babe." He kissed down my neck while he rubbed his hard cock against my center. "What am I going to do with you?" he groaned in my ear. While lowering his mouth down to my aching nipple, his beard brushed my skin and sent a bolt of lightning straight to my aching core.

He lavished my breasts with attention, licking, sucking, and kneading. I didn't know where this was going or what we were doing. My brain was screaming that we should stop and have an adult conversation about this. But my body didn't care. I needed to take control of this situation before things got completely out of hand again.

I pushed back on his shoulders. "Slow down, tiger. I need some coffee."

"And I was planning on making you some. Until you whipped out these gorgeous tits and now I need to be inside you again." He groaned as he snaked his hand down my stomach and gently stroked my needy slit.

He growled and I clenched. "Oh my God, Cecelia, you are soaked. You want me, don't you?"

He gently probed my slit with his index finger while slowly circling my clit with his thumb. I arched my back under him. "Yes, Liam."

"Is that yes, you want me inside you? Or yes, you want coffee?" He laughed evilly while torturing me with his incredible fingers.

I could feel the need building up inside me, low in my belly. I don't know how I could be so close so fast, but I knew what I needed. "Both, Liam. I need both."

I panted as he slipped a second finger into me. "But I need you to fuck me first," I added.

"As you wish, princess." With that he pushed back on his hips and flipped me over so I was lying on my stomach. He quickly smacked my ass cheek, and I arched my back up for more.

"Look at that beautiful pussy. You need me so badly, don't you?"

"I do."

"Tell me. Beg me."

I heard the tear of a condom wrapper, and I looked over my shoulder. He was kneeling behind me, looking so large and imposing, slowly stroking his massive dick.

It was an out-of-body experience. I had been reduced to nothing but aching need. Gone was my usual self-consciousness, gone was my desire to strategically hide my body parts. Instead, all I could think about was how badly I wanted this man and the orgasms he was definitely going to give me.

I opened my mouth and words came out. I am not even sure if my brain was working correctly. "Yes. Please. Please. I need you."

"Do you need me or my big dick?" He smirked, perfectly in control of this situation, the bastard.

"I need your big dick. Please give it to me."

He draped his large body over mine, pushing my legs open wide. He slowly entered me from behind, while I lay flush against the bed. His body was on top of mine and he breathed into my ear.

I gasped from the intrusion at this angle. "You like that?"

"Yes," I hissed. "I love it."

He started to move gently, slowly. The angle was intense. He was only able to manage short, hard strokes, but my God, I could feel him hitting my G-spot. I arched up to try and meet his thrusts while his body weight held me down.

"I am not going to last long like this, babe. You are gripping me so tight. Reach down and touch yourself for me."

Wait, what? That was not something I did. Well, it was something I did regularly since I was fifteen, but not with a guy. That seemed really...intimate.

But I had to say, it sounded pretty damn good right now. Liam had scrambled my brain and I would give him anything he wanted.

"Okay."

I gently snaked my hand under my body and found my needy clit, I slowly stroked, circling the tight bud.

"Oh my God. You just got tighter."

I moaned. It was too much sensation. Every cell in my body was on fire.

I felt dirty and desired and liberated. I felt my ass jiggle every time he pounded into me, and I didn't care. I liked it. I wanted this fast and dirty sex with this delicious man. I wanted to desire and be desired. I didn't want to live in my head. I wanted to give in to my body for once and enjoy it.

"You got this, girl. Rub yourself. I can feel you squeezing me. Tell me what you need to get there."

"Harder. I want it harder."

He picked up his pace, slamming into me while his strong arms caged me in. Every thrust got me closer and closer. Within seconds I was detonating. Just completely coming apart. The pressure, the intensity, being pinned down—all the sensations were washing over me and I was powerless. I screamed and bucked and flailed as every muscle in my body contracted. I could feel him swell inside me and heard him growl in my ear as he found his release.

I was spent. I should have probably found my clothes and left, but after disposing of the condom, Liam climbed back into bed and pulled up the fluffy comforter. So instead of fleeing, I let him curl his arms around me, and I sank into his body heat. I closed my eyes, inhaled his scent, and allowed myself to drift away on a cloud of orgasmic bliss.

———

I woke to the blaring of my phone. Liam's arms were still curled around me protectively as I disentangled myself and jumped up, searching for my purse. He sat up and I got another eyeful of his exquisite chest.

"Everything okay?"

I finally found my phone on the floor under my bra. "Hello?"

"Where the hell are you, Cecelia?"

*Oh shit. Oh shit.* My mom. I should have texted her last night. My mom rarely got angry. She was pretty zen most of the time. But given what happened with my dad, she was obsessed with our safety. Not calling and telling her I wasn't coming home was a huge offense to Grace Leary.

"Hi, Mom. Don't worry—I'm fine."

"I thought you were dead."

I wasn't even sure how to respond. Sorry didn't seem like enough, but at the same time, I was thirty-one years old.

"Or in jail. Or had been kidnapped."

"Mom, stop. You know I was at the brewery late last night."

"I texted you dozens of times. Could you at least return your mother's texts? Is that too much to ask?" Oh Lord, she was laying on the guilt.

"Mom, I'm sorry I didn't call or text. I was just so tired after the long day."

"Your sister says I'm overreacting and you are a grown woman. But this is not like you, Cecelia. You were always the dependable one who texted."

"Mom, I'm really sorry, okay. I was tired and I crashed."

"Where? Where did you crash?"

"Um…" I wracked my brain about what to say to her.

"Do not even think about lying to me. I called Nora, and I know you aren't at her place."

*Shit fuck shit.*

"Well. We had to stay late cleaning the brewery last night, and there was a lot to do. So I ended up crashing at"—I took a breath—"Liam's."

"Liam Quinn?"

"Yes, Mom. How many Liams do you know?"

Her tone changed. I could practically see the grin on her face over the phone. "Oh, really? This is so interesting."

"No, it's not, Mom. He is my boss and my friend."

"Huh. I mean I certainly thought this was possible, especially the way he looks at you. But, wow, I figured he would be too chicken to make a move. Good for him."

"Mom, stop. It's not like that. I can hear the wheels turning in your head. Don't go there. I just slept here, and I am going to be home soon. I am so sorry for worrying you."

She had clearly gotten over her "dead in a ditch" theory pretty quickly. She sounded like a cat who got the canary. "Well, I have a lot of things to do. I assume you will come home for fresh clothes at some point?"

"Yes, Mom, I live there." This was beyond embarrassing. I'd rather have her yelling at me about being irresponsible than giddy over the prospect of me and Liam. "And what things to do? It's nine o'clock on a Sunday morning. I know you. You are going to hang up with me and then call everyone you know."

She huffed with faux indignation. "I would do no such thing." She was blatantly lying. I knew she was sitting in the sunroom with the cat on her lap, positively vibrating with her need to gossip. She would love nothing else than to call up my second-grade teacher, my softball coach, and the owner of the shoe store to tell them I was boning Liam Quinn.

"So, just out of motherly curiosity, does this mean you and Liam are an item?"

"What does that even mean, Mom? And no. We are not an item. Why aren't you hearing me?"

It was then that I realized I was standing in the middle of Liam's bedroom, stark naked, and yelling at my mother on the phone like a teenager. I looked over to where Liam was leaning in the doorway smirking. He had the good sense to put on a pair of gray sweatpants but was thankfully still shirtless.

I looked at him with exasperation. He strode over to me, all cocky and confident, and plucked the phone out of my hand.

"Hello, Mrs. Leary." I could hear her voice go up an octave on the other end.

He started pacing. "Well, thank you. I appreciate that. It was a big success, in large part due to the work Cecelia did. She really pulled it off, don't you think?"

After a pause, he continued. "Yes. Thanks for the feedback. I will speak to the caterers about adding a vegan schnitzel option next year. That's an excellent suggestion."

He vigorously nodded and continued to pace around the small room. I could see his shoulders tense.

"Yes, Mrs. Leary. I understand. Yes, it was irresponsible. No, it was my fault. I made her stay very late to clean up. Things were a mess, and there was a lot of work to do. Of course I will fairly compensate her for her overtime. No, I am not an unfair boss."

I couldn't make out what she was saying, but she was using her lecture tone of voice. *Good luck, Liam.*

"Please don't report me to the Department of Labor."

"Yes, I understand."

Liam grew more and more exasperated by my mother on the other end of the phone.

"Yes, my intentions are honorable. No, I would never dream of hurting your daughter. She is my most valued employee."

I could see him flush. He was starting to sweat. Served him right. He thought he could handle my mom? Cocky bastard.

He finally hung up and tossed my phone on the bed. He ran his hands through his hair and looked up at me. "Holy shit, she is intense."

"Yup."

"She totally knows about us."

"Yup."

"And she's going to call my mom."

"Yup." I started to laugh. The entire situation was completely ridiculous.

"Well, so much for casual. Now the entire town knows." He shrugged and smiled. "I guess we can go out for coffee and breakfast then." He walked over to his closet and started fumbling around for a shirt.

"Wait. Shouldn't we talk about this?" I began to panic.

"What is there to talk about? I like you, you like me." He went back to his quest for a shirt.

"Yes. But what are we doing? Is this a one-time thing?"

He paused and walked over to me. He ran his hands up and down my arms, and I felt my vulnerability seep out of my pores.

"I respect your decision, but not for me. I got a taste, and now I want all of you, Cecelia."

Jesus, he was making it hard to be calm and cool right now. Especially because I was freaking out while buck naked. We agreed on casual last night. I was good with casual. Casual was my happy place. I couldn't fall into a full-on relationship with Liam Quinn. I had to go back to New York in January. That was my plan. This was just a sexy distraction while I figured my life out. Just because he was gorgeous, kind, and great in bed did not mean I could get attached to him.

He gathered me in his arms, looking all hot and sexy, and laid a sloppy kiss on my mouth. His hands roamed down the sides of my torso and then firmly gripped my ass. I didn't know what to say. I didn't want a relationship. But I would be lying if I said I didn't want to spend more time with Liam, both naked and clothed. In a matter of minutes the entire town would know, so I guess I could get some caffeine in my system and figure it out.

"You need to put some clothes on. Because I need coffee to recover from that phone call."

"Well, you need to let go of my ass cheeks in order for me to put clothes on."

"You drive a hard bargain, Leary."

## 22

LIAM

I FELT INCREDIBLE. WHO KNEW THAT ALL I NEEDED was some great sex with a gorgeous, sarcastic woman to break me out of my funk? Oh right, everyone.

Between the revelation that Cecelia Leary was even sexier than I imagined and the incredible success of Oktoberfest, I was on cloud nine. It was as if, after four years, I could finally breathe. The daily panic that sat on my chest like a weight was finally gone, and I could just be me again.

It also didn't help that she was completely adorable. We had decided to go out and get coffee and some food when she realized all she had was her beer wench costume from Oktoberfest. As much as I would love for her to parade around in it, we decided it wouldn't be the best look at ten on a Sunday morning.

So I gave her some sweats and a Binnacle brewery T-shirt. She had to roll the sweatpants up on her waist, and it was pretty cute. Standing on the street corner in my clothes, her wild curls all over the place and beaming at me, I felt an instantaneous warming in my chest. Like something had burst open inside me.

I realized then I could never go back to the way things were before. I could never go back to being just friends or just coworkers. In less than twenty-four hours, this woman had turned me inside out, and I had never been happier or more confused. Our physical connection was incredible, but I just loved spending time with her. She challenged me on every level and pushed me to be my best. I wanted to talk to her and joke with her, and yes, of course, fuck her senseless every chance I got.

We made our way through town, past the common and the wharf. There were people everywhere, enjoying the fall colors and a few days of unexpected warmth. A boot camp group with a few people I knew ran by and waved.

"Was that Grace Hawkins? I think she was friends with my sister in school."

"Yeah. She is married to Billy Forte. She owns the fitness studio on Water Street now. These outdoor boot camps are super popular."

Her eyes traveled up the street where several senior citizens were lagging behind the main group. "I can see that. I'm glad things haven't changed in Havenport. If people weren't running charity road races and brewing kombucha in their backyards, I'd be concerned."

"Yup. The elderly population continues to put us young guns to shame every chance they get. It also doesn't help that a few of them could drink me under the table."

"I wish I could say I didn't believe you, but I've seen my grandmother and Nonna Riccio put away sambuca."

I grabbed her by the elbow and steered her into High Tide Coffee. An old-fashioned storefront on Main Street, it was already wall to wall with customers needing their morning caffeine fix. As a town in Massachusetts, Havenport was obligated to have at least two Dunkin Donuts, and there was a Starbucks off the highway. They mostly attracted the tourists, while locals came to High

Tide to caffeinate, gossip, and eat Miss Betty's award-winning scones with clotted cream. High Tide was owned by Leah and Dave Bell, a punk couple in their midforties. They were covered with tattoos and piercings, and Leah had purple hair. They moved to Havenport and took over the business from Dave's Aunt Betty, who operated it as a tea house for almost thirty years after emigrating from Surrey. After Betty retired, they convinced her to keep baking scones and include some vegan and gluten-free options, and Havenport turned out every morning to get the first batch.

As a result, High Tide was a dizzying combination of grunge-era Seattle coffee shop meets prim New England seaside bed and breakfast. Industrial style stools and large chalkboard signs warred with cabbage rose print wallpaper and framed watercolors of seabirds. The effect was a little disorienting but also extremely fun. Several generations of Havenport citizens were already lined up for sustenance.

When Dave saw me walk in he shouted, "Liam, the usual?"

"Two," I signaled back.

"You don't have to wait in line?"

"Nope. Dave's a friend. He comes and hangs at the brewery a lot."

She looked impressed, and I stood up a little taller.

"He is a client of Callum's as well. So he is basically family."

We found a small table in the corner and crammed ourselves into the tiny chairs. Dave came over and personally delivered our coffees. "Cheers. Great to see you, Liam."

"I hope you don't mind an Americano."

"No, not at all." She took her first sip and a slow smile spread across her face. "This is so good. Given how little

I've slept in the past two weeks, I probably need about ten of these."

"You can have as many as you want, gorgeous." I take a big sip but I didn't even need it. Staring into the hazel eyes of Cecelia Leary was like a shot of espresso.

"So," she said, looking awkwardly at her coffee cup, "we should probably talk about last night."

"Um…sure. If you want to."

"Well, I do. It was amazing."

I lowered my voice to a whisper, aware the people in this town love to gossip. "Fuck yes, it was amazing. This morning was also pretty great too." I winked and took a sip of my scalding coffee.

She leaned in closer. "So amazing." Her eyes sparkled, and I wanted to throw her over my shoulder and run home for another round. "But—"

"Stop right there," I said, blatantly interrupting her. "I want it to happen again."

She pushed her hair behind her ears. "And so do I. But I am not in a place to start a relationship right now. And I know you aren't either."

I nodded, not sure what to say. On the one hand, she was right, I probably was not in a good place to start a relationship. But on the other, I woke up next to Cecelia this morning and all was right in my world. I would make it work if I had to. I needed to play it cool. "So what do you want to do?"

"Well, I hate the term friends with benefits." She shifted uncomfortably and avoided my eyes.

I tipped her chin up to meet my gaze. "No. Absolutely not. You are my friend, and I think we both enjoy the benefits. But I am not doing that. We have a connection, Cece. You know it, I know it, the entire town knows it." I gesture around to the dozen or so people sitting quietly staring at us.

"Okay, okay. But I can't do anything serious. I am leaving soon, and you have to stay focused on the brewery."

"I understand, but I think we need to at least give this a chance. Also, the town is going to start planning our wedding, and there is no way to avoid that."

She looked around, registering the faces absorbed in our hushed conversation. I swear I saw Burt snapping photos with his phone.

I continued. "So if people ask, we are dating casually and seeing where it goes."

"But it can't go anywhere, Liam."

I wracked my brain to give her some reasons why it could work. But I knew I had to tread carefully with her. "You say that, but let's give ourselves a chance. Let's enjoy this time and have some fun. It's not even October yet."

She seemed comforted by that. "Okay, you're right. I would be honored to casually date you, Liam."

"Back atcha, babe."

We sat in silence for a few minutes, drinking coffee and staring. Our chairs were pushed up against one another in a crowded corner, and my arm rested lightly around her shoulders. I leaned in to catch a whiff of her hair, and she nuzzled into my chest. Sitting with her was just so perfect. When was the last time I felt so giddy and at peace at the same time? I leaned in and kissed her temple. It was an intimate gesture, especially in such a public place, but I couldn't help it. I craved her.

Unfortunately, the peace was short-lived. All of a sudden, a large figure descended on our table. My brother. "What's up, guys? Enjoying your coffee?" Declan grabbed a chair, flipped it around, and straddled it right next to Cece. I could feel my face fall.

"What are you doing here, Declan? I assume you need

coffee. The line is over there." I tightened my grip around Cece's shoulders.

"Callum and I stopped by to see you, actually."

"Really?"

"Yup." I sat in silence contemplating how I could drag his Neanderthal ass out of here without making a scene.

"Mom called us." He smiled. "And she told us that you are dating the lovely Ms. Leary here, so we just wanted to come and confirm with our own eyes."

Just then, Callum walked over looking like he stepped off the cover of a magazine. "Declan, don't scare the poor girl."

He handed him a large cup of coffee. "Here you go, Dec. Black like your soul."

"Ah, just the way I like it."

"So, now that you guys are together…"

I needed to stop this immediately. "Actually guys, Cecelia and I are just casually dating. She is my friend and my employee. Please don't pressure her. In fact, just leave now, and we'll be good."

Callum rolled his eyes at me and turned his attention to Cece, who had been sitting silently. He gave her a big smile, and I was half afraid he would kiss her hand or something stupid like that. "We're here to formally invite you to family dinner next Sunday. Mom insists you join us."

"No," I shouted a little too loudly. "She is not coming to family dinner."

Cece seemed offended. "It's not a big deal, Liam. I can come."

Declan and Callum exchanged evil smiles. "The Captain is so delighted and is going to wax the boat this week to make sure she is shipshape for you."

"Sorry. I'm not following." She looked at me with total confusion, and I knew I was sunk.

"Our family does family dinner on my dad's sailboat. It's family tradition when the weather is nice. We go out on the boat, and my mom packs a picnic and it's a whole thing. You do not have to come."

"That sounds fun." She turned back to Callum. "Please tell your mom I accept."

"Cece, you don't know what you are agreeing to. We will be out on the ocean. There is no escape." My heart was racing and I was panicking. These assholes were going to ruin this for me. I finally met the woman of my dreams, and they were going to ruin it.

She ignored me as I started to sweat. "I would love to come. It's been years since I've been out on the water."

I want to punch those fuckers in the face. This was so typical. They had been ganging up on me my entire life. I finally got one good, amazing thing all to myself and they came here to make me look like a jackass.

Cece was, of course, not fazed at all. She handled everything with good humor. When she excused herself to go to the ladies' room, I decided to lay it down for them.

"You assholes need to get out of here. You are going to scare this nice girl away."

"I think you can do that yourself, dumbass."

"Shut up. You two are dicks, you know that? Let me have this one good thing in my life."

They stared at me, clearly not connecting the dots.

"And she's not coming on the boat. The last thing this poor girl needs is to be in the middle of the ocean with our crazy family. We are not serious. She's not staying."

"You say that, but the way you look at each other indicates otherwise." Callum said.

Declan nodded sagely. "Hey, this way you know if she's for real. If she really likes you."

Callum patted Declan on back. "Yes. And you know

Mom will be nice. She's a Leary. Trust me, she is thrilled that you are dating the daughter of her best friend."

"Casually dating," I remind them.

"Sure thing, bro."

"It's not serious," I insist.

"Then what are you doing?" Declan snapped. And just like that, they turned on me.

"Yeah," Callum piled on, "the Learys are good people. You can't mess around with Cece. Especially after what happened with her dad."

Declan piped in, "Yeah. She is pretty and nice and smart. Don't fuck with her, dude."

"I don't plan to. I like her a lot. We just haven't discussed anything, and she's planning on leaving in a few months."

"Well, find your balls and ask her to stay."

I sighed and shook my head. I couldn't win with these two.

"Obviously you're not me. You don't have my skills. You also don't have Cal's looks. But you're okay, you're a good guy, and your beard is very full."

Callum hit him and took over Declan's misguided pep talk. "She's clearly way out of your league, but she's here with you in public, right? So that's a victory."

I glowered. "You guys need to leave. And for the record, you should not be giving out love advice. Cal, you're divorced."

"But at least someone wanted to marry me."

"And Dec, you can't keep a woman around for more than one night."

"Don't need to. There are always more out there." Declan nodded in the direction of the line, where at least three different women, ages eighteen to eighty, were staring at him with blatant lust. I clearly had to change tactics.

"Please just go home. I promise my intentions are honorable. I like her so much, and I've never felt this way before. Please, please, please, don't fuck this up for me."

They looked at each other and then got up to leave. "Okay, okay, bro. We love you. And you are probably going to fuck it up for yourself. You won't need our help."

"OOH. I'M SO GLAD YOU'RE HERE. I HOPE YOU DON'T
mind I invited Emily. She was in the store yesterday asking
about you, so I told her about our Monday breakfasts."

Nora gestured to Emily who was standing at the
counter. She smiled and waved. "I just dropped my kids
off at camp and I am dying for some adult time." Emily
looked casually beautiful in some kind of expensive
looking sweatpants that may have actually been pajamas, a
T-shirt that said "Wine Mom," and a messy bun on the
top of her head. Regardless, she made slouchy mom chic
work for her.

Since Nora worked crazy hours in her shop, and my
schedule at the brewery tied me up during nights and
weekends, we decided to make Monday morning breakfast
at the diner our weekly catch-up time. Nora's store was
closed on Mondays, as were most businesses in downtown
Havenport, so it was a great time to get our fix of caffeine
and girl talk.

We found a booth and flagged Jackie over. Jackie was a
helmet-haired septuagenarian who took no shit and
suffered no fools. She had owned Wheeler's Newsstand

and Luncheonette with her husband, Joe, since the 1970s, and knew everyone and everything that happened in Havenport.

She arrived wearing a frilly powder-blue apron and clutching a coffee pot. "Hello, girls. I am so happy to see you again. And Emily. You look lovely. When are you going to bring those beautiful kids here to see us?"

"Soon, Jackie. I promise."

"Good. Nora, sweetie. That nice Thompson girl was in here yesterday with her mother. What's her name?"

Jackie turned around and let out an ear-piercing scream. "Joe. Joe!"

"Yeah," Joe answered from the kitchen.

"Joe, what's the name of the Thompson girl who came in yesterday with Marie?"

Joe shouted from the counter. "The one who had the weird mole as a kid?"

"Oh, Jesus." She turned to us. "I swear he's senile."

"No, Joe. The other one, the younger sister."

Joe shrugged. "I don't know." And went back to his paper.

Emily hesitated. "Violet Thompson?"

"Yes, that's the one." Jackie slammed the coffee pot on the table for emphasis, and I was terrified it was going to shatter. It looked like it was manufactured in the early eighties. "Nice girl. Married a bad guy and had a couple of kids. She's divorced and is feeling pretty sorry for herself. I told her to come down to your store and you would get her some new duds to make her feel good."

Nora nodded, sipping her coffee.

"Keep an eye out for her, okay?"

"Of course, Jackie. I will give her the friends and family discount too."

"Attagirl. Your grandma taught you right." Jackie was the lifelong bestie of Nora's grandmother, Nonna Riccio.

They had been knitting, drinking gin, and gossiping together for many decades.

Jackie filled up our coffee mugs and went back to yelling at Joe behind the counter. The place had changed a lot since I was a kid. The newsstand area had shrunk to a corner, understandable with the death of print and all. Gone were the racks and racks of international magazines and newspapers and a whole wall devoted to comic books. Instead they had expanded the luncheonette into a full-fledged diner with tables and booths in addition to the counter.

Back in high school, Nora and I would come in here, read fashion magazines, and eat piles of grilled cheese while gossiping about boys. It has always been our special place where we could just let go and be ourselves. Jackie and Joe had known us since we were born, and I loved them like extra grandparents.

The menu had also changed to reflect the Havenport spirit. The old standbys were still there. But now you could also get avocado toast and tofu scramble with your corned beef hash or tuna melt.

The bells above the door jingled, but I didn't look up from my menu.

"Don't be mad, but I invited your sister."

I popped my head up. "What? Maggie? Nora, you should have told me."

"I'm telling you now. When your mom called me thinking you were dead, I texted her. Given your recent sex fest with the hot brewer, you need all the feminine wisdom you can get."

Maggie strolled in, immaculately dressed in a blue sheath dress without a hair out of place. She warmly greeted Jackie and Joe and waved to some of her patients seated at the counter.

She plopped into the booth beside Emily, in a most un-Maggie-like manner.

She removed her sunglasses, and I could see dark circles under her eyes. "Would you judge me if I ordered a mimosa? I'm not on until one p.m."

We all shook our heads and decided to join her. Monday breakfast was nothing if not a tolerant and open-minded event.

Nora put her menu down. "Now that we're all here, it's time to start talking, Ms. Cecelia. Did you have sex with Liam?"

"Nora, keep your voice down."

"She totally did. Look at her face. Her skin is glowing," Emily said, while stirring ten sugar packets into her coffee.

Maggie was massaging hand sanitizer into her palms. She always had several varieties in her designer purse. "We all knew it would happen. I'm surprised he didn't drag you behind a brewing tank during Oktoberfest." She raised one perfectly manicured eyebrow at me, and I shrank back into my seat.

They were all insane. "What? You guys are exaggerating."

"Did you seriously not notice how that man looks at you? It is incredible." Emily giggled into her coffee.

Nora jumped in, "I would kill for someone to look at me that way."

Maggie looked strangely sad. Since coming home, I had noticed that she seemed off. I had no idea what was going on, but I could see she was hurting, and I wanted to help her. I wanted her to confide in me, trust me to help and support her. But I also knew she would never say anything in front of Nora and Emily.

"Guys," Nora said, "let's focus. Skip the true love bullshit. Let's talk about the fucking. How was his dick?"

"Nora!"

"What? I assume he's packing. But I want all the deets." She took a big swig of mimosa and gave me her best innocent face.

"I'm not sharing anything."

"Come on. Use your hands and just show us."

"No. This is embarrassing. Jackie and Joe can hear you!"

Of course Jackie chose that exact moment to walk up to take our order. Pen poised on her pad, she was completely nonplussed. "Nothing I haven't heard before, sweetie. You get some. You deserve it after the way that bastard ex of yours treated you, what with the dick pics and all."

"How does everyone know my business?"

"Because this is Havenport," everyone chanted together.

We turned our attention to placing orders with Jackie. Maggie ordered a second mimosa, which was extremely strange. Maggie almost never drank, and she certainly never day drank. I needed to get her alone and find out what was going on with her.

Jackie took our menus. "Do you need a coffee warm-up? Of course you do. I'll be back in a jiffy."

Silence descended over the table. I wasn't going to speak first. I prayed Emily would bust out some charming anecdote about her wild kids.

But I should have known better. Nora was like a dog with a bone. "So how was the sex?"

"Don't mind me, girls," Jackie said, pouring coffee.

I sat and stewed in my humiliation for a moment. I loved everyone here, but I forgot how nothing was ever private in this damn town. For the first time in weeks, I missed my anonymous New York life.

"And," Jackie said, still pouring, "it's an important

question, Cecelia. You are all young and beautiful. Don't waste your lives with men who can't deliver in the sack." She had raised her voice and was on the verge of shouting. I looked around and didn't recognize anyone here, thank God.

"I'll drink to that!" Nora said, raising her glass. Emily toasted her and giggled.

"Trust me. Joe might be a moron, but he knows how to treat his lady right in the bedroom, which is why we've been married forty-nine years." We all laughed uncomfortably, but it wasn't surprising. Jackie and Joe screamed at each other for twenty-three hours a day, but everyone in town had a story about how much they secretly loved each other.

After she walked away with the coffee pot, Nora whispered, "My brother Dominic worked here in high school. Said he used to catch Jackie and Joe making out in the back office all the time. Said they would scream at each other and then go at it like teenagers."

Maggie sighed audibly and looked like she was going to burst into tears. I needed to intercept her second mimosa. She was a lightweight and a very dramatic drunk, if memory served.

"Orgasm count?"

"Stop, you are embarrassing me."

"Oh, so it was bad?" Nora took a sip of mimosa and gave me a pitying look. Emily held my hand, as if offering moral support.

"Oh my God, you guys it was amazing, okay? Incredible. He is a sex god and I might be obsessed with him. Are you happy now?"

Nora and Emily held up their hands for high-fives. I reluctantly returned them. Maggie just sat there looking miserable.

"So, like, two then?" Nora pushed.

"Derek's record is three. If you beat that I will pretty much hate you forever," Emily said smugly.

"In one round? Damn, Derek. After three kids he can still throw down? I'm impressed." Nora reached out to offer Emily a high five.

Emily blushed and beamed. If she wasn't such a beautiful, kind person I would punch her.

I needed to end this conversation. "Let's just say that it was a respectable amount and leave it at that."

"You are no fun."

Emily made a pouty face. I hadn't pegged her for a pervy girl like Nora, but hey, people surprise you. "Anyway…so are you guys together now? I thought you weren't staying."

"I'm not. I'm going back to New York in January. We're just having fun. Seeing where things go. He doesn't want anything serious because of the brewery, and I just got out of a long-term relationship."

"So you are friends with benefits?"

"No. I don't think so. I hate that term. We just decided to keep it casual."

"You need to have an RDT—relationship defining talk." Nora nodded sagely.

"First of all, we are not in high school anymore. And second of all, no. I had fun, I am having fun. I have spent years of my life having no fun. So I am not going to stop the fun or change the fun. I just want sexy fun." I sounded like a spoiled toddler, but after years of hard work and disappointment, it was nice to have something special, even if it was just temporary. I certainly wasn't going to jeopardize this. It went against my very nature as a cautious planner, but I loved the idea of just having fun with Liam.

"Sure, sure. Keep telling yourself that." I took a swig of

Maggie's second mimosa to try and distract from this conversation.

Maggie sat quietly stirring her coffee. "I think you're going to marry this guy." She didn't look up, just sat and stared into the mug. I had not expected that from her.

"Maggie, stop. That's not going to happen."

"I think you will. He seems obsessed with you. And he is exactly the type of guy you need."

I stared at her.

"Look at you—starting a new job and totally crushing it. You got up in that German outfit and danced with the brass band. I have never seen you like this. You are so confident and positive and full of life. Liam Quinn is good for you. This job is good for you. And this town is good for you." She finished her monologue and went back to idly stirring her coffee.

Nora looked at me with eyes the size of saucers. "Damn, Mags, you are permanently invited to Monday breakfast."

Maggie laughed. I could tell she was finally enjoying herself a bit. My sister did not loosen up often, but I could see it happening slowly.

I would not have guessed that this combination of women would work, but what did I know? Maggie and Nora knew each other well, but I didn't get the sense they had ever hung out in my absence. I assumed Maggie forgot that Nora shared everything with everyone and generally held nothing back. Emily wasn't batting an eyelash, so there must be a lot going on beneath that sunny preschool teacher exterior. But she was fitting in and having fun.

I was suddenly overcome with gratitude for these pervy, snarky women. I felt a lot less alone knowing they had my back.

# 24

CECELIA

Trent leaned on the bar, gently drying glassware, his large body almost balletic behind the bar. Every movement was deliberate and efficient.

"You are really good at this, you know. "

"Thanks. I've been bartending for a long time."

"How long?"

"Well, I started as soon as I turned twenty-one. Before that I worked as a barback in high school. As soon as I got a work permit at sixteen I went and applied for a job. Then I graduated up to bartending once it was legal. Bartended full time while I went to Tech and then started working here four years ago with Liam and have never really stopped. Pulling pints is a hell of a lot easier than mixing complicated drinks though."

"Well, you clearly know what you're doing."

"Thanks."

"What about you, Cece? Do you know what you're doing?" His ever-present smile faltered a bit.

"Behind a bar? Mostly. I have bartended a bit, mainly in college and in my early twenties."

"No, I mean with Liam."

"I am not sure what you mean." I started to feel defensive. Why was he asking me about Liam?

Trent stopped cleaning the bar and propped himself on his elbows. He stared directly into my eyes, his face serious. "Listen, Liam is my best friend. The Quinns are the closest thing I've ever had to family in my life. I love them all deeply. Liam is a good guy."

"I agree."

"So don't buy his bullshit. He is crazy about you, and I just don't want to see his heart get broken when you leave town."

I wanted to be offended. I wanted to get mad. But Trent, with his good-natured manner and sweet dimpled smile, was just a loyal friend. And I knew he had a hard time growing up and was extra protective of the people he loved. In fact, I admired him for it.

"I appreciate your concern, Trent. But it's not like that. Liam and I are just casually hanging out, and he knows I'm planning to leave. I am helping out here while I figure things out."

"We are grateful for your help. Things have improved significantly since you came in and started making changes. It's hard for him to admit he needs help, but he really respects and values you."

I could tell what he was thinking, so I beat him to the punch. "Because I'm sleeping with him."

He at least had the good sense to look offended. "Jesus, woman, no. It has nothing to do with that. You are smart and dedicated, and we all respect the hard work you're putting into improving this place. I don't know what he's paying you but I guarantee it's probably a fraction of what you're worth. So thank you."

*Put away the knives, Cecelia. He is being kind.*

"You're welcome. What about you, Trent?"

"What about me?"

"What's your plan? I know you are a machinist. What are you doing brewing beer?"

"I went to technical school and got certified, and I use that certification frequently. But I had an opportunity to do something I love and support my best friend, so I learned to brew, and I'd like to think I'm pretty good at it."

"No complaints here. But what else? It's awesome that you are supporting Liam's dream. But what about you? What is your dream?"

He went back to wiping down the bar, probably to avoid answering my question. I sat and waited until he replied. "I'm not sure. It probably sounds crazy to you. But I really want to go to college and finish my degree. When I aged out of foster care, I had very few options. Mr. and Mrs. Quinn kept me on the straight and narrow —helped me graduate high school and get into technical school. I am so lucky compared to most kids like me."

"But you want more."

"Of course I do. Doesn't everyone?"

"Probably. But you could do it."

"I know I could. I take one online class every semester. I am studying business administration. But I would just love to have more time to devote to it. Actually earn my bachelor's, you know?"

"Of course. I get it. What's stopping you? I know Liam would be flexible here."

"I know. I just feel embarrassed. I have a good life, I have a good job, things are fine. I feel greedy asking for more."

Trent was one of the most loyal, hardworking people I'd ever met. "You deserve so much more and you don't even realize it. Portsmouth State is a really good school and only twenty minutes away. I am sure you could apply for January admission if you want."

"I'll think about it." He continued wiping, avoiding my gaze.

"You know, if you need help applying or getting your paperwork together to transfer your credits, let me know."

He looked up and smiled. "Really?"

"Yeah, you know me. I'm a nerd who loves paperwork."

"You're okay, Cecelia Leary."

"Why, thank you," I said, giving him an exaggerated bow.

"Just don't break my best friend's heart and we'll be good."

I smiled at him and nodded, feeling a weight settling into my stomach. What if he was right? What if Liam was getting attached to me when he had insisted he wanted casual?

———

After my unnerving conversation with Trent, I went searching for Liam. For reasons I could not explain, I needed him. I eventually found him in his office with his head in his hands.

I walked over, and he pulled me into his lap and wrapped his strong arms around me.

He nuzzled my neck and asked, "Do you feel like some coffee? I need a fresh cup."

"Sure. I'll grab it for you."

After coming back from the kitchen, I settled onto the couch in his office and waited. Something was clearly bothering him. His back was slumped, and those gorgeous blue eyes lacked their usual sparkle.

"Tell me what's going on."

He looked at me quizzically. "What do you mean?"

"You seem really stressed, and I want to help. Spill it."

I blew on my mug of hot coffee and waited patiently. I
knew Liam enough by now to know he held everything
tight to the vest, but I also knew that it would feel better
to unburden himself. So I settled in and waited.

He seemed to be debating with himself. "I don't want
to bother you."

I shot him a look. "Really? Because you didn't have a
problem bothering me at five a.m."

"Well, yes, my cock was aching for you. It was worth
it, no?"

I gave him a big smile. "Definitely worth it. But I'm
not sure about the shower afterwards."

He jumped up from his chair, sloshing coffee on the
hardwood floor. "What? You were screaming my name for
like five straight minutes while I went down on you with
the shower head."

I laughed. "Calm down. I was just kidding. And you're
right. It was incredible." Actually, his tongue plus the
shower head was a religious experience, but I didn't want
him getting too big of an ego. My two orgasms seemed
like enough of a pat on the back.

"Thank you," he said, puffing up his chest.

"So now that I've got you all worked up, how about
you just tell me what's going on?"

He grabbed a paper towel and began cleaning up the
spill. He was detail-oriented both inside and outside the
bedroom, which was such a turn-on.

After finally sitting down on the opposite side of the
couch, he sighed. "I'm stressed about brewery business.
Things have improved a lot, thanks to you."

"Thank you."

"We are finally getting to a place we can sustain, but
we have a lot more to do before we can really grow and
expand."

"How can I help?" I still didn't know a lot about the

science of brewing, but I had learned a lot about the beer industry and its customer base. We were doing well, and I had big plans for next year lined up already.

"You've done so much. And it's not something you can help with. We are just stuck."

This defeatist attitude was very out of character for him. "I don't believe you. Whatever it is, we can fix it."

"The brewery itself is going amazing. Our numbers are way up, and our events are providing so much income as well as exposure, it's incredible. But on the distribution side of things, it's just so hard."

I let him continue. "The big distribution companies are hard to work with. We are such a small brand that they spend all their time and effort pushing the large national and international brands. It's very hard for craft breweries to get wider distribution for this reason. It's an old-school wholesale model, and these companies and account reps take advantage of the little guys. Lifetime contracts, lots of limiting regulations about selling your own beer, and loss of control."

"Is there any way to get around this?"

"Not that I know of. The other problem is that there is a huge legal gray area. A lot of the big distributions engage in pay to play."

"You mean you have to pay them to sell your product?"

"Yes. In addition to the huge percentage of the sales, we have to pay them kickbacks on top of that just for placing our product, and sometimes even kickbacks to the retail store or bar for stocking the product. When you are small like us, it makes it really hard to compete. A corporate manufacturer can line everyone's pockets to make sure they are fully stocked everywhere. We don't have that luxury."

I was pissed. This was some dishonest bullshit.

Binnacle's product was great. They deserved to be served everywhere.

"We're trying to work within the system. But it's so expensive and not really sustainable. I've met so many brewers who didn't make it because they got screwed over by unethical distribution companies."

"But you can't grow unless you widen distribution."

"Exactly. So we are stuck between a rock and a hard place. Shane is great. He is an awesome sales rep for the brand, but we can only afford him part-time, and his contacts only spread so wide."

He took a sip of his coffee. "It's just not a level playing field."

"Well, have you thought about playing on another field?"

"What do you mean?"

"You can't play with the big brands—I get that. Competing with them for distribution is difficult, especially if the people you pay to distribute your beer don't have your best interests at heart. So create a new field. For yourself and others like you."

I got up and started to pace around. Liam was smart and savvy and had a professional network of other craft brewers. He had the knowledge and the contacts to actually do something about this problem. "Why not build your own distribution company? You know every microbrewery on the eastern seaboard. What if you all got together and did it in a way that benefits small breweries instead of disadvantaging them?"

"I have no idea how to even do that." He didn't seem remotely interested in my idea.

"I bet it's easier than you think. These distributors, I doubt they are business geniuses."

"No, they are not."

"You are smart and you have connections. Doesn't your family business involve distributing perishable goods?

He smiled. "Oh, right. Declan does oversee the distribution of fish all over the Northeast."

"Bingo!" I shouted. "He could help. He knows all about distribution networks."

"I can't ask for his help." His face was firm. For a few seconds, it had seemed like he was into what I was saying and then he just shut down.

"Why not? He's your brother, and judging by how much time he spends here, he loves your beer." I didn't know Declan well, but underneath the gruff exterior was a guy who loved his family. He clearly supported Liam and his business, so I couldn't imagine him not wanting to help in some way.

Liam sipped his coffee. His body language was closed off, and he seemed annoyed with me. "It's a good idea, I'll give you that. But I don't know if I could do it. And I don't have the time or the energy."

"You could give Trent more responsibility at the brewery while you work on this. He is really smart, and I think he wants to do more."

Now he looked really annoyed. "So now you are an expert on Trent?"

"No. It's just he's capable of a lot more than you think he is."

"We have been best friends since we were five. I think I know him."

I started to feel guilty. I had clearly overstepped, and Liam was reacting badly. I just really wanted to help him. I wanted him to see what I saw. I think he could do much more if he opened his mind and accepted more help and outside expertise once in a while.

"Okay, okay. It was just a suggestion."

He got up from the couch and went back to his desk.

"Thanks for your input, but I got this. I'll figure something out. We have enough coming in from the taproom and events to float things while I figure it out."

Was he brushing me off? After everything that had happened between us? Or was he just in a bad mood and I pushed him too hard?

I excused myself and headed home. I had a lot of thinking to do.

# 25

LIAM

FAMILY DINNER WITH THE QUINN FAMILY WAS NOT A normal affair. I had been stressing about this for the past week. I had finally found a cool woman who I wanted to spend time with. Someone who understood me and understood my business. I didn't want to share her. I wanted to spend every spare moment I had with her in my bed, or my shower, or on my sofa. Anyway, the last place on earth I wanted to be was on a goddamn vintage sailboat with my parents and brothers.

Making matters worse, I had acted like a total dick a few days ago, shooting down Cece's admittedly good idea and making her feel shitty. I don't know why I did it. She was just trying to help, and honestly, doing her job.

Her idea was great, but impractical. In my wildest dreams I could never grow a distribution operation. I would have to bring on a lot of help and lessen my ownership and control. I couldn't do that again. I couldn't expose myself to that kind of risk. She also had a point about Declan. He might be a grumpy bastard, but he was a shrewd businessman and knew the ins and outs of this type of business. Beer and fish were not that different.

I loved that she wanted to help. I loved her creativity and enthusiasm. But she didn't know she was picking at an open wound. She poked at my insecurities, and I reacted badly. I didn't want to argue. I wanted to gather her in my arms and kiss her until everything was better.

Fortunately, she wasn't much of a grudge holder and allowed me to do just that. I apologized and begged her forgiveness and she obliged. It helped that I gave her two orgasms first, so she was in a forgiving mood. But things felt weird, off-balance somehow. I knew I liked her, and I wanted to see as much of her as possible, but there were other things going on too. Instead of just enjoying this casual fling, I found myself anxious and unmoored.

An afternoon stuck in the middle of the ocean with my family was certainly not going to help matters.

My mother stood on the dock, wearing an enormous hat and shouting orders at everyone. I picked up a large cooler and carried it on board. "Mom. I really don't think we should force Cecelia to come with us."

"Put that in the stern between the seats. What? Why? We have known her since she was a child, Liam."

"Mom. You know what I mean."

She leveled me with one of her mom looks. "I certainly do not. You are dating. And she is a family friend. Why not take her sailing?"

"Mom, we're not dating. We are casually seeing each other, and she works for me. We didn't go out for a sail with Callum's ex-wife until after they got engaged."

"And look how that turned out!" My mom was still very salty about the divorce. She composed herself. "We will have a lovely day. You really need to relax."

She patted my cheek and smiled at me. "You know, Liam, in my day, when a man wanted to impress a pretty girl, he shaved and put on a collared shirt." She looked down at my jeans, T-shirt, and fleece. "It wouldn't kill you to make an effort." My mom loves to twist the knife.

I ignored my mother and hauled the rest of the gear on board and said a silent prayer that my family would not traumatize Cece. I had texted both my brothers and told them they'd better be on their best behavior or I would cut off their free beer supply. In our family, that was like threatening death or dismemberment, so I felt moderately confident they would at least try to behave.

My mother, on the other hand, was a different story. Annie Quinn was a very tiny, but very terrifying woman. She had to be, raising the three of us. It was because of her we grew up to be marginally productive members of society. She took no shit and gave no fucks. She was bluntly honest and never hesitated to tell us when we were acting like idiots. I loved these things about her, but she had a tendency to be very intense when it came to the girls we brought home.

Turns out I had nothing to worry about. Having grown up in Havenport, Cece was comfortable on the water and completely charmed my parents. She showed up wearing proper footwear and layers and bearing a container of freshly baked chocolate chip cookies. She wasn't wearing any makeup, and her freckles shone in the sunlight. She let the Captain give her a historic tour of the downtown from the water, droning on about significant moments in the Revolutionary War. Most importantly, she gushed over the boat, a Sparkman & Stephens from the 1960s, which the Captain had painstakingly restored over the course of the last decade. This boat was his passion project and the one thing that kept him out of my mom's hair during retirement. He lectured Cece about the type of varnish he used, and she was polite and engaged. I felt bad for subjecting her to this, but she seemed to actually be having a nice time.

She chatted with both my brothers and asked insightful questions about their businesses, complimented my mother on raising such entrepreneurial and hardworking men, and raved about the food my mom brought. She also talked up the brewery, bragging about my beer and management style, while proudly smiling at me. She was relaxed and happy and looked like a beautiful sea goddess, with her wild hair blowing in the wind.

I, on the other hand, spent the entire time in the throes of a minor anxiety attack. My mother kept shooting me meaningful glances, basically trying to telepathically say "Propose to this woman and give me grandbabies." I did my best to ignore her, studying the water and contemplating if I could jump ship and swim to shore.

It helped that the weather was beautiful. Cool and sunny with a strong breeze. We were able to get the sails out and really enjoy the day on the water before motoring back to the dock. We were able to catch a spectacular sunset. I took the opportunity to wrap my arms around her and hold her tight. "Thank you," I whispered into her ear. She turned and smiled at me and my heart soared.

It did not escape my notice that she fit in perfectly with my family. I had never really cared about what my family thought about someone I was dating before. I loved my family, and we were, by most standards, pretty close. But seeing Cece with them, having fun on the boat, made me realize how much I wanted to be with someone who loved my family and enjoyed spending time with them. Her mom was my mom's best friend. Holidays would be a blast. We would never have to fight about where we were going or stress about the rude relatives. Our kids could play with Callum's kids—I sincerely doubted Declan would ever procreate—and go to the same school. I could see a future with her, backyard barbecues, Sunday dinners on the boat, strolling arm in arm at the town festivals.

*Pump the brakes. Why am I thinking about kids? I have never given any thought to kids before. I am clearly having some kind of breakdown.*

Cece was unlocking all kinds of new thoughts and feelings within me. She was forcing me to confront what I wanted and needed, and I was a better man for it. For so long, I believed that I had to put my life on hold for the brewery. But it was becoming more clear every day that I didn't. That I could be focused on my business and make room for someone special.

I needed to tell her everything, get all the truth out. Lay myself bare and make my intentions known. I wanted something real with her. And in order to earn that, I had to be honest with her and myself.

I was ready. Ready to get serious. Ready to take this to the next level. But was I ready to take a chance and tell her I wanted more? And was she even interested?

## 26

LIAM

"WHAT DO YOU MEAN? WHAT HAPPENED WITH THE last brewery?" She settled down next to me on the couch and pulled her knees up to her chest. I knew if this relationship was going to progress I had to tell her what had happened. I wanted her to know everything about me, even the bad stuff.

She had her hands wrapped around a mug of tea and looked too perfect on my couch. I had to fight the urge to ask her to stay here forever. After another busy night at the taproom, I was able to talk Cece into spending the night with me. The thought of going home without her filled me with dread.

"Liam. Please tell me."

Part of me didn't want to share my shame and embarrassment. But at the same time I didn't want to lose her. This wasn't casual, no matter what she said. And I knew I needed to be honest with her if this was ever going to go anywhere. And for the first time, I felt like I had a teammate, a confidante, someone who had my back. And I wanted to share this story, I wanted to unburden myself.

"Well, right after I finished my apprenticeship after

college, I started brewing and networking with other brewers and business types. I met this great guy, Eric, who was an investor, who had built some other breweries and distilleries in New England. We ended up developing a friendship and a partnership." Looking back, Eric was bad news. Early forties, twice divorced, sketchy finances, and a tendency to lie and exaggerate. But I had a dream, and he said all the right things to get me on the hook.

"My girlfriend at the time, Delilah, was really involved with the project. She's an interior designer and helped design the space with Eric and me. It took two years of planning, but we finally opened up just outside of Portsmouth, New Hampshire. It was beautiful. Not super functional, because she didn't care much about the actual brewing of beer. But everything was state-of-the-art and top-of-the-line." Cece sat silently, absorbing every word. I wanted to reach out and take her in my arms and forget all about this embarrassing chapter in my life. "I sunk every penny I had into it. At one point, I sold my car to pay for equipment. This was my entire life."

I took a breath, studying her reaction. "Wow. I had no idea. And Delilah, was it serious?" She asked.

"I don't know. Looking back I don't think so. But at the time I thought it was. And I thought we would get married and build our empire together. She was so supportive and so involved in every detail. Turns out it was because she was cheating on me with Eric." I hated saying this part out loud. Being swindled by an unethical business partner was one thing, but also getting cheated on at the same time? Even thought this was six years ago, it still chafed.

"Oh my God. I am so sorry."

"Thank you. So, as you can imagine, our business relationship soured. We fought and then we ended up going under. The beer was just okay, he had way too much input in the brewing aspect, and our finances were a mess. He held himself out as an expert, but he was an idiot who overspent on our space and all these amenities so we were deep in the red when we opened. We were destined to fail. We ended up having to auction off everything just to pay back the debts. I lost literally everything I had as well as my pride. It took me a long time to even consider brewing again." In some ways Delilah did me a favor. And by fucking my business partner behind my back, she sped that process along.

"I was depressed for a long time. I considered giving up and pursuing a different career. Everything was shit. I had no money, no references, and no plan."

"So what did you do?"

"I wallowed for a while. Declan had just gotten out of the navy and let me live with him for six months while I worked my shit out. And he and Callum basically verbally and physically kicked my ass until I decided to try again." It was a dark time. But I got through it. I made changes. I trusted my instincts and brewed how I wanted to. "I bought this crappy old warehouse and made smart money choices while building it out and buying equipment. And I didn't take on partners or investors. I wanted to do it myself. I *had* to do it myself."

"I'm so sorry. It must have really hurt." She squeezed my hand and I instantly felt better. I had never unburdened myself like this before and it felt good to have this kind, smart woman in my corner.

"You would think, right? But at the time, I was way more upset about the professional betrayal than my girlfriend cheating on me. I realized that I didn't love her because I was devastated to lose my dream but not as devastated to lose her." And that is when I realized that if I was going to try again I could not lose focus. I had to give everything I had to making my dream come true and my personal life would have to wait. "So I wasn't really in love with her."

She sat silently, contemplating what I had shared. I loved that she never felt compelled to fill the silences.

"And I learned a valuable lesson—that personal stuff can't get in the way of my dream."

She sat up and stared at me. "Really? So you don't think you can have a personal life and a successful brewery?"

"I don't know. But I certainly never envisioned someone as beautiful, brilliant, and talented as you showing up at my door." I smirked and grabbed her, pulling her onto my lap. She squirmed around, torturing me with that gloriously round ass for a minute before I hugged her tight and buried my face in her wild hair.

"Fair point, Quinn."

"So what about you? Did you love your dick pic ex?"

She laughed. "Definitely not. I knew I didn't love him." That was interesting. I am glad she didn't, obviously, but I sensed there was more to the story.

"Then why did you stay? Why did you live with him?"

"The crazy thing is that I would have married him if he asked."

"But you didn't love him?"

She got a sad look on her face. I wanted to kiss it off her. "In hindsight, I'm not even sure I liked him."

"Jesus, Cece. No matter what happens between us. Please promise me you will never sell yourself short like that again. Never settle for someone you don't love or even like. Never settle for some shitty soul-sucking job. You are incredible and you deserve incredible things." I wrapped her up in my arms and held her close.

She didn't respond for a few moments. Her eyes were teary, and I hated myself for asking so many questions. "It's just…losing my dad suddenly at thirteen destroyed me. It crushed my whole family. You just never come back from that. And since that day, I always promised myself I would be safe and protect my heart. Because that loss, it lives within me to this day."

I squeezed her tight. I wanted her to know that I was here for her. "And so I always took the safe path. I chose a safe major, got a boring corporate job, dated boring guys who I didn't really like. So if it didn't work out, and it usually didn't, then I wouldn't be crushed. I wouldn't have to live with more loss."

My heart broke for this poor girl who lost her dad and then decided to settle for the rest of her life. I didn't know what to say—nothing I could say would be enough. Instead I just held her.

"I know it sounds dumb. But it's like my heart hasn't matured since I was thirteen and just wants to protect itself." The grief in her voice gutted me. I vaguely remembered when Mr. Leary died. I know my mom made us get dressed up and attend his funeral. But I guess I never connected the dots. That the Leary kids would grow up without a dad.

To be sure, the Captain was a pain in my ass, but he was a damn good father.

I wanted to tell her no one would ever hurt her again. That I would protect her with my life. That with me around, nothing would ever upset her again. That I would vanquish pain, loss, and grief like a knight in shining armor. But I knew that wasn't realistic, nor did she want it. She wanted casual.

"It's not dumb. It makes sense. But that's the thing. You have me now. I will share the burden with you. I will help you carry that loss and I will always have your back." I wrapped her up in my arms, savoring her sweet scent and the way she allowed herself to sink into my chest. I wanted to protect her heart. And I would. If she was willing to give it to me.

A few minutes passed, and she began to relax. I could feel the tension melt off her body as we sat here in silence.

"But my cock is way bigger than his, right?"

She lifted her head off my chest and smiled at me. "Oh yes. Way bigger." She wiggled her hips more, making my erection ache.

"And he never went down on me," she added.

"Wait. What?" I shifted her off my lap so I could look her in the eyes and give my aching cock a moment to breathe.

She nodded.

"That is a crime!"

"He said it tasted weird and it made his neck hurt."

"That bastard. You have the sweetest pussy on earth. I can't believe he made you feel like that. I want to punch that asshole in the throat."

"Stop. I don't care. He was terrible at it anyway. I had to fake it so it wasn't worth the effort." These words scrambled my brain. How could any man have the most beautiful woman on earth in his bed and not die trying to please her? It was inconceivable.

"Okay. We are fixing this right here." I pulled her to the edge of the couch and started to unbutton her jeans.

"What? Here? On the couch?"

"Yup. I obviously have to make up for your previous terrible experiences. I am going to make you come so many times you forget about that asshole. And trust me, my tongue is more than up for the challenge."

## 27

CECELIA

I was still smiling as I walked briskly down Main Street toward High Tide Coffee.

The sun was shining, it was cool with a light breeze, and everything seemed good. I had a job, my family, and a really hot guy who spent all his free time giving me life-changing orgasms.

I reached into my backpack and pulled out my camera. I had taken it to get professionally cleaned at the camera store last week and was happy to find it was still in perfect working condition. I snapped a few photos of my coffee, the harbor, and a huge flock of seagulls perched on the boardwalk. It felt good to have the camera in my hands again—the weight and feel of it, the heightened senses of seeing things through its lens.

I couldn't remember when I stopped taking photos. It was after college, I think. I had just landed my first entry-level corporate job and was bartending on weekends to make my impossible Brooklyn rent. All of a sudden, the architecture, the energy, and the feel of the city didn't excite me anymore. I didn't race home to get my camera after a long day to capture a gorgeous sunset or rain bouncing off the city streets. The camera collected dust, and I ended up packing it up and sending it back to my mom's house along with a bunch of other things I couldn't use in my tiny city life—old clothes, artwork, books, kitchen gear, and impractical shoes.

But for the first time in ten years I felt inspired. I looked around my everyday life and I saw beautiful moments that I was compelled to capture.

Things had certainly turned out differently than I had expected. Havenport wasn't the prison I had envisioned. I had been astounded by the community and the love its citizens had for one another. They had accepted me back immediately and made me feel welcome. The town had come together to support the brewery and, by extension, Liam and me.

I thought I loved New York. I thought I loved the anonymous big city atmosphere and the breakneck pace, but standing in the sunshine while breathing in clean ocean air was pretty freaking great too.

As I sat and sipped my coffee, my mind wandered to last night with Liam. We promised each other we were going to take it slow and then ended up ripping each other's clothes off and fucking on his couch. Then we decided to clean off, and I went down on him under the drizzle of the rainfall showerhead. He made me feel delicious, desired, and totally insatiable. I wanted him all day, every day, in every conceivable position. I wanted to fall asleep with him and wake up next to him every morning. How was I going to survive this? How was I ever going to leave this man? The thought made me sick to my stomach.

I'd spent years lying to myself, and I'd like to think I was pretty good at it. But even I couldn't deny the fact that I was falling in love with Liam Quinn and it was terrifying. My mind, my body, my soul craved him every moment of the day. When I was with him, all my neuroses and anxieties faded into the background and I could just be myself.

And I knew that I was becoming a better version of myself. I was more confident, smarter, and more ambitious. He was making me better. My entire life I had assumed that men would drag me down and that being in a relationship was a sacrifice. I thought I would have to change who I was to make a guy like me and want to keep me around. I thought I had to dim my light to make room for a man. Turns out I was wrong. The right man made my light shine brighter than ever.

But this was a dangerous path. Could I leave him? Could I leave Havenport? I was beginning to feel like I belonged here—with my family, at the brewery, and in Liam's bed. I loved seeing Nora and my family every day. I loved my morning run down by the docks with a stop at High Tide for an Americano on the way back. I loved that I was taking photos again, that I was meditating and reading and spending quality time with the people who were important to me.

Me, the person who had never fit anywhere—the person who had to contort herself to fit—might have finally found her place.

*But I don't want this life. I want to be back in the city, in an office. Kicking ass and taking names in expensive shoes. Don't I?*

I told myself I wanted a corporate career. I wanted to climb the ladder.

I wanted a 401k and stock options and yearly exotic vacations.

I wanted to live in the city and soak up art and culture and museums.

But, if I was being honest with myself, I had lived in New York for almost nine years. And how much did I really do? I worked too much to ever appreciate anything or go anywhere. And the cost of living was so high that in the event I had the time, I certainly didn't have the money to do anything exciting. I didn't have any significant friendships there, I had no time for hobbies, and I felt continually trapped and suffocated by my life.

So maybe it was time to put on my big girl pants and be honest. Did I really belong there? Just because I had built up some unrealistic fantasy in my head didn't mean it was true.

I had no delusions about Havenport.

I had no delusions about Liam.

But I had found a place that accepted me entirely and welcomed my quirks. And instead of having to change or adapt to fit in, I was finally embracing who I really was.

Maybe this was who I really was meant to be. Maybe there was room in this town, and in Liam's heart, for me—flaws and all.

———

"Excuse me, Cecelia?"

I removed my earbuds and saw Leah Bell standing before me in all her early morning punk glory. The fuchsia High Tide apron clashed with her lavender hair and black leather leggings, but somehow she made it work.

"Hi, Leah, how are you?"

"Great. Busy...tired. Our twins just started kindergarten and I have been so stressed about it."

"Well, that's exciting. I didn't know you and Dave had kids. My mom taught kindergarten here for thirty years before she retired."

"Oh yes. I love your mom. She is such a hoot. They actually have Mrs. Foster this year."

"Lucy? She is an old friend of my mom's. Trust me, they are in great hands."

"Thanks for saying that."

She tucked her hands in the pocket of her apron. "So I don't want to bother you. But I wanted to ask you if you would be interested in doing some freelance marketing and branding work for us?"

I almost spit out my coffee.

"Um, me?"

"Dave and I have seen what you've done with the brewery, and you are so talented."

I wasn't sure how to respond.

"We've been doing well here since we opened, but we want to take things to the next level and potentially expand. We want to upgrade our website, logos, social media, the whole thing. Maybe even start a blog or e-book with Aunt Betty's recipes. Obviously, this would just be a few hours of your time, but we would love to pick your brain and get some ideas from a professional."

"Wow, I am so flattered."

"Do you have a business card?"

"Ha…no. But let me give you my cell."

"It would mean so much to us if you would consider it. I know it's small potatoes for you."

"No, no. It's not at all. I love High Tide, and I want you to succeed. I am not planning to stay in town much longer, just till after the holidays, but let me mull it over and get back to you?"

"That would be great. Thanks so much."

Well, that was strange. Strange and super flattering. I was not a marketing guru. As much as I would love to help Leah and Dave, I needed to find a real job at some point. I am not an entrepreneur, and I'm certainly not creative enough to do branding and marketing work for people. The brewery was just a one-off. I was a corporate person, and even if I stayed in the area, I would have to find a corporate job at some point. I couldn't live with my mother forever.

# 28

LIAM

I was running on about four hours of sleep, but I felt more energized than I had in years. That was the power of Cecelia Leary. We had been working nonstop with new events, social media promotions, and themed nights at the taproom. In addition, she had me making long-term plans for next year already. We were totally in sync, both in and out of the bedroom. Our days were spent poring over spreadsheets and analytics, and our nights were spent wrapped around each other in my apartment. She consumed my thoughts and body. I had spent years avoiding this situation because I assumed I would be too distracted to do my job. What an idiot I was. If anything, a beautiful, challenging woman was just what I needed.

"So I can only guess from the shit-eating grin on your face that things are going well with Cecelia?" Callum leaned on the bar, coiffed and pressed to perfection. It was Tuesday night, and my brothers and Trent were here, chatting and drinking. I was in such a good mood I even stopped by the gourmet dog store on the way to work and bought Ginger a grass-fed organic bone. She took it from me without growling, so that felt like a win.

I smiled at him, too happy to even pretend to be annoyed by his intrusive question.

Declan snapped at him, mainly out of habit. "Why are you dressed like that? Are you running for office?"

Callum instinctively snapped back at him, "We can't all be as stylish as you, Dec. Is that ripped hoodie designer? Did you let Ginger use it as a chew toy?"

I laughed—that was a good one. Declan definitely took dressing down to new levels.

Declan rolled his eyes and drank his beer. Trent shot me a look. Watching these two argue was always entertaining.

"Have you thought about our offer to invest yet?" Callum innocently asked.

Oh God, not this again. My brothers had organized and were pressing me to consider taking them on as investors to build and expand the business. I appreciated the offer, but it was truly the last thing I wanted to think about right now. I had a nagging feeling in the back of my brain that I should tell them about Cece's distribution idea —just to see what they thought and if it was even possible. But I shut that feeling down. I had to stay focused on the present and my goals. At some point maybe I would bring it up.

"No, but I will. You guys know I don't want your money. Things have picked up significantly. The expanded hours, the festivals, and even the larger social media presence is helping. Traffic to our website has exploded, and we are selling out of T-shirts. Orders are up and things are humming along. It's only been two months and we are already seeing big improvements." I couldn't help but smile. It was the truth.

"Oh my God, look at him. He's so far gone." Callum smirked.

"It's about time."

"Fabio is right. I never thought I'd see the day where Liam was mooning over a girl," Declan added.

And then they started doing the charming thing they do where they talk like I'm not actually in the room with them.

"I mean you know he's going to fuck it up."

"Of course he's going to fuck it up."

"Guys. He will not." God, Trent was such a good friend. I was so grateful to have him in my corner.

"Don't be a moron, Trent, you know Liam. He is pretty much guaranteed to fuck up a good thing." Declan gestured at me with his beer stein.

Trent shot me an apologetic look.

I had to defend myself. "Guys, I have no intention of screwing this up. I wish you would have a little more faith in me." Of course it made no difference to my brothers. They just kept piling on.

"Poor Cecelia does not deserve whatever Liam is going to do to mess this up."

"I know. And mom will be so mad too."

"Seriously, Liam. Get your head out of your ass. We all know that you are more likely than not to screw this up. I'd stop being so complacent if I were you," Callum mused.

"Good point."

"For God's sake, Mrs. Leary was your kindergarten teacher. She was so kind to you that day you pooped your pants. That woman is a saint." Declan loved to retell that story.

"Jesus, guys. I was five years old and had a stomach bug. Can we please let this story die?"

"Nope, never." You could always count on my brothers

to carefully catalogue every embarrassing moment of my life and continue to bring it up, even twenty-eight years later.

"Guys, it's too early. We are friends, and she is my employee. We hooked up, and she's planning on leaving after the holidays. We have a good thing right now. It's casual." I kept telling myself that. I thought if I repeatedly used the word "casual" then eventually my heart, brain, and dick would get the message. So far, it had not been successful.

My brothers exchanged "can you believe this guy?" looks.

Callum walked behind the bar and helped himself to a refill. "Don't talk like that. That woman is beautiful and smart and the daughter of your mother's best friend. You need to get your shit together."

"Plus she listened to the Captain drone on about his boat. That was awesome. We didn't get one lecture about varnish and viscosity."

"Good point, Dec."

Callum shook his head at me. "Cecelia Leary is rare and special. She is the type of woman you marry. If you don't marry her, I will."

"Or I will," echoed Declan.

"Or I will."

"You too, Trent?" That one stung.

My best friend shrugged at me. "Sorry, dude, I'm with the brothers on this. I don't think you can see how much she has changed this business and changed you. You would be an idiot not to lock that down."

"Trent gets it." Declan clapped him on the shoulder and they clinked glasses.

"I was married and so I know firsthand how hard it is to find an amazing woman. You will never get this lucky again in your life." Callum almost looked regretful. I only knew bits and pieces about what happened with Becca, but I know it wrecked him.

"Get out of my head, guys. I am an adult and I have no intention of screwing it up." I was really not in the mood for getting picked on by my big brothers tonight. I knew they loved me and I knew they meant well but I could not deal with their judgment tonight. I just wanted to work on brewery business and obsess about Cece.

She was in my head. And my dick had taken a liking to her such that he perked up at the sound of her voice— even, inconveniently, during staff meetings.

I was a prideful idiot, but even I could admit she had changed things at the brewery. Hell, I could admit she had changed things for me. I could not imagine this brewery without her, and I could not imagine my life without her. Having a strong, sassy woman to challenge me, support me, and put me in my place when I deserved it was the best gift I'd ever been given. And I didn't want to give her up.

"You say that. But do you have a plan?"

"Yes. You need a plan, since you are obviously in love with her."

"What are you going to do about it?"

I felt like I was being cross-examined. I needed to do something. The thought of losing her made me nauseous and dizzy. I had to tell her how I felt. How I really felt. I was in love with her. I was crazily, madly in love with her and I needed her in order to function. I needed to wake up next to her and work alongside her every day.

"Are you going to tell her? Are you going to ask her to stay and get serious?"

I knew in that moment, looking at the faces of Trent and my brothers, that I had to man up, acknowledge my feelings, and tell her how I felt. "I hate to say this, but you guys are right. I need to talk to her."

"Ok, but don't go in half-cocked. Make a plan."

"I'm working on it. I want to get through Gourd Fest this weekend, then we can talk and figure things out."

Declan was clearly a bit tipsy and feeling emotional. I made a mental note to stop drinking so I could drive him and Ginger home. He stood and we all raised our glasses. "To love and may we stubborn, idiotic Quinn brothers find it someday."

"To love."

# 29

THE 33<sup>RD</sup> ANNUAL HAVENPORT CHARITY GOURD Festival was in full swing. The streets were shut down, and vendor tents and tables lined the cobblestone sidewalks headed down toward the ocean. HavenFire, our local folk band comprised of members of the Havenport, West Haven, and Havenfield fire departments, was tearing up the town square with an acoustic version of the Backstreet Boys' "I Want It That Way," while revelers warmed their hands at strategically placed outdoor heaters to take some of the early November chill off.

People were dancing, eating, drinking, and shopping. It was chilly but not cold, and the sun was just beginning to set. Business was booming at the Binnacle Brewery tent. Liam and I were pouring beers from the taps we had hooked up to the keg refrigerators, and Trent was changing kegs stored in one of the refrigerated trucks. We had Gourd Fest T-shirts with the brewery logo on over our fleece jackets.

As in many things in life, success at any Havenport street festival was all about location. Thankfully I had sweet-talked the clerk at city hall to get us the space next to the Nonna's Kitchen tent. It was one of Nora's family's restaurants, and the line wrapped down the street. Nonna Riccio was famous in Havenport, and there was always a high demand for whatever she was serving. People were naturally coming over to grab a beer while waiting for their meatball and eggplant parmigiana subs. So we were killing it. Despite the day starting off in the high fifties, it had chilled considerably, and I was grateful that my mom had loaned me a pair of gloves. I had been pouring beers, chatting with friends and neighbors, and laughing at ridiculous gourds and hilarious gourd-inspired artwork all day.

The Gourd Festival, or Gourd Fest, as it was known locally, was an annual Havenport tradition. Always held on the first Saturday after Halloween, it started off as an excuse to celebrate the harvest. But that was deemed "too mainstream" by Havenport so instead it became a perverse celebration of ornamental seasonal gourds. The legend goes that one year, Milton Snow's pumpkin crop failed so he submitted an enormous yellow pimpled gourd to the pumpkin competition because he didn't want to end his win streak. He was disqualified, but apparently the idea of Gourd Fest was born. Somewhere along the line it morphed into a charity fundraiser and the legend spread near and far. And then about fifteen years ago the town got serious. There was now an official judging panel, a lengthy screening and entry process, and over a dozen categories including ugliest, largest, most likely to succeed, and best conceptual art piece. There was a separate entry for gourds bearing a resemblance to famous people or town residents. People were still talking about the speckled swan that bore a striking resemblance to Warren Buffet that took top prize last year. The town square was lit up and decorated and featured a large stage where the judging panel was currently reviewing the submissions in the children's category. This year the entire town, plus thousands of tourists, had descended to eat, drink, listen to live music, and feign an interest in some really ugly gourds. Local businesses donated fun prizes, and every year the entry fees and license fees for vendors were donated to a featured local charity. Most Havenport businesses participated in one way or another. It was classic Havenport—welcoming, fun, and more than a little bit bizarre.

It had taken some persuasion, but I had talked Liam into participating this year. It took some time for us to figure out how to set up taps in a tent and maintain a supply of fresh beer, but it was worth it. While several bars and restaurants had tents, as well as one local vineyard, we were the only brewery and so business was excellent. It also helped that Lucas Kim was the honorary MC this year and had tweeted to his hundreds of thousands of followers about the event and even name-checked the brewery. I still couldn't understand why Nora hated the guy so much. He was surprisingly decent for a rich, semi-famous tech genius.

Speaking of Nora, she had stopped by earlier to see us. She had been chosen as a judge this year and took her duties very seriously. She was even wearing a pumpkin-orange coat with a matching hat for the occasion. I forgot to ask her how one objectively judges an ornamental gourd, but knowing Nora, she had probably prepared a spreadsheet of scientific criteria. Most of our friends and family had also stopped by to say hello and grab a beer. Emily and Derek came over with all three of their kids, who went crazy for Karl's root beer. Declan had even volunteered to help break down the tent and pack up later tonight, which was surprising. He was the last person I expected to see at a town festival.

I worked side by side with Liam all day. We were busy

and engaged and having fun. But I couldn't touch him the way I wanted to. And there were so many things I wanted to do. My brain, my heart, and my lady bits were on fire for this man. I could not get enough. I don't know when I turned into such a sex fiend. I'd heard that women reach their sexual peak in their thirties—maybe that had something to do with it. But I had never wanted a man as much as I wanted Liam every waking moment. I needed to feel his bare skin against mine, feel the weight of his body on top of me, feel his glorious cock inside of me, hammering away...

"Cecelia? Cecelia, are you okay, honey?" I violently snapped out of my horny daydream to come face to face with my mom. She was bundled up and wearing a hand-knit scarf. Captain and Mrs. Quinn were standing behind her, and right next to her was Chief Wilson, fully decked out in his police uniform. *That's weird. I didn't know they were friends.*

"Hi, guys. Can I get you all a beer?"

"Ooh yes. Please," the Captain said, studying the taps at our table.

"Off duty tonight, Chief?" I inquired innocently, still confused about his presence.

"Unfortunately no, never off duty during town events. But I'm taking a little break to stroll with some friends." He looked slightly embarrassed and took a big step away from my mother.

If I didn't know better, I would think Chief had a crush on my mom. Obviously not returned by my mom, as she was deeply committed to being single forever. My dad's death did a number on her, and she had sworn off men many years ago. But he was looking at her with such intensity, it was unnerving. I had known Chief Wilson since childhood. He was a good guy, kind and empathetic, but with an air of authority. I know his wife died a few years ago from cancer, but I just never saw him interested in my mom. For a guy in his late fifties, he was tall and fit and handsome. He even had a graying mustache, which looked pretty good on him. He had a real Sam Elliot vibe. It was too bad my mom had no interest in dating. He would actually be good for her. He was quiet and thoughtful and would probably admire her crazy schedule and lifestyle. I don't know how he felt about meditation and quinoa, but I'm sure he'd probably be amenable. I wished my mom could get out of her own way and give him a chance. I almost wanted to warn him he was barking up the wrong tree, but that just seemed cruel.

"Well if you can't drink on duty, Chief, we have house-brewed root beer."

"Oh yes, please. I'll take one. Sounds good."

I poured beers for my mom and the Quinns and signaled Liam to pour the chief a root beer. They were all happily chatting about some of the interesting artwork they had viewed and speculating about who would win the gourd contest.

The Binnacle tent looked pretty darn good. My mom and I had designed a scarecrow made entirely of gourds wearing a Binnacle Brewing T-shirt and holding a stein of beer. As a former kindergarten teacher, she owned several hot-glue guns so I knew she was the woman for the job. We set "Gourdy" up so people could take photos with him and post to social media for a small donation to the featured charity. After much protest, Liam even agreed to let me create the #binnacleoutofmygourd hash tag, and people had been flooding our socials with funny pics all day.

Figuring out the logistics of this type of festival was a blast and would hopefully pay off in the future. Liam agreed the brewery should participate in all town festivals, as it was a great way to sell some beer and market the brewery. I was already brimming with ideas for next year. *You won't be here next year. Someone else will be working with Liam on these events.* It was painful to think about. I had grown so attached to this job and the future of the brewery. Not to mention its hot, bearded owner. *And let's face it, Liam will probably be sleeping with someone else next year too. Probably even getting serious if the brewery is doing well.*

The thought made me throw up in my mouth a little. I had been having such an amazing time, and now I wanted to go home and curl up on my childhood bed and sob. This town that I loved so much, these people that I loved so much, would all be here next year and the year after, having fun and keeping our wacky traditions alive —without me.

Liam bumped my hip. "You okay, gorgeous?"

"Yeah. Just distracted." *Distracted by envisioning my lonely-ass future without you and this town.*

"Well, our shift is almost over. Kyle and Shane are taking over at six. That way we can get some food and have a bit of fun."

I gave him my best brilliant smile, trying to hide the shakiness in my voice. "Sounds awesome. I'm starving."

## 30

AFTER PIZZA, GRASS-FED BURGER KEBABS, AND SOME gluten-free whoopie pies, Cece seemed more like herself. I wanted to get her alone, ravage her, and tell her I was falling for her. Beg her to stay with me—at the brewery and in my bed—and be mine forever.

We walked and chatted about other potential festivals we could participate in. Every minute I spent with her was so much fun. Watching her come out of her shell was such a privilege. She brought an infectious enthusiasm to everything— pizza toppings, nineties rock, or string lights for the patio. I loved what I did and I loved her passion for the brewery. She was making all the hard work worth it.

She was taking her place in this town, in my business, and in my family. All these years there had been a hole and I hadn't even realized it. Having her here made me finally feel whole.

I wasn't quite sure how I was going to broach the subject, but several beers and Declan's emergency whiskey flask were making me feel courageous. Tonight was the night. Every minute since our first kiss, I had been falling more deeply in love with this woman, and I needed to tell her. Better yet, I needed to show her.

I was done with casual dating. No woman would ever compare, and I was not letting her get away. I was done with this idea that she was going to pack up and leave town when she was thriving here. I wanted her to be mine.

I wasn't dumb enough to propose. At least not yet. But we would obviously get married. How could I let her slip away?

For once, my idiot brothers were right. I had to lock her down.

I was going to lay it all out.

We walked slowly back to my apartment, laughing and chatting about the weird gourds we had seen. Everything was more fun when I got to talk to her about it.

I unlocked the door and led her up to my apartment. I had spent the morning cleaning furiously and preparing for this moment.

"Liam, what are we doing here?"

"I just wanted a minute alone with you, and this seemed like a good place for that." I opened the door and let her walk through.

She gasped. "Liam, what is all this?"

In addition to thoroughly cleaning my apartment, I had lit a bunch of flameless candles and set them all over the space. I also had a massive bouquet of roses in a fancy vase on the coffee table for her. The lights were low, and there was soft music playing. I wanted to set the scene for romance, and judging by her reaction, I had succeeded.

"This is incredible."

I took her coat and hung it up. I was struggling. Could I do this? Could I really share my feelings? I was a man—a Quinn for Christ's sake—and we didn't do that. But I had to lay it out for her. I couldn't lose her and then hate myself for not being honest. "I have to tell you something."

She turned and crossed the room, wrapping her arms around my neck and tilting her head up to look at me. Her hazel eyes glowed softly in the candlelight, and her lips glistened. Those wild curls were escaping from her ponytail. She looked so beautiful I couldn't stop myself from kissing her. It was a gentle kiss that began to intensify. I wrapped her in my arms and felt her entire body pushed up against me.

I finally tore myself away from the kiss. *You can do this. Tell her how you feel.*

"Okay. You have my full attention." She gave me a wink and an electric current shot straight through me.

"Today was amazing. Tonight was amazing. You have done so much for me, I don't even know how to thank you."

"Liam, stop. It's literally my job."

"No. You have gone so far beyond. You are so talented and creative. You don't even know how incredible you are."

She rolled her eyes and tried to brush me off.

"No," I said forcefully, grabbing her by the shoulders. "You are fucking amazing. I look at you and I see the most brilliant, beautiful woman I've ever seen, and it scares the shit out of me."

Her eyes flashed and next thing I knew she was kissing me. I lifted her up and she wrapped her legs around my waist. Her kisses were both rough and soft. Every single cell in my body lit up as I carried her over to the large leather sofa. Her hands were in my hair as I kissed a trail down her neck to her collarbones. We quickly shed our winter layers as we scrambled to touch each other and taste each other as much as possible.

Cece was dominant tonight, grabbing at me and

practically ripping through my layers of clothes. She pulled my shirt over my head and slowly unbuckled my belt and unzipped my jeans. She was careful, deliberate, taking care not to touch my straining erection. She was clearly trying to kill me and I loved every second of it. Once I was standing in only my boxer briefs, she removed the rest of her clothes and stood before me, a naked goddess, lit by the glowing candles and the moonlight through the window. I was overwhelmed by her beauty but also her confidence. A confidence that was hard-fought and well-earned. My heart was pounding. "You are so beautiful," I whispered.

She began to kiss and lick my collarbone and chest, like she was trying to memorize every bump and ridge of muscle as she made her way down to the promised land. By the time she got to the waistband of my boxers, I was shaking and growling with need. Slowly she peeled them down and dropped to her knees. I almost fainted from the visual.

She grabbed the base of my cock and slowly lowered her mouth to the crown, pausing before licking the tip gently with the flat of her tongue.

"Holy shit."

She maintained eye contact, her eyes hooded with lust. "I'm just getting started." She slowly lowered her mouth and took all of me.

Cece worked me thoroughly and reverently, alternating between deep and shallow strokes and swirling her tongue in the most incredible way. My vision was blurry, but I looked down and saw her playing with her nipples. The sight of this naked goddess, on her knees with her lips wrapped around my cock while pinching her nipples, was almost too much to take. I almost detonated on the spot. I had to regain control. This night was about her.

I slowly removed myself from her mouth and pulled her to standing before planting a big messy kiss on her swollen lips. "Cece, that was the most incredible thing I have ever experienced. But I need to slow down and take care of you. I need to be inside you."

"I need it too," she whimpered.

I carried her to the bedroom and set out to grab a condom.

"Liam?" she asked demurely. "I want you. I want all of you. I don't want anything between us tonight."

My brain started to short-circuit. I had never had sex without a condom in my life. But there was nothing I wanted more than to feel every single inch of her and give her every single inch of me.

"I'm on birth control. And I'm clean. I was tested after Xavier."

I nodded, incapable of formulating words. "Me too."

She wrapped her arms around me, kissing me deeply and pushing me back onto the bed.

I watched in awe as she positioned herself above me and slowly lowered herself onto my aching cock. The feel of her silky walls against my bare cock almost pushed me over the edge. We were joined, touching the most intimate parts of one another, and I felt overwhelmed, not just by the physical sensations, but by emotional ones as well.

When she finally began to move, gently rocking her divine wetness against me, I had to bite my tongue to keep from screaming out "I love you." My hands caressed her breasts and landed on her hips as our rhythm grew wild. I was thrusting with everything I had, exploring her body and teetering on the edge.

Watching her body on top of mine, watching her chase her pleasure while giving me the most I had ever experienced in my life, was world altering. I held on long enough to watch her come apart, throwing her head back in an epic climax. Her body shook, her inner walls trembled, and her riotous hair cascaded around her like a wild, dirty angel. It triggered my own climax as my body finally released, pouring myself into her, giving her absolutely everything I had.

We collapsed, sweaty and breathless, on the bed. My mind and heart were racing, but one thing was certain. I wanted this woman forever.

# 31

LIAM

In our postcoital bliss, Cece and I wrapped ourselves in my comforter and made our way to my deck. We stood there, my arms wrapped around her, keeping her warm, as we stared out at the choppy ocean. It was a clear night, and we had a gorgeous view of the lighthouse, perched on its rocky peninsula shining its light out to sea. I could have stayed like this forever. She smelled like beer and sugar cookies, and her wild hair blew around my face. She was so warm and soft in my arms, and I wanted this moment to last forever. I wanted her forever.

Just as I was getting up the courage to tell her, I heard a strange vibrating noise coming from inside my apartment.

"What's that?"

It was coming from my jacket, which I had thrown on the floor in my haste to get naked.

I walked over and found my phone.

"That's weird. I have a bunch of missed calls from my brothers. Hold on." I gestured to her as I answered an incoming call and she wrapped herself up tighter.

"Callum, what's up?"

"Where the hell have you been? Why didn't you pick up?" He sounded distraught and out of breath.

"I was walking with Cecelia and didn't have my phone on me. What's going on?" I was beginning to panic. Callum was always calm and cool. Very little rattled him.

"It's Dad. He collapsed at the festival and had to be taken to the hospital by ambulance."

"Holy shit. Is he okay?"

"We don't know. They haven't said anything. Mom said the EMTs stabilized him. They said it was some kind of cardiac event." The words "cardiac event" hung in the air. I felt like I couldn't breathe. I sank onto my couch, willing this to be a dream.

"Are you there? Where's Mom?"

"She went in the ambulance with him. And she's waiting at the hospital alone. Dec and I are driving right now. We'll be there in five minutes. It's hard because most of the streets are closed."

I sat speechless. How did this happen? What could I do to help? I was spinning out of control.

Callum broke my panic spiral. "Get your ass to the hospital."

"Okay, okay. I'm on my way." I started to gather my clothes up off the floor and inventory what I needed.

After a minute of silence, I looked up at Cece. Her face was as white as a sheet and she was shaking. "Is he okay?" she asked, her eyes wide, blinking back tears.

"Callum doesn't know anything yet. I've got to get to the hospital now."

She nodded and wordlessly started getting dressed.

How could this happen? Nothing made sense. My dad had a heart attack? My dad, the naval captain and fishing tycoon? The self-made badass who could still probably beat me in arm wrestling? He's not some old, frail man. My dad was basically a healthy guy. My mom made him eat vegetables, and he spent his life doing a physically demanding job. He was only sixty-one. That was way too young for a heart attack.

Cece handed me my coat, face determined. "I'll drive."

I wasn't going to argue with her. I was in no state to be behind the wheel right now.

She held my hand as we made our way down the stairs. I caught a glimpse of her beautiful face, and just the simple act of her touch grounded me, keeping me calm and levelheaded. "He's getting medical attention. We just need to get you there," she said.

My mind and body were reeling from the whiplash. One of the best nights of my life had morphed into one of the worst. My mom, dad, and two brothers were my world. We were the Quinns, and aside from the woman holding my hand right now, there was no one on earth I loved more. The helplessness and fear consumed me. I was conscious only of her firm grip on my hand as we walked to where my car was parked.

No sooner had we pulled onto Main Street, than we were confronted by the street closures for the festival. The entire downtown area was closed off, and we had to get to the other side of town where the hospital was. I started to panic.

Cece squeezed my hand. "Don't worry about it. I can handle this."

She drove up to the next intersection where a police officer was stationed. She rolled down her window.

The cop peered into the car. It was late and I couldn't make out his face. When he got closer, I let out an audible "oh shit." It was Marcus Flint. There was no way that asshole would help us.

Cecelia turned on a megawatt smile. "Officer Flint. So great to see you," she purred.

"Hello, ma'am, this street is closed for the festival. What can I do for you?"

Cecelia placed her hand on his forearm that rested on the windowsill. I wanted to get out and punch him for even being in close proximity to my woman. I hated this guy.

"Well. Captain Quinn had a heart attack. I've got to get Liam to the hospital as quickly as I can."

Flint gazed at me in the passenger seat. "I'm so sorry to hear that, man." He turned his attention back to Cece. "Say no more. Let me see what I can do."

Then, the most extraordinary thing happened. He grabbed his radio and started talking to the other officers. He came back to the car and leaned in. "Okay. Take the next right onto Spring Street. Officer Mitchum will meet you there in his cruiser. He is going to escort you to the hospital."

"Oh my God, thank you!" Cece gushed.

"No problem, ma'am. Liam, I hope your dad is okay."

"Thank you."

Huh. That was weird. I was too dazed thinking about my father to realize that Marcus Flint actually just did me a favor. I guess it was just another bullet point on my list of crazy today.

# 32

CECELIA

WE GOT TO THE HOSPITAL IN RECORD TIME THANKS to an assist from the Havenport Police Department. Officer Mitchum put his sirens on and led us through town at high speed. I was going to have to bake some thank you muffins and drop them off at the police station this week.

We got to the ER and found Mrs. Quinn slumped in a chair next to Callum while Declan paced around the waiting room like a feral animal.

Liam looked dazed. I squeezed his hand.

"What's happening?"

"They just took him to surgery."

"So it was his heart?"

Mrs. Quinn looked up with tear-filled eyes. "Yes. The doctor didn't say much. Just that they needed to operate before his heart sustained too much damage. Those wonderful EMTs gave him CPR." She could not contain her tears and began to weep. Growing up, Mrs. Quinn was always a very stoic woman. Seeing her like this, so small and frail and scared, broke my heart.

Liam walked over and embraced his mother. Callum put his arm around them and then Declan came in and completed the family hug. It tugged at my heartstrings to see the four of them so scared yet drawing strength from one another.

I vividly remembered what it was like going from a happy family of four one day to being a grieving family of three the next. I sat down, not wanting to call attention to myself. This was the same ER where we sat after my dad's accident. With the same flickering fluorescent lights and the same ripped pleather couches. Where we waited and waited for any crumb of information we could find.

We were sitting down to dinner when we got the call. I was a moody thirteen-year-old going through my goth phase, and I remember painting my fingernails black at the dinner table while my mom made dinner and asked us about our days. My dad had been driving home from work when his car was T-boned at a stop light. The other driver was drunk and unharmed. They were trying to stabilize Dad, but he had lost a lot of blood.

My mother sat on that couch with my head on her lap for almost two days. I was thirteen, but I curled up in mom's lap like a baby. I remember my grandmother coming and trying to take us home, but we refused to leave. We refused to give up hope. Sitting in this room eighteen years later, I could still feel the numbness that consumed my body. Sometimes, I would sleep in a weird position and I would wake up and my arm was numb. Sitting in the waiting room, I remember feeling that numbness throughout my body. I couldn't move, couldn't walk. I could barely get up to go to the bathroom. It was like every cell in my body shut down. Grief shut me down.

When the doctors came out to pull Mom into another

room to tell her he had died, I remember they wanted Maggie and me to stay in the waiting room. But we refused. The three of us got the news together. They told us they did everything they could, including multiple surgeries and blood transfusions. But the internal injuries were too severe. He was gone. And just like that our entire lives changed.

I fought back my own tears. I was drowning in my own grief, and I wanted to leave so badly. I hated this place. It was too hard to sit here. But I couldn't leave Liam. I cared about him too much.

Callum was scrolling on his phone trying to research every potential diagnosis. Declan paced and occasionally growled, shooting him dirty looks. And Liam bustled around fetching cups of coffee, texting family and friends, and locating a phone charger for his mother. Typical Liam —he could not sit still, instead wanting to fix everything and help out as much as he could. Even in times of crisis, Liam just wanted everyone to be safe and comfortable. At this point, I wouldn't be surprised if he picked up a mop and started mopping the floors, just to keep busy.

"Maybe we can request he be airlifted to Boston. I just researched the best heart surgeons and there are a few possibilities."

Mrs. Quinn shushed him. "Don't get ahead of yourself, Callum. Let's see what the doctors have to say."

I sat there awkwardly, watching them all cycle through hope, confusion, and fear.

"Cecelia, come here," Mrs. Quinn gestured, pulling me into a hug. "Thank you for getting Liam here so quickly, and thank you for being here with us."

She pulled me closer and then whispered into my ear, "I know how hard this must be for you."

I nodded into her bony shoulder and tried to keep my

tears from exploding out of my eyes. Liam grabbed my hand and we sat there, hugging, crying, and hoping for good news.

———

After several hours and a dozen cups of shitty coffee, we were finally given an update.

A weary-looking doctor called us into a dingy office at the end of the hall. Mrs. Quinn signaled for everyone to file in quietly, and no one objected.

"Mrs. Quinn." He took a deep breath. "Your husband suffered cardiac arrest due to a massive blockage of the left anterior descending artery. This caused his heart to stop beating normally and go into cardiac arrest. This blockage prevented his heart from receiving oxygen-rich blood, which resulted in damage to his heart tissue."

He paused to let this news sink in.

"The good news is, we were able to remove the blockage in surgery and inserted a stent into the artery."

"That's wonderful!" Mrs. Quinn exclaimed.

"Is he awake yet?"

"Should he be transferred to a cardiac ICU in Boston?"

The doctor tried to contain the rapid-fire questions. "Please let me continue. Although the surgery was successful, we do not yet know how extensive the damage to his heart is. He is still under anesthesia, and we will need to do more tests and perhaps another surgery to determine his future prognosis."

"Because he received prompt medical care, his odds are good. In common parlance this incident is referred to as a 'widow maker' because it is one of the most deadly types of heart attack."

All the faces in the room fell, processing the gravity of what could have happened. "Oh my God." Mrs. Quinn fully broke, descending into tears. Liam held her in his arms as she sobbed and shook.

"How soon can we see my dad?"

"He is in recovery now, and he will be transferred to a room in the cardiac unit in the next hour or so. I will have a nurse escort you up to that waiting room."

Callum reached out to shake the doctor's hand. "Thank you, doctor. Thank you." Declan walked a shaking Mrs. Quinn out the door.

I slipped my arm around Liam's waist and felt him exhale. He held me close and rested his chin on the top of my head. We stood in the hallway, clinging to each other for a few minutes. "Liam, I am so sorry."

He slipped his arms around me and pulled me into a tight hug. He gently kissed the top of my head, and I briefly closed my eyes, feeling the last of my defenses crumble. "Thank you for being here. For me and for my family. It means so much to me."

"There is no place I would rather be." And I meant it. I wanted to be by Liam's side forever. There was no use pretending I hadn't fallen in love with the man. That I was not head over heels for him. I knew in my bones that he was it for me.

And I was fucking terrified. My heart slammed in my chest as the realization spread throughout my body. This man was going to break my heart, and there was no going back. He held me close, so close that I could feel his heart beating beneath his sweatshirt. But my mind was so far away. All the emotions I had bottled up for years were bubbling up inside me, threatening to escape. My mind was reeling, my heart was racing, and I could not keep up.

I had no idea if he felt the same way. I knew he liked me and liked being with me. But he was clear, just as I was, that this was a casual short-term thing. And at the very core, we were friends. And I loved his friendship. And I knew he appreciated mine, especially right now. But that didn't mean he wanted more. I couldn't dump all these wild emotions all over him while his father was in the hospital. I couldn't force him to talk about the future when he didn't even know if his father would live. So I had to do what I'd always done—lock it down and pretend everything was fine.

He straightened up and looked at me. He gave me a weary smile and then took a step back, putting a wide gulf between us. "It's after one a.m. You should go home and sleep. I'm going to stay here for when he wakes up."

And just like that I felt dismissed. I felt sidelined. Of course he doesn't need me here. I stumbled. "Sure. If that's what you want. But I could stay if you need me."

"No. I think we're good now. I'll text you once he wakes up with any updates."

And just like that every insecurity swirled up within me. *Of course he wants me out of here. I'm not family. I'm not anything. I'm just his casual fuck buddy. I need to go home and regain my dignity.*

I adjusted my purse on my shoulder and turned to say goodbye to the Quinns.

"Oh, Cece, one more thing."

"Yes."

"Can you stop by the brewery tomorrow and check that Trent and Kyle cleaned and sanitized all the equipment? And can you email me the latest numbers from Gourd Fest?"

*And just like that I'm an employee again.*

"Okay, will do."

I start to walk down the long corridor toward the parking lot. "And Cece?" he called out, and my heart leapt into my throat. I turned around.

"Thank you for everything."

I wanted to run into his arms and tell him I loved him. Tell him I wanted to stay with him forever. Tell him I would hold his hand through the good times and bad forever and ever. But instead I nodded and walked to my car.

## 33

### CECELIA

I was curled up in my favorite chair in the sunroom—a giant recliner that my mother had reupholstered with mustard yellow and pink floral fabric during her crafting phase. It was objectively hideous but oversized and fluffy like a marshmallow.

I saw the kitchen light flick on, and my mom tiptoed into the room.

"I saw you were still up and thought you could use some tea."

"Thanks, Mom."

She went back into the kitchen, and I could hear the rattle of mugs and her turning on the kettle.

She came back and sat down next to me in a much prettier but far less comfortable armchair.

"What's on your mind, hon?"

"Nothing. It was a stressful night. The Captain's not out of the woods yet."

"I know, sweetie. But I have known Captain Quinn for almost forty years. He is a fighter, and so is Annie. I am going to the hospital in a few hours to sit with her and bring her fresh clothes. I know everything is going to be okay."

I nodded.

"Are you sure you're okay? Is something else bothering you?"

"The last twenty-four hours have just been really overwhelming." That was an understatement. I was drowning in feelings. I was feeling sad and hopeful and confused and excited all at once. The event had been so successful. We were making real progress with the brewery. I was proud of the work I had done. And then there was Liam. My feelings for him were so much bigger than I knew how to handle. I knew I was in love with him, and I was terrified. I had been the one to insist on casual. I had been the one to put on the brakes. What if he didn't love me back? The thought made me sick. I didn't do this. I didn't jump into the deep end without a plan.

"Of course, hon. And I'm sure it has brought up some difficult feelings for you."

"Yes. I miss Dad. And I wish he was here. And I was so scared because I don't want anyone to live with the loss like I do. I would not wish that sadness on anyone. Seeing another family potentially lose someone just really shook me up."

My mom threw her arms around my neck. "Oh, sweetie. I love you so much. And your father did too. It never gets easier, does it?"

"No. It still hurts, Mom."

"I know, sweetie. It hurts me too."

The kettle started to whistle, and she went back to the kitchen and returned with two steaming mugs of Sleepytime tea with big slices of fresh lemon. Just like my grandma used to make when we were upset.

She sat back down and the two of us sat in silence, sipping tea. It was nice to have her here. One of my mom's best qualities was her ability to be quiet. She has this stillness and this peace about her and has for as long as I can remember. My mom seemed to be able to just sit with things and really feel them. I decide to follow her example. I sat and felt sadness over the loss of my father, and I felt fear about my future and Liam, and I felt my insecurities swirling around in my brain. And it wasn't awful. And so we sat, sipping tea and gazing out into the darkness.

Feeling bold, I turned to her. "Mom, why have you never dated? It's been eighteen years since Dad died."

"Because I still love your father. And I took vows, and losing him damn near killed me. That loss is so great, and it was worse because I had to watch the two of you grow up without him. We had been together since high school, sweetie. I didn't know how to live without him. I still don't know if I do. I simply can't open myself back up to that kind of love and the potential for that kind of loss."

"But shouldn't you be brave? Isn't love worth it?"

"It was worth it. It was incredible, and I am so grateful for the time we had. But I will never find that again, and I'm just not brave enough to try." I nodded. For once, my mother was really making sense.

"Not like you. You are brave."

"No, I'm not. And I'm honestly feeling unsure if I'm doing the right thing."

"What do you mean? You love Liam. I can see it on your face."

"I think I do. but I'm just not sure, Mom. And honestly, I'm afraid to stay and find out. Being back in Havenport has opened my eyes to so many things. But I'm not sure I am ready for this." What I couldn't say out loud was that I was not ready to risk my heart. Especially when it was all so sudden, and my life was out there waiting for me to go and find it.

"You have made quite a life for yourself here over the

past three months, sweetie. You have blossomed and tried new things and taken risks. I am so proud of you."

"Thanks, Mom. And I think this experience has given me a lot of confidence about the future." But I wasn't sure whether that future was here.

"You are a smart girl, and you guard your heart. It's probably my fault that you do. But I have confidence in you, Cecelia. You have a big, beautiful heart, you just have to listen to it. You have to trust yourself." She got up from her chair and yawned. "I'm going to hit the hay."

"Okay. Love you, Mom."

"Love you, darling." She leaned over and kissed my head, taking the empty mug from my hands.

I pulled an old afghan around my shoulders. Today had been intense. On many levels. I felt completely mixed-up and turned inside out. Gourd Fest was awesome. I was incredibly proud of what we accomplished. I did that. I planned and executed it, and it went better than expected.

But on the flip side, the event and its success made me think more about what I was doing with my life. I was proud of the work I had done at the brewery. Yes, it was not what I had envisioned for myself, but I was having fun and developing new skills. Hell, Nora wanted to hire me for projects, and Leah at High Tide has inquired as well. I could make a career here. But doing so would mean giving up my city life and my corporate job. And right now, when everything in my life was so uncertain, I wanted to cling more and more to old Cece and her carefully curated existence.

And then there was Liam. We were riding a high of a success at the festival and shared a truly incredible physical connection back at his apartment. We connected so deeply and so viscerally. Our entire relationship had shifted and changed in a few short minutes.

And then we got the call about the Captain.

It was just too much too soon. I needed time to sort through my feelings for Liam and my feelings about Havenport. I needed to figure out my career and where I was going to live. The thought made me hyperventilate.

My feelings for Liam were so intense. I had fallen for him. There was no question. Our friendship had evolved and turned into something explosive and intense and undeniable. I knew he liked me. And being with him was so wonderful. Working with him was a blast. He challenged me and pushed me and made me better and more creative. And he trusted me and helped me learn to trust myself.

But we were both clear from the beginning. The entire point of this arrangement was to avoid heartbreak and hurt feelings. His priority was the brewery, and mine was starting my next chapter. We agreed on casual. The problem was that the feelings I was having were anything but casual.

An incoming text pinged my phone.

Liam: Thanks for tonight. It meant a lot to have you there with me.

Cece: No problem. I am happy to help. How are things going?

Liam: No change yet. He's stable. I'll text you.

Cece: Keep me posted. I'll be thinking about you all.

Liam: I am so lucky to have you. Goodnight.

I wasn't sure how to interpret his messages. He was exhausted and terrified and living a nightmare right now. Hopefully we could talk sometime soon.

I needed to know what he was thinking, and if he maybe loved me too.

I came back to Havenport to find answers. But over the last three months, all I had found were more questions.

## 34

CECELIA

"GRANDMA, GRANDMA, CAN WE SHOW YOU OUR paintings?"

My mom put her dishes down and gathered both kids into her arms. Every time I saw my niece and nephew, they seemed so much older than I remembered. I had seen them last week and Jack already looked taller. Getting to see what interesting little people they had become was a joy and one of the unexpected benefits of being back in Havenport. Ava was eleven going on thirty. She was serious like her mom, almost as tall as me, and a bundle of tween angst. Jack was eight and full of boundless, happy-go-lucky energy.

Unfortunately, the last thing I wanted to do right now was celebrate. But I had to step it up. It was Maggie's birthday and the first time in a decade we had celebrated together. My mom was bursting with excitement and thrilled to have both her kids home to celebrate for a change. Since it was a school night, my mom prepared Maggie's traditional birthday dinner and cake and we drove over to her house.

Birthdays were a big deal in the Leary household. We

always had parties with decorations, games, and lots and lots of cake. My mom hosted so many sleepovers and oversaw so many crafts and games—she really was a marvel. Especially after Dad died, Mom went out of her way to make us feel special. Birthdays were sacred. We could have all the gluten, sugar, and butter we wanted. Mom would cook our favorite meal and top if off with cake and movies. While we were away at college, Mom would send elaborate birthday care packages and balloons. It was just one of the many ways my mom showed her love.

As much as I love family birthdays, I was not in the mood for family festivities. I was just spent. I had an emotional hangover from this weekend. The highs of Gourd Fest and my time with Liam plummeted to the lows of being back in that hospital waiting room. I was not in the right headspace to be in my sister's perfect house with her perfect husband and perfect children. I loved them all to bits. But there was nothing like a visit with Maggie to make all my insecurities flare up. The good news was that the kids were a great distraction. I wouldn't have to talk about anything substantial and I could just talk about BTS with Ava.

Maggie's house was the complete opposite of where we grew up. New construction, neutral color palette, immaculately clean and organized. In fact, it sort of looked like the show unit at the apartment complex where no one actually lived. Except this was a three thousand square foot colonial on a cul-de-sac. And her home was not the only perfect thing about her.

Maggie was a nurse practitioner in town. She practiced family medicine and owned her own clinic with Dr. Peters, who was our family doctor growing up. When Dr. Peters hit her sixties, she hired Maggie to help and eventually made her a partner. Maggie bought into the practice and made a whole bunch of changes including an online patient portal, web-based scheduling, mobile flu clinics, and other updates. Maggie now runs the place, overseeing a dozen nurses, physician assistants, and office staff. She was both a health care provider and a businesswoman. In addition to her successful career, she was a loving, hands-on mom, a frequent volunteer, and ran two marathons every year, one in the spring and one in the fall. She and Josh, her surgeon husband, were still madly in love almost fifteen year after they met in college. I had idolized her since I was born and had never grown out of my inferiority complex.

My mom was busying herself heating up the lasagna and setting the table. The kids were rapid-firing questions at her and running around excitedly. I grabbed the balloons and presents from the car and headed back into the kitchen. Maggie gestured at me with a wine bottle and I nodded. Alcohol would definitely help me get through this night. Despite being the birthday girl, Maggie did not look thrilled about this either. I was a bit worried about her. She seemed off.

My mom was busy assembling the salad. "Maggie, dear, where is Josh?"

"He's working, Mom. He's not going to make it." She said it so breezily, I did a double take. I knew Josh worked a lot—being a surgeon is pretty demanding—but he never missed a Leary birthday. My mom even had special traditions for his birthday. I caught Maggie's eye, and she just smiled at me and took a gulp of wine.

———

I had forgotten how good a cook my mom was. We were stuffed with lasagna, garlic bread, and red velvet cake. My mom took the kids to the basement to watch *Beauty and the Beast*, and left us with the dishes. Maggie topped off my wine and we began to clear, rinse, and load the dishwasher.

"Are you okay, Mags?"

"I'm hanging in."

"I'm always here if you want to talk. Is there something on your mind?"

"Let's finish up and make some coffee."

After we finished the dishes, Maggie sat down gracefully on the immaculate white couch, balancing a fresh cup of coffee. My sister was never without her precious fair trade, organically grown caffeine. Usually you could find her toting it around in a stainless steel travel mug that matched her outfit. Today she was drinking out of a plain white mug. Who buys plain white mugs?

She seemed distracted, so I opened the cabinet to pour myself a cup. Sure enough, the cabinet was filled with perfectly organized plain white mugs. There is nothing that says "World's Greatest Mom" or "Havenport Annual 5k 2012" anywhere. Not that I'm remotely surprised. Maggie would never. Since we were little, Maggie has always been perfect. In every freaking way. She always looks amazing, everything she says is intelligent and thoughtful, and her home is tasteful and sparkling clean. If I were to go in her bathroom, I could guarantee that all the towels in the closet would be the same color. She is successful, beautiful, and generous, and it exhausts me.

We aren't even physically similar. Maggie is taller, thinner, and has deep chestnut waves and piercing blue eyes. I, on the other hand, am shorter, curvier, and inherited my mom's insane curls. She tanned, I burned. She ran, I read. It was a tale as old as time, the shiny amazing big sister and the average, normal, and not super exciting little sister. I made my peace with it a long time ago, and I loved her dearly. But sometimes it made it difficult to relate to her.

"So I need to tell you something."

I steeled myself, my brain swirling with every terrible possibility.

She took a deep breath and exhaled. Her shoulders slumped slightly, betraying her usual military posture.

"Josh and I separated. He moved out two weeks ago."

I was gobsmacked. How could this be possible? Maggie and Josh were the perfect couple. "Are you okay?"

"I'm trying to be."

My mind was spinning. Maggie and Josh were perfect for each other. They were married and parents and have a whole beautiful life together. If my beautiful, perfect sister couldn't make love last, what chance did the rest of us have? "Do you mind me asking what happened?"

"I don't really know what happened. Things have been getting progressively worse for the past few months. If we weren't arguing and fighting we were ignoring each other. I'm just so exhausted all the time, you know? My plate is full with the kids, my career, the house, Mom, and everything else."

I didn't know what to say. She was clearly in so much pain.

"I've known for a while that things were bad and just tried to push forward."

"So he moved out?" I asked.

"Yes, a few weeks ago. Josh came home and announced he is a finalist for a prestigious fellowship in New York. He had never told me he applied or mentioned that he wanted to relocate. We got in a big fight about it."

"Okay. And then what happened?"

"Josh said we'd grown apart and weren't in love anymore. And I agreed. So, a few days later, he packed up and left."

My heart broke for her. "Oh my God. Are you okay? Are the kids okay?"

She hesitated. "We are all...processing. The kids are shocked and a bit confused, but I am keeping them in a stable routine, and hopefully things will normalize soon." She spoke clinically, like a robot.

"What about you, Mags? How are you?"

"I don't know. I am just really confused. Our marriage wasn't great, and we were both so busy all the time that I haven't really noticed that he's gone yet. The kids and I are still trucking along without him. I can't tell if this was the best or worst decision of my life."

"Well, are you still in love with him?"

"I don't know. It's been so long since I felt romantic love that I almost can't remember it. Like, I love my kids, and I love you and Mom, and I love a lot of things. But that special love that Josh and I had a decade ago? It's long gone. And maybe that's okay?" She dabbed at her eyes with a tissue, and I was so confused.

Maggie and Josh had met at Boston College freshman orientation. They were both Pre-Med and hyper-competitive students. They were inseparable best friends while acing every test and nailing every lab report and being all around awesome. Josh didn't get up the courage to ask her out until sophomore year and then they became *that* couple. The beautiful, accomplished couple who were so outrageously in love you wanted to vomit. After graduation they both got accepted to medical school and immediately got married. When I was younger I used to go to bed praying every night I would meet a guy who looked at me the way Josh looked at Maggie. I loved my sister and I loved my brother-in-law, and it broke my heart to think of their family breaking up.

I chose my words carefully, as Maggie's tears flowed

freely. "Okay. So it's gone for now. But could it come back?"

She blew her nose. "I mean, I'd like to say yes, it could. But I don't know. How do you get it back? Is that even realistic?"

"Don't look at me, I have never had a successful relationship. What does he want to do?"

"He wants to be separated and co-parent while we figure things out."

"What do you want to do?"

She paused and thought for a moment. "I think I want to get divorced so I can resume my life without disruption. Because he is right. We can't go back to the way things were for the past few years. Looking at it now, it sucked. We weren't married, we were colleagues who were raising kids and sleeping in the same bed."

I looked at my sister. While still beautiful and more put together than I would ever be, she looked so defeated. As she stared into her coffee cup, I could see how the years had worn on her. She delayed starting medical school when she got unexpectedly pregnant with Ava. She had planned to go back but then ended up enrolling in a two-year nurse practitioner program so that she could support Josh through his grueling residency. She had built an incredible career for herself, but I could see the years of sacrifice in her slumped shoulders and tired eyes.

I held her hand. "Mags, I don't believe you. You don't have to be tough, perfect Maggie for me. You can be honest."

She sighed and looked at me skeptically. I could tell it was a struggle for her to take off the mask of perfection. "I don't want to get divorced. I want my husband back. I want my life and my happy family back. I just don't know where it went. And I can't even pinpoint when it left.

Everything is a weird blur right now. It feels like getting divorced is inevitable at this point."

"Divorce isn't inevitable. Maybe there is a way forward that is better?"

She shot me a strange look. "When did you become such an optimist? A romantic?"

"I'm not. I'm just being your sister, and I can help."

"You already admitted you know nothing about relationships."

"Yes. But what I lack in practical knowledge I make up for in sarcasm and wine. And love for my big sis." I pulled her into a hug. "Maggie, I am a realist. You and Josh are both amazing people who love those two kiddos more than anything on earth. I am your sister and I am on your team no matter what. I love you, and I know the past few years have been weird but I am here now for whatever you need."

She started to sob into my shoulder, and I held her tighter. "I love you."

I started to cry as well. "I love you too."

We sat, crying and hugging for a few minutes. It felt good, cathartic even. Our lives were in disarray, but we had each other, and that made me feel a lot better.

"Seriously," she said, wiping her eyes, "I love having you back in Havenport. And the kids love it too. We were apart for so long."

"I know. I love seeing them grow up."

"Do you enjoy being back?"

"I do, actually. I feel more like myself these days." And it was true. I had spent years being miserable and didn't even realize it. My life was filled with some things I didn't care about and a few things I actively disliked. It was like I had been asleep for the past decade. It took crash landing in Havenport and sleeping in my childhood bedroom to finally wake up. Since being here I had reconnected with my family, friends, and community, found a random but exciting new job, rediscovered yoga, cooked some fabulous meals with my mother, and had actually been chipping away at my reading list. I couldn't remember the last time in my city life I had sat down to read a book.

"I know you are planning to leave, but maybe you could stay?" She looked at me, her tear stained face full of hope.

Her question hit me like an arrow to the heart. The longer I stayed, the more I felt like I belonged here. Like people needed me here. It felt good and comfortable and also scared the shit out of me.

I smiled at her. "I'm working on it, Mags."

I thought this would be weird. I thought it would feel like failure, but it was turning out to be an awakening of sorts. Maybe Nora was right, maybe my next chapter had already started…

## 35

---

### LIAM

THE LAST THREE DAYS HAD FELT LIKE THREE YEARS. I was finally back at the brewery catching up on everything I'd missed. We had camped out at the hospital for two straight days before my mom kicked us all out. I think we were driving her crazy, and she wanted some peace and quiet. The waiting room felt smaller and smaller as each day went by. We chugged bad coffee and doomscrolled on our phones. Callum and Declan bickered endlessly, and I stared at the generic soothing artwork, trying to make sense of everything that had happened.

By the time Tuesday rolled around, the Captain was out of the woods and recovering nicely from his second surgery. The doctors were very optimistic that with medication and some lifestyle changes he would make a full recovery. It was a tremendous relief. But there was still a lot of work to be done. The good news was that my mom was such a hardass, I knew she could whip him into shape. And if she was busy policing my father, she would have less time to obsess over our love lives.

Despite my darkest fears, the brewery was not a disaster. Trent stepped up and had kept everything moving. He'd maintained our brewing schedule and managed the few deliveries we had. Cecelia had worked up the analytics from Gourd Fest and we had done better than expected.

So I should have been happy. My dad was recovering, having dodged a major bullet, and my business was growing stronger every day. Yet I was restless and confused.

I had so many thoughts swirling in my mind. The time spent at the hospital was mind-numbing, but it gave me a chance to think. To reflect on my priorities and my values and wrestle with my own mortality. It was pretty messed up that it took my dad having a major heart attack for me to slow down and actually think things through. I wasn't particularly proud of myself.

I smiled when Cece walked into my office. She rushed over to me and gave me a huge hug. I took a moment to smell her hair and enjoy the feel of her in my arms. It had only been a few days, but my body missed her. "How is the Captain doing?"

I took a step back and sat down at my desk. "Better. He has to do a few months of rehab and vastly change his lifestyle, but he's alive and kicking." I felt bad for my mom, having to put up with him. Getting him to cut the red meat, whiskey, and cigars was not going to be easy.

She perched on my desk and gave me a tentative smile. "Good. I'm really glad he's okay."

"Thank you. And thank you for everything you did at the hospital. Having you there helped a lot. I didn't realize it at the time, but it must have been hard for you."

She avoided my gaze. "It was."

"I'm sorry." I wasn't sure what else to say. I know losing her dad was really traumatic, and it could not have been easy to sit in that waiting room with me.

"Not your fault. I'm just glad the Captain is okay."

She got up and started walking toward the door, like she couldn't wait to get out of this room. She seemed too jumpy, so anxious today. "Do you want to get dinner tonight?" I had to see her, I had to hold her and wake up with her. My entire world was spinning out of control, but I knew the one thing that could ground me would be Cecelia in my arms.

She gave me a tentative smile. "Sure."

She made her way toward the door, pausing as if she was debating whether or not to say anything else.

"Hey, Cece."

"Yeah?"

"Do you miss your dad?"

She held my gaze. "Every day."

———

I decided to take Cece to our favorite Thai place for dinner. Most nights we got takeout and hung out at the brewery, catching up on work, or at my apartment. But this felt different. If I wanted a real future with this girl, I needed to start treating this like a real relationship. It was hardly a fancy place, but they did have a live pianist playing, which was nice.

The restaurant looked out at the harbor, and the lights from the incoming boats reflected beautifully on the water. I was feeling introspective, so I didn't really want to talk. But I wanted to be with her. She sat and listened to the music and sipped her water. She seemed anxious, but given the insanity of the past few days, that was hardly surprising.

But as we sat in awkward silence I couldn't shake the feeling that something was bothering her. She seemed to be a thousand miles away. She fidgeted nervously with the cloth napkin as we waited to place our order. I placed my hand over hers, giving her a gentle squeeze and smiling. "I'm glad you're here."

She smiled weakly. "Me too."

I wanted to talk to her, have her confide in me. I wanted to hear all about whatever was going on and to do my best to make it better. I wanted her to trust me and depend on me. But I also understood that sometimes people needed to be left alone. I hated when people intruded while I was working something out. So I gave her another gentle squeeze and let her go back to wherever she was in her head.

———

After some yummy Thai food and green tea ice cream—her favorite—we headed back to my place. She still seemed out of sorts while we caught up on brewery stuff. The only time she cracked a smile was when she told me funny stories about her niece and nephew. She clearly loved being an aunt. She was so honored that Jack invited her to his soccer game next weekend. It was adorable.

We ended up watching an episode of *Succession* and then falling into bed. She had some stuff here—a toothbrush, pajamas, that kind of thing. I didn't mind. If anything, I wanted her to feel totally comfortable here. Watching her go through her nighttime routine, I was struck by a warm feeling of contentment. It was so domestic, and so nice. We chatted while we brushed our teeth and plugged in our phones. I didn't ever see myself as the domestic type, but having her here just made sense.

I kept trying to open my mouth and have a conversation with her. Tell her how I felt, talk about the future, but I just couldn't. I opened my mouth and nothing would come out. It didn't help that something was clearly wrong. She seemed distracted and anxious. She responded to my questions with one-word answers. Maybe she was getting ready to dump me.

It was only November, but it felt like I was counting down the minutes until she left. Had she mentally left me already? We had our fun and now she was checking out? I decided to take a shower, since I wasn't falling asleep anytime soon.

By the time I got out of the shower, Cecelia had dozed off. I stared at her peaceful face, her thick lashes, those beautiful lips, and the wild mess of hair cascading all over her pillow and mine. I wanted her like this forever. But I was too chickenshit to ask for it.

By the time I fell asleep, I was so distracted that I didn't even realize this was the first time we had slept in the same bed without having sex. I also didn't notice until after she left the next day, she had packed every single possession she'd left here into her backpack.

It was as if she wasn't planning on coming back.

# 36

CECELIA

I WAS BOOKING EVENTS FASTER THAN I COULD TYPE. People wanted to use the brewery for graduations, retirement parties, and even a 1$^{st}$ birthday party. I was busy drafting proposals and emailing caterers. The new year was shaping up to be a busy one at Binnacle.

I was so busy event planning, I was way behind on scheduling my social media posts. As expected, the custom hashtags were blowing up. I had hundreds of photos to upload, edit, and post. It was going to be a long night.

It was hard to believe it had only been three months. I had accomplished so much and had so many more plans for this place. Liam had shared that the finances had improved, so things were really looking good. Week to week, numbers had gone up. We had a lot of weekend traffic and our specialty weeknight activities were also generating some sales. Trivia had been a big hit, but the biggest surprise was Senior Night. Every other Wednesday we hosted Senior Night where the senior citizens of Havenport could join us for discount drafts and themed appetizers. Tonight we were hosting a very popular bingo caller and were expecting big numbers. I had worked with a local bakery to offer bingo ball cake pops and cupcakes, and we had hundreds of bingo markers and colorful balloons. It was embarrassing to admit how excited I was. The old folks were a loyal and reliable customer base. They showed up, had a good time, and didn't get too rowdy. I loved planning events for them. Our Rat Pack themed night last month was a huge success. Burt showed up in a fedora and danced with all the ladies to the rotating soundtrack of Frank Sinatra and Dean Martin songs.

I was uploading photos from Gourd Fest onto the brewery's website when Liam stomped in and slammed the door. He was wearing my favorite jeans, the ones that make his ass look bitable, and a backwards brewery hat. Goddamn, he was fine.

"You're taking Monday off to go to an interview?" It wasn't a question as much as a growl.

"I emailed you the details. I don't think it's that big a deal." I busied myself packing some folders into my tote, making sure to take home the notes of our latest brainstorming meeting.

"What the fuck, Cece?" I jerked my head up and almost dropped my bag on the floor. What was his problem? He was standing with his fists clenched, and his jaw was set. I had never seen him like this.

"I have everything ready for the staff meeting presentation on Monday about plans for the spring festivals. All you have to do is press play on the laptop."

He tossed his hat on his desk and proceeded to run his hands through his thick hair while pacing. If I wasn't the target of his anger, I would have been really turned on right now.

"I don't understand why you are interviewing."

"Because I want to." That wasn't the entire truth. Marissa, who I had worked with for years, had recently started as head of hematology at a huge biotech company in Boston. She was building a team and wanted to see if I was interested. I wasn't particularly excited about the opportunity, but I felt obligated to go out of professional courtesy. "My old boss called me and I like her a lot. It sounds interesting, so I thought I would go. See what's out there."

Liam looked up at me, his blue eyes burning. "But it's in Boston." He said "Boston" like it was a four-letter word. How dare he have an opinion on where I could go and what jobs I could pursue?

I was starting to get really pissed. "Yes. It is less than an hour away. The same city where your brother works. It's not Antarctica, for Chrissake."

"I just can't believe you are going back to that."

"Going back to what? Gainful employment?"

He stared at me blankly, as though he was shocked by my behavior. What had gotten into him?

"I'm not going back to anything. I'm going to an interview to learn more about a potential opportunity. I thought as my friend you would be happy for me."

He crossed his arms and glared at me. So I kept talking.

"I am evaluating my options. I am learning more. This is what I want. And you don't get to tell me what to do. This is the first job in a while that interests me. And I am sure as hell going to go and see if it's a good fit."

"I know you, Cece. You will hate it."

"Maybe I will. But that's for me to decide. You don't know me. You don't know what I want. You don't know what's best for me."

He looked defeated. "You're right. I have no idea what you want." I suddenly got the feeling we weren't talking about this job anymore.

"I came to Havenport to figure my life out, and that's what I'm doing. If you don't want to be a good friend and support me, then get the fuck out of my way." I was pissed. He could not come in here and alpha male all over my career. If I wanted to go to an interview, I would go.

Sensing the intensity of my rage, all the anger drained from his face.

"Cecelia, I am sorry. So sorry. I don't know what came over me. I know we agreed you would work here until the end of the year, and you deserve to pursue any career opportunities you want. If you're excited, then I'm excited."

*What? That was a total one-eighty. What is going on with him? Why won't he talk to me? Maybe I should talk to him? Tell him why I'm really going.*

He paced around, not saying anything. I wanted to slap him and then hug him, preferably in that order.

"It just feels like you are trying to run away."

"Going to a job interview is not running away, Liam."

"You packed up all your stuff—at my apartment the other night—like you were never coming back."

"I live out of a suitcase at my mother's house, Liam. I don't have that much stuff. What does it matter where I keep it?"

"It matters to me."

I threw my hands up. "Why, Liam? This is casual, remember?" I gestured between the two of us. *This is what he wants. He told me he didn't have time for anything serious. He was honest that the brewery comes first.* I was lashing out at him because I was upset. I would love to have an honest conversation and talk about our feelings, but the mixed signals I was getting from him were making my head spin.

"This was never casual for me," he said. The words hung in the air, and I didn't know how to respond. On the one hand he had said the words I'd been needing to hear for weeks. On the other, why couldn't he just grow up and talk to me? "I need to go set up for senior night," he grumbled. And he walked out the door without another word.

I walked over and sat back down at my laptop. What had just happened? Liam and I occasionally argued, but nothing like this. Did he think he could control me? This was a casual relationship. He had never asked for more. He had never indicated that he had anything beyond casual feelings for me. He couldn't walk in here and tell me not to pursue a promising new job.

I had spent the last few weeks wrapping my mind around staying in Havenport and making a life here. I wanted to stick. I wanted to be a part of this community. But getting my heart stomped on by Liam Assface Quinn was making me want to jump in my car and speed off into the sunset.

I knew my feelings were messy right now, but I had not expected Liam's would be messy too. I hated messy. I had to figure out how to clean this up.

## 37

## LIAM

"N 45. I REPEAT, N 45."

"Bingo!" The crowd groaned as Joe from the diner won another round. Apparently he was some kind of bingo genius. His wife Jackie laid a huge kiss on his mouth, and everyone groaned again. I knew I was a fool in love when their constant hot and cold antics seemed sweet instead of weird to me.

Bingo night was shaping up to be one of the most rowdy nights in brewery history. We had drawn a huge crowd. Over one hundred seniors were wall to wall in the taproom, drinking beer and munching on charcuterie boards and bingo-themed sweets Cecelia had ordered. It was wild. People had come from surrounding towns, apparently excited for this type of event. I learned quickly that the elderly took their bingo very seriously.

Mel, the bingo man, or whatever the hell he was called, wore a tuxedo and was an incredible master of ceremonies. He entertained, called numbers, learned people's names, and kept the crowd engaged. We were selling lots of beer and food, and a few months ago I would have never imagined this type of crowd on a Wednesday.

As happy as I was about business, I was still reeling from my argument with Cece. I had acted like such as asshole, and I felt badly about it. But at the same time, I was right. How could she just go out and interview without even telling me? I mean, technically she told me, but before that she hadn't even mentioned she was looking for a job in Boston. I got blindsided and reacted badly.

But as much as I could recognize that I was in the wrong, I was still angry. Why was she keeping stuff from me? We were a team, both inside the brewery and out. It would suck to lose her as an employee, but I'm not going to hold her back. She deserved to do whatever she wanted. I guess I was just hoping she would stay closer to home.

I also had to apologize to her. I knew that. She had been stomping around all night and avoiding me. She was chatting with the guests, making sure everyone got what they needed, and helping with crowd control. These seniors could get unruly. I had expected this to draw a modest crowd and end early. Now it looked like I would be here all night, and the cleanup would be brutal. I shot a look at Cecelia who was laughing with a group of ladies. I was so grateful to her, but why had she packed so many events in? I still had to brew and run this business. I couldn't be here until one a.m. cleaning up from bingo. I was exhausted. We had been hosting a ton of events, and with Thanksgiving next week, we were headed into a packed holiday calendar. Add to that our brewing schedule —I had to actually make the beer after all—and my dad's health issues, and I was completely spent. I was feeling overwhelmed and out of control and I was panicking.

Maybe the best thing would be to cut back on some of the events and get things under control. I was barely managing. I had to keep a lot of balls in the air and couldn't afford to drop anything at the moment. And Cece was eventually going to leave and take another job. Maybe next week or maybe in a few months. But it would happen. Without her here to keep everything running smoothly, we would be screwed. I need to talk to her, get her to understand that the schedule is just too ambitious right now. Get her to slow down, focus, and talk about the future, talk about us. I don't care if she works in Boston, but I need a minute to catch my breath and at least talk to her about it. That's what I need. Just to slow things down.

———

"I don't understand. You want me to cancel the band?" I had the bright idea to grab Cece and have a quick chat in my office during bingo. It was not going well.

"Yes. No. I'm not sure. There is a lot going on right now, and I'm struggling to keep up."

"Well, the rest of the team is ready for this weekend. We'll be fine." She was completely brushing off my concerns.

"But the band is expensive, and I don't want to do the music thing this weekend."

She glared at me, and I took a step back. "Why not? They have a huge social media following and people are really excited about the show. I rented professional sound equipment and we are expecting huge crowds, including people from out of state. Also we signed a fucking contract."

I sighed and cursed myself for even starting this conversation. I was not in the right headspace to have this fight with her right now. And her unwillingness to listen to me was really starting to piss me off. She clearly had not cooled down from our conversation this afternoon.

"I told you it's a bad idea. We are not a music venue.

We are a brewery. I don't want a ton of hipsters buying one beer and sitting at my bar all night listening to shitty music. This isn't what I want for my business."

"Excuse me? The goal has always been to get more people in the door, make them customers, sell them beer, and then send them out into the world to buy your beer at liquor stores and restaurants. I am not following."

Godammit, I forgot how smart and logical she was. "I didn't approve this. You can't go behind my back and just make these plans. I am the CEO. I need to be able to manage everything we do."

"No, you don't. You have employees for that, dumbass. I have worked here three months, and in that time you have trusted me enough to plan and execute many events. How is this different?"

I struggled to give her an adequate answer. Truth was, I didn't know. My head was foggy from exhaustion, and I was mad, sad, and frustrated with the world. I wanted to tell her lots of things, but apparently the only words that could come out of my mouth were shitty ones.

She put her hands on her hips. Damn, she looked sexy when she was mad. "You are just pissed because I told you about the interview."

*No. I'm not mad about that. Was I? Of course not.* I wasn't happy about it. I wanted her to stay here forever, but this was a totally separate thing. This was my brewery. I needed to be kept up to speed and not blindsided by concerts and rental equipment. "No, this isn't about that. This is about you being all up in my business. This is my brewery. I succeed alone and I fail alone. I gave you a chance, and you've done a good job."

She stood there speechless. Logically, I knew I should stop talking, but the word vomit kept flowing. "But there is a reason I don't take on investors or partners. I call the shots."

The words hung in the air between us. I could see her shaking with rage. *What did I do? God, I'm an idiot.*

After a few minutes of tense silence she spoke. "Look around, Liam. You are so fucking lucky, and you don't even realize it. You are surrounded by people who love and support you. People who want to help—who are desperate to help—and you won't let them because you are too stubborn."

I didn't know how to respond. Her voice was eerily calm as she continued. "I don't know why you have this obsession with doing everything yourself. It's not working out for you. Wake up."

"I would wake up if I wasn't so exhausted. I work twenty hours a day, Cece. I can only do so much."

There was a knock on the door. Trent popped his head in, and he looked sweaty and disheveled. "Sorry to interrupt, guys, but the IPA is tapped and I can't leave the bar to change the keg. These old people are relentless. I can barely keep up."

"You okay, Trent?"

"Yeah. It's just busy and some of the ladies are making me uncomfortable."

Cece laughed. "Yup. Give these folks some booze and they start getting inappropriate really fast."

"Mrs. Goldman just told me she was going to 'eat me like a snack'" Mrs. Goldman was in her eighties, widowed, and had been our elementary school crossing guard.

Cece intervened as I laughed. "Don't worry, Trent. I'll be right out. I will make sure no one sexually harasses you."

"Thanks, Cecelia." He ran back to the bar, leaving us at a standoff.

I wanted this conversation to be over. I wanted to take her in my arms and kiss her and forget about the past few days of weirdness and go back to the way things were. The friendship, the banter, the intimacy. What we had was incredible. So why was it slipping away?

"You are totally projecting. You are too chickenshit to admit that trusting me improved your business. We both know sales are up. We both know our engagement on social media is up. This place is filled every single weekend, not to mention the events and festivals. I have this space booked through next summer. We have enough staff to keep things running smoothly, and there is even enough wiggle room to bring on a part-time bartender or two. You just refuse to admit things are going well because you have help."

"Some of that is true, but you don't understand the pressure I am under."

"Then let's sit down with the team, make a plan, and execute it. We can work through any problem if we plan ahead and work as a team. But you don't want that, do you? You are such as asshole. You can't admit that trusting me and giving me the reins to make changes worked. You can't admit that you can't do it on your own. That you need me just like you need Trent, and your brothers, and your parents. It's okay to need people, you ass."

Deep down I knew she was right. Deep down I knew that things had only improved once I'd stopped controlling everything. But I wasn't going to back down from her. This business was all I had. She clearly didn't want me like I wanted her, so I had to cling harder to the one successful thing I had built. "This has nothing to do with needing people. I'm just trying to keep everything together."

"And don't put this on me because you are too scared to embrace all the changes we've implemented or to consider launching your own distribution company. We both know it's a great idea. We both know it would make a huge impact on the industry. But are such a control freak that you can't get out of your own way."

I advanced toward her, my body reacting to her anger. "Don't talk to me like that. I am your boss. And I am the expert here." *Wrong! Wrong! Don't wave a red flag at a raging bull, dumbass.*

"Wow. I guess that's how you really feel." She turned around and grabbed her camera off the table and started shoving it into her backpack. "You are the CEO and you do call the shots. But respectfully, I quit. I don't want to work in a place where I am not trusted or valued."

She grabbed her stuff and started to make her way to the door.

"Cece, stop. We should talk about this."

"There is nothing to talk about. You freak out about my interview, you apparently have opinions about where I keep my toothbrush, and now I'm trying to mess up your business. You are clearly trying to push me away. Congrats, you succeeded. I'm leaving."

"I'm sorry. I am stressed. Let's sit down and talk about this like adults." *I have to stop her. I can't let her walk out the door.* Everything was happening in slow motion and I couldn't move my fucking feet.

"Too late, Liam. Good luck with the seniors."

And she walked out the door. I collapsed on the couch and tried to replay the conversation. How had things gone so wrong? Why had I said those things? Why was she pushing my buttons so hard?

I looked at the ceiling and a realization washed over me. I had pushed Cecelia away. I had been scared and defensive and lashed out. And now she was gone. I had never told her how I really felt. I hadn't told her how amazing she was and how much better she made me.

And now she might never give me that chance.

# 38

CECELIA

THAT BASTARD. WHO DID HE THINK HE WAS?

I thrashed around my room, packing up clothes, books, and camera equipment. Where was I going? I had no idea. But I was overcome with the urge to run away. To leave Havenport and put this entire mess behind me.

Everything hurt. I had done the one thing I promised I would never do. I opened up my heart. I exposed myself, and I got what I deserved. I had spent thirty-one years protecting my heart, and the one time, the *one* time, I let my guard down, Liam Assface Quinn stomps all over it.

I was so busy raging around I didn't even notice my mother standing in the doorway.

"Sweetie, I don't want to push you."

"I know you don't."

"But I do need to know you are okay. And if you're not, that's fine too. But we are going to get you better, I swear."

"Mom, I'm fine."

"No, you're not. You haven't been fine for a long time. It's my fault. You were always my easy kid. You go along to get along and never cause a fuss. Your sister scared the shit out of me with her compulsive perfectionism and her surprise pregnancy. I never had to worry about you. But looking back, I should have paid more attention. I am so truly sorry."

"No, Mom. Please don't say that."

She tried to blink back tears. "Sometimes I worry I failed you kids."

"That's not how I remember it. Not at all. I remember you being totally involved and positive and upbeat. You kept us moving, kept us busy. You sat and did physics with me every night junior year when I almost failed. You showed up to every game, concert, and play even though you were hurting."

"I could have done more. I could have been stronger."

"No, Mom. You did the right thing. You showed us how to be vulnerable and showed us how to push through pain and grow from it. You are a real human being and I am so grateful for that."

We sat on my bed, and she stroked my hair. I loved my mom. Even though my heart was broken, I loved having her here. I loved knowing she had my back no matter what.

After a few minutes of sniffly silence she looked down at me. "Cecelia, I love you completely no matter what. If you want to go back to New York, I support you and will be proud of you. If you want to go to the moon…same. I want what's best for you. And I want you to be confident enough in yourself to figure that out."

"Thanks. I'm trying do that."

"I know, sweetie."

"I just don't want to disappoint you."

"There is nothing you could do to disappoint me. If Liam is not the right guy for you then that's fine. If this new job is not right for you, that's fine too."

I nodded as the tears started to flow again.

"But I don't want you to walk away from something or someone wonderful because you are scared. If you do then I really did fail you. Because I did not empower you to trust yourself and your choices. I didn't create a safe place for you to take risks, fail, and get back up and try again. And that breaks my heart more than you moving away ever could."

I couldn't hold back now. I sobbed and sobbed. Curled around my pillow on my bed, I just let it all out.

"Mom, how did you get so wise?"

She kept rubbing my back. "Pain. baby. Lots and lots of pain. Hey, I have an idea. Let's go bake some cookies. It always helped you feel better when you were little."

I nodded, happy for any distraction.

My mom was a master of misdirection. No sooner had I preheated the oven and creamed the butter and sugar than she restarted her interrogation.

"So do you want to leave Havenport? Is it too small for you?"

"No. I love it here. I love it more than I ever thought I would. It's smaller than New York, obviously, but there is a lot going on here. It's vibrant and busy."

She smiled at me while rummaging around for the vanilla extract.

"I love you and Maggie and Nora and the entire community."

"And you love Liam." God, she was sneaky.

"Of course I love him, Mom. But love isn't enough right now."

She slammed her hand on the butcher block countertop. "What a preposterous thing to say! If love isn't enough, then what is?"

I was kicking myself for saying that. "I don't know, Mom. A plan? Security?"

My mother threw her hands up.

"Mom, you don't get it. He dismissed me and the work I've done. He just brushed me off and didn't listen. That hurt more. Having him not respect my intellect and my hard work? That's where I draw the line."

She nodded sagely. "I hear you Cecelia. And I am with you. But he was surprised and overreacted."

She wasn't wrong. But I was not exactly in an understanding mood. "Yes, I may have pulled away and I should have told him about the interview sooner, but he still hurt me deeply. And it wasn't just the hurt, it was the realization that I was no closer to figuring out my future.

Earlier this year, my life was great on paper, but not so great in reality. When I lost my job, boyfriend, and apartment this summer, I thought my life fell apart. But I am beginning to realize it was just starting to come together. I came to Havenport to get myself back on track. Get focused, get organized, and finally manage to get it together.

But the irony was that coming back here made things messier. I had no interest in the career that I had carefully cultivated over the last decade. I fell in lust and then in love with someone who did not love me back. And now I was back where I started, but with a broken heart.

He didn't ask me to stay. He didn't even ask me to consider it. I wasn't expecting him to ask me to move in or even to keep working at the brewery, but I thought he would want to be with me. I was willing to do anything to make that happen. I had developed real feelings for him. I'd fallen for him and it scared the shit out of me, but I couldn't deny it. I had spent so many years lying to myself, I had to face the truth. He didn't love me like I loved him.

"I know you are hurting, sweetie. But he might be hurting too. Did you consider that?"

"Of course, Mom. But he got so mad about my interview, and I can't understand it. I took the interview so

I could build a life here, a life where I could be with him. I did this for him. I wanted to get settled into my career so that he and I could have a shot long-term."

"Are you sure about that?" Damn my mom and her stupid perceptiveness. "Are you sure you aren't just scared and grasping for security?"

"Of course I'm scared. But right now I have to get my life together. I have to figure out my career and my next steps. This interview is important, and I have to focus on that. I can't be distracted by Liam right now."

"So you're not going to return any of his calls?"

"How do you know he's called me?"

"Because you have your phone on vibrate, and I can hear it buzzing constantly. I know it can't all be Nora. Give him a chance, Cecelia."

I shook my head. I would not be returning any of his calls or texts today. I had to work things out for myself first.

# 39

## CECELIA

My suit was scratchy and my heels were pinching my feet. I hated this. I hated pantyhose. They were the work of the devil. I swear to God, pantyhose are an invention of the patriarchy intended to oppress women. Yes. I am so smart. This is a great idea. I should write a book about this. The feminist war against pantyhose. I got out my phone and started typing in my notes app so I would not forget this brilliant idea.

"Can I get you another?"

"Yes, Fran, you can. Please and thank you."

Fran busied herself behind the bar, clearly stalling on pouring my next drink.

"I appreciate you, Fran. You are a feminist and a badass. And you make good drinks." I love Fran. I love this bar. I wish Christian and Dante could make over my life. It would be like Havenport Queer Eye. They could probably fix my crazy hair and find me a job. And then they would talk to me about my deep-seated problems while gently building up my self-esteem. Ooh. I need to pitch this to them. I'll put it in my notes app too.

Just as I was congratulating myself on my creative

brilliance, I felt a cold burst of air as the door opened. Nora swept in looking enraged and wearing a bright purple wool coat and matching purple knee-high boots.

"Here you are! I have been looking all over for you."

"What are you doing here?"

"Looking for you. Maggie is worried, your mom is worried. What happened today?" She sat on the barstool and shrugged off her coat. "Did the interview go badly?"

Fran finally returned with my refill. "No, it went well." I took a huge gulp and it burned so good.

Nora and Fran exchanged looks. *Weirdos.* "Ok…so if it went well, why are you sitting here drinking whiskey alone in the middle of the afternoon in a powersuit?"

I turned on my barstool to face Nora and accidentally splashed some whiskey on my skirt. "Because I hate everything and I just want whiskey. I like the way it burns my esophagus on the way down like it's mad that I actually drank it. Makes the rest of me hurt less."

"Oh, Jesus." Nora put her purse down and rolled up her sleeves. "Fran, can you get my dumbass friend a water, please?"

"Sure thing, Nora." It was curious, Fran moved a lot faster to get what Nora asked for. I was beginning to feel outnumbered here.

"Cece. You are acting insane. What happened?"

"They offered me the job, on the spot."

"Okay…"

"And I don't want it," I spat out. Just talking about this was making me mad again.

"Okay. Well, there are other jobs."

"I mean, I do want it." I hiccupped loudly and took another gulp of my whiskey. For the expensive stuff, it really tasted like burnt ass.

Nora gently took the glass out of my hand and slid it across the bar to Fran. "Okay. I'm not following."

I decided not to yell at her for taking my drink. "It's a good job. More pay and better benefits than my last gig and a chance to lead my own team."

I took a gulp of the water she handed me. *This isn't whiskey but it also isn't setting my GI tract on fire, so that's a plus.* "But I don't want that life anymore. I walked into the fancy Cambridge high-rise and had a panic attack. I hate fancy office buildings with TVs in the elevators."

I had hated every minute I was in that building. "Everyone was dressed up and walking and talking and clicking away on state-of-the-art laptops. There was constant talk of "saving lives" and "putting patients first". The same generic corporate speak I'd been throwing around for years. I despised it and wanted no part of that world. "I hate the idea of having six bosses again and trying to get anything done in another soul-crushing bureaucracy."

"Sounds like a nightmare." She nodded sagely.

"You get it!" I screamed, sloshing my water over the rim of my glass.

"So are you here drinking and feeling sorry for yourself about the job? Or about Liam?"

"Stupid Liam and his stupid handsome face. I hate him."

"Sure you do." Nora patted my head like a child, and I stuck my tongue out at her.

"He is a controlling jerk who can't admit he needs help. That he needs me. He acted like I did nothing, like I added no value."

"Are you sure? Cece, everyone knows what an incredible job you did at the brewery."

"Right!" I kicked the underside of the bar with my uncomfortable shoe and Fran shot me a dirty look. "Sorry, Fran." I smiled at her weakly. "He's just a big dick control freak who couldn't handle all of my awesomeness. He was scared of my professional brilliance and what an amazing casual dating kind of girlfriend I am."

"Okay. I can't unpack that right now. So what you are saying is he was a dick to you and you're mad?"

"Not just a dick, Nora. A big dick. A big dick who happens to also *have* a big dick. Ugh. There is nothing worse than a big dick with a big dick. Amirite?"

Nora laughed. "We should put that on a bumper sticker."

"Oooh, good plan. I'm going to put that in my notes app."

"So what do you want, Cece?"

I was afraid to tell Nora what I really wanted. *I want Liam. And I want the brewery. And I want to be with him and work together and build something of my own. Something I can be proud of. I want to help other small businesses market themselves and grow. I want to have Monday breakfast with you at the diner and watch my niece and nephew grow up. I want to spend more time with my mom because she is amazing and I've been too self-absorbed to realize it. I want to be happy and loved and challenged every day of my life.*

"I want Liam. And I want to stay in Havenport. And I want to be challenged and have fun and see the people I love every day. But I don't want to want those things. Well, not all of those things, but I don't want to want *some* of those things so I am confused and mad." I took a deep breath and slumped on the bar. "That speech took a lot out of me."

Nora patted my hand. "I'm sure it did, sweetie. You can have all of those things."

"No, I can't. Liam pushed me away. He doesn't want help. He doesn't want a partner." *He rejected me. Not just me as a girlfriend but me as a professional, and that really hurt.*

"I think you may be overthinking this. It was one fight." I hated when Nora was the rational one in this relationship.

"But there's more to it. I don't know if I can love him."

"You already do."

I was shocked. "You don't know that!"

Nora looked at me like I was a toddler throwing a temper tantrum. "Um...news flash, Cece. Everyone knows that you're in love with him. You are being a dumbass."

I stared at her. She was totally wrong.

"Back me up, Fran."

'Yup," Fran deadpanned, "you are a huge dumbass"

"Just admit you love him."

"I can't, Nora. It's not that easy. Imagine how much worse it will be if I love him for years or decades? I don't think my heart can handle that. You of all people should know that, Nora." I gestured to her. Nora was as anti-monogamy as you could get. She was the queen of hit it and quit it. She did not let anyone hurt her. She had to understand what I was going through.

But instead of agreeing with me, she just looked pissed. "Stop it. You know I believe in love. My Nonna and Puppa loved each other for life. It's been eight years, and Nonna still wears black to mourn him. My parents love each other and made a big, messy, amazing life with six kids and two restaurants. I am not anti-love for anyone. I just haven't met the right guy yet." She stared me down and I shrank in my seat a bit. "And the difference is you have. And if you let him get away, you are a dumbass."

*Fuck. Nora is right. I am a dumbass. And apparently the entire town knows this and I have been blissfully unaware of my dumbassery. This day keeps getting better and better.*

"So what do I do?" I needed to get my shit together and I had no idea how.

"Well first, let's get you home and sober. And then

after a long shower and a good meal we can formulate a plan. I am taking you to the diner. I'm going to stuff your face with grilled cheese until you see sense."

I checked my watch. "The diner isn't open. They closed at three."

Nora patted my cheek. "Yes, darling. But Jackie and Joe owe me several favors. I'm texting them now."

After I paid my tab and thanked Fran, Nora dragged me up the street to the diner. The door was locked but Jackie came over and opened it for us.

"You weren't lying," Jackie said to Nora, "she looks like shit."

"I would never lie to you, Jackie. You have known me since birth. We need to get this girl some grub and then yell at her until she sees sense."

Jackie smiled. "Well then, you came to the right place." She turned around and started yelling towards the kitchen. "Joe. Turn the grill back on. We got orders."

After three grilled cheese sandwiches with tomato and bacon—and a pot of coffee—I was feeling more like myself. Nora licked her fingers. "These are so fucking good."

"I know. Reminds me of when we were kids." When Nora and I were in middle school we would save our allowance money and then come to the diner after school. We would sit at the counter and eat grilled cheese and French fries and drink Diet Cokes while reading all the high-end fashion magazines from the newsstand. It felt so good to be back here with her, eating grilled cheese and talking about boys.

I reached out and grabbed her hand across the table. "Thank you for being my best friend."

"You're welcome."

"No, I mean it. Thank you for making me get it

together. Thank you for not letting me wallow in self-pity. You are an incredible friend."

"Oh, I know I am. And you're welcome. So now we need to figure out what you are going to do about Liam."

Jackie came over and sat in our booth with a cup of coffee, and I told them all about our fight and the things we had said. I told them about how I had been pulling back because I had been so afraid of my feelings. They listened and nodded, encouraging me to keep going.

"So you guys are right. I am going to talk to him and be honest. Tell him how I feel. If he doesn't feel the same way, at least I tried." I was feeling really good about this plan. "And I want to stay here. I don't want to go back to New York. I don't want to live in Boston. I want to be here in Havenport."

"Good. It's about time you got your head out of your ass." Jackie saluted me with her coffee mug.

"Thanks, Jackie."

"It's worth it, you know?" She looked at Nora and me. "Take risks. Because getting to spend your life with your soulmate is wonderful. I would know." She looked wistfully at the counter where Joe was reading the newspaper.

Nora and I looked at each other and smiled.

Jackie narrowed her eyes at us. "Now don't ever tell anyone I said that, okay? No one. If you repeat one word of that you will never get an after-hours grilled cheese again. Understood?"

## 40

---

LIAM

IT WAS MONDAY NIGHT, AND APPARENTLY MY brothers were coming to drink at the brewery tonight rather than waiting until our usual Tuesday night. Instead of looking forward to seeing them, I was dreading it. I am sure the news of Cece and I breaking up had already spread all over town, and I didn't want to deal with any of it. I felt like shit. I was shit. I was the biggest piece of shit on the planet.

At least I can be honest with myself about that. At least my dumbass stupid ego can admit when I've really fucked up. That is personal growth, right?

Trent came in and interrupted my inner monologue. "You look terrible, bro."

God, Trent was such a good friend. He was yet another person I didn't deserve. He was being kind too. I looked like shit. I hadn't showered since Thursday and had basically been drinking my face off and sleeping in my office.

I couldn't help that I had no motivation to do anything but wallow. If I went home and slept in my bed I'd be tortured by memories of Cece in that bed with me.

And then I would probably do something stupid like punch a wall and break my hand. This was far smarter and far safer. *I will just sleep here and keep drinking beer until it stops hurting. I feel like I'll probably be fine in, like, two to three years.*

I didn't even get a chance to respond to Trent before two large goons descended on me.

"You are a fucking moron." Declan slammed the bar for emphasis. He was wearing a ripped hoodie and his hair was down past his chin.

"Mom is going to disown you." Callum, although dressed in a suit and carrying an expensive leather messenger bag, was just as pissed as Declan.

I snapped back at them. I was not in the mood for my big brothers to gang up on me. "I was never her favorite son anyway. So it's not like I can fall further."

Callum rolled his eyes at me. "Yeah. But you were a solid number two. She can barely tolerate Declan."

Declan shoved Callum. "Hey, I'm standing right here. And Mom made me pumpkin bread last week, so shut the fuck up."

Both Callum's and my head snapped around to stare at him. My mother was an incredible baker but rarely felt motivated to utilize her talents. She only gave us baked goods when she was really happy with us for some reason. "Wait, what? She made you pumpkin bread?"

Declan smiled. "Yup, with chocolate chips, assholes."

"Shit. I didn't get any."

"Maybe she doesn't love you anymore, Cal," I offered.

"Yup. It's cause you are losing your looks." Declan always went for the jugular.

Callum looked like he was going to throw up. "Shut up, assholes."

"She made me pumpkin bread too." All three of us

turned to look at Trent, who was loading glassware onto the shelves behind the bar.

"What?"

"Yup. I went to visit her and see how the Captain was doing and ended up changing the bulbs in the recessed lights. She made me tea and we chatted."

Callum threw his hands up. "So Trent is a better son than we are. Fucking great."

That was probably an accurate statement. I wasn't sure anyone loved my mom like Trent did. I had no problem sharing her. But special pumpkin bread was another matter entirely.

I could tell Trent regretted telling us that information. "Guys. We need to refocus. Your brother is a moron who screwed up the best thing in his life and is now suffering. We need to help him."

"Well, he deserves to suffer for being such a dumbass," Callum lobbed in.

Declan nodded and looked at me. "We told you to marry her."

Jesus, would they ever get off my case? "And I was going to, asshole!"

I took a deep breath and ran my hands through my, admittedly, very dirty hair. "But then Dad had a heart attack and she got scared, and I got scared. And she got a job interview and I just freaked out. I blew up at her and fucked things up so badly she will probably never speak to me again."

At least they were listening. Declan walked behind the bar and started quietly pouring beers. I'm glad he understood the gravity of the situation.

Once all four of us had a full beer, we were ready to focus. Callum tried to be kind. "It can't be that bad."

"Oh, it's that bad," I said, taking another sip of beer.

"How can we fix it?" Declan was a fixer, but this wasn't the engine of a boat or an end table.

"We can't."

"We're Quinns. Of course we can fix it."

Callum put his arm around my shoulders. "The Captain has fucked up so many times. We could ask him how he gets Mom to forgive him."

"I don't know if I want to know the answer to that."

He shuddered. "Probably not."

I looked at the three of them, so clueless about women. "Guys. This is not a flowers and chocolates type of situation. She is literally going to leave town, get another fancy corporate job, and probably marry some boring-ass lawyer."

They stared at me blankly. "And not only have I lost the love of my life, I've lost an incredible partner who made my business better. Hell, she made me better."

"She definitely did. She made you way more tolerable."

"Agreed. Just her presence made you seem less like a dumbass."

Trent looked annoyed. "Stay focused." He was such a good friend.

My brothers exchanged a look before Callum turned his attention back to me. "So do you want us to yell at you? Or do you just want us to sit with you while you get drunk and be sad?"

"I don't know."

"Cause we are sure as shit not talking about your feelings." Declan finished his beer.

"Nope. No fucking way," Callum chimed in.

I smiled. "You guys are the worst."

"It's interesting that she's single now..."

"Stop it, Callum!" I snapped at him. It was too soon for him to joke about stealing my girl.

"No, seriously, Mom is so hung up on her one of us should marry her. She is beautiful."

"And smart."

"And really fun to hang out with."

"And she puts up with Liam's shit so any one of us would be a walk in the park by comparison."

"Agreed!" All three of them clinked their glasses and I saw red.

"I hate you all right now."

Declan mussed my hair. "We love you too, little brother."

"Actually, while I have you all here, there is something else I need to talk to you about. I've been thinking about the future of this business and I have an idea."

———

Several beers and a couple of pizzas into this boys' night, we were ready to make a plan.

"So how do I fix this?"

Everyone was quiet for a few moments.

"Don't you think maybe you should just speak to her?"

"Jesus, Trent, no. He's got to make a grand gesture." Callum was insistent.

Trent was dubious. "But I know Cece, and she probably just wants him to be honest and open with his feelings."

Declan rolled his eyes. "Who brought this guy? You have to sweep her off her feet."

Trent ignored him and continued, "Liam, you and I have been friends since kindergarten. I have been by your side for every girl you have ever dated or even crushed on. We both know that Cece is different and that she is the one for you. I believe in you and I believe in her, and I believe that together you can build something beautiful together."

Declan was impressed. "That is really fucking poetic."

"I agree with Trent," Callum mused. "But first, you have to get your head out of your ass and deal with whatever your problem is."

He took a long sip of beer and pressed on. "So she applied for a job? What's wrong with that? She is an accomplished woman with goals and dreams, so why shouldn't she be out there interviewing? It has nothing to do with her feelings for you or your relationship."

I stared at him. That wasn't how I saw it. When she told me about the interview, it felt like she was trying to run away from the brewery, from me, from us. I panicked. I had spent weeks coming to the realization that I had fallen in love with her and then all of a sudden she was running off to some shiny new life.

"Yeah, man. And she didn't interview in New York," Trent reminded me.

Declan seemed confused. "So what's the problem if she works in Boston? Fabio over here goes to Boston a few days a week,"—he gestured to Callum with his beer—"and we deliver to restaurants there every day. She's not leaving you. It's just a job and a crappy commute."

Trent shook his head. "It sounds like she was trying to stay local for you. Wasn't she supposed to go back to her apartment in New York soon? Now she is trying to rebuild her life nearby. Did you even consider that?"

Declan snorted. "And not only did you act like an ass, you literally gave her a great reason not to."

Shit, they were right. I didn't even ask. I was too chickenshit to share my feelings and see if we were on the same page. What if she was interested in this job so she could stay in Massachusetts and be with me? She was probably going to move back to New York now.

Was I pushing her away because I was afraid? Afraid that she didn't want me as much as I wanted her?

"Talk to her. Tell her. Don't be such a baby."

I knew Callum was right, but it felt impossible. "I'm a man. And a Quinn. It's so hard to talk about this stuff."

He cut me off. "In a real relationship you have to. That's what makes it last. It's what makes it all worth it." My normally calm brother seemed agitated and upset. I could see the hurt in his eyes. I knew we weren't only talking about Cece right now.

As much as I hated to admit it, my brothers were right. That fear, the fear that she would know how I feel and leave anyway, was crushing me. I had to grow up, face my fears, and tell her everything. I had to show her how much I loved her and wanted to be with her. But I couldn't talk to her, because she was ignoring all my texts and calls. I even sent roses to her mom's house and got no response. I just wanted a chance to speak to her and tell her how I felt. I just needed a chance.

"You should call Nora." Was Declan reading my mind?

"Why?" I asked. "She scares me."

He nodded sagely. "She scares me too. But the word on the street is that Nora picked up drunk Cece at the Tipsy Whale this afternoon and then they were spotted at the diner together, crying and eating grilled cheese."

Callum was incredulous. "How did you know that?"

"I know what's up."

"But you don't speak to anyone or socialize."

Declan shrugged. "I work with a bunch of gossipy guys who spend lonely days on boats. I hear things. I also heard Violet Thompson just got divorced and is living back on the family farm." Declan gave Callum a pointed look. Callum ignored him and pretended to be fascinated by his phone. There was a story there, but despite all the sharing we were doing, I doubted I could drag it out of him.

While my brothers squabbled, I began to formulate a plan. I had to see Cece and talk to her. Tell her everything, lay my soul bare, and let her decide what she wanted. Because as badly as this hurt, not telling her would hurt so much more.

I wanted her. I wanted her forever. I wanted her in my brewery and in my home. I wanted to wake up next to her, drowning in that wild hair for the rest of my life. I wanted to build a business and a home and a family with her.

I wanted more. I wanted everything. I could see it—holidays and birthdays and warm nights snuggled up in front of the fireplace. Teaching our kids to sail and then disappearing below deck to make out like teenagers. I wanted it all.

But I had fucked up. I had pushed her away when she was at her most vulnerable. I knew she was tough, so how am I going to convince her to give me a second chance?

# 41

## CECELIA

I woke up hungover and depressed to the sound of my phone ringing. Who called this early? Whoever it was, I hated them and would never speak to them again. I was sober when I went to bed. What happened? Being in your thirties sucked. It was going to take me a week to recover from my whiskey adventure yesterday.

It was Nora calling. Of course it was Nora calling.

"Hello."

"Good morning, bestie." She sounded really chipper, and it made me more irate.

"Nora, I was asleep."

"It's nine a.m. kid, get your ass out of bed. You have things to do today."

"No, I don't."

"Yes, you do. You are going to shower, get dressed, and come meet me at the diner. We have a lot to talk about."

"We talked plenty yesterday. Please let me wallow in my depressed hungover state."

"Nope. Don't make me come over there and drag you myself. You know I'm super strong since I started doing those Krav Maga classes with Yael."

Shit. I knew she would do it too. Nora was an incredible friend, but she would not hesitate to walk in here and throw my sorry ass in the shower. "Okay, fine. Give me thirty minutes."

"Let's make it an hour so you have time to do your hair and put on makeup, okay?"

"Fine." I didn't want to put on makeup for breakfast at the diner, but it was easier to just go along than to fight with her right now. Besides, gallons of coffee and some bacon sounded pretty amazing right now.

"Great!" she trilled. "I love you to the moon and back! See you in an hour."

———

After a shower and an attempt to mask my poor life choices with makeup, I stumbled into the diner. Maybe Jackie could get me that coffee in an IV.

The doorbell jangled but I didn't hear anyone. The diner was completely empty. That was weird. The place was usually packed. I doubled back and looked at the door. There was a huge "closed" sign hanging there. I was so confused.

I started to leave when I heard Jackie's voice from the kitchen. "Cecelia, sweetie, we'll be right out. Have a seat at your regular booth."

Weird…they were expecting me.

I walked around the counter to my regular booth and was greeted by a familiar face. Liam. *Oh, shit.*

My eyes were probably the size of saucers. I was not ready to see him right now.

He stood up. "Cece, I just want to talk to you for a few minutes. Sit down, please." He looked rough. Like he hadn't been sleeping either. He had dark circles around his eyes and his beard was in desperate need of a trim. He still looked stupidly handsome, which annoyed me.

I debated leaving. But Nora had clearly set this up and was colluding with Jackie and Joe who had obviously closed the diner for me. I owed all of them to at least sit and listen. "Fine. But I need coffee first."

As if being summoned by a genie, Jackie appeared, pot in hand. "Good morning, sweetheart. And Liam, so nice to see you! Joe and I had a fabulous time at bingo night last week." She threw him a very unsubtle wink.

Liam gave her a megawatt smile and thanked her profusely for the coffee.

As soon as she had disappeared into the kitchen, he started. "Cece, I am so sorry. I was such an idiot. I know you are mad, but I can't let you take that job and leave town without at least knowing how I feel."

I was stunned. "I didn't take the job."

"You didn't?"

"No. You were right. I hated it. They offered me the job on the spot but I turned it down."

He stirred his coffee. "That's interesting."

"Yeah. I'm done with corporate America. I want to try some new things."

He smirked. "Is that so?"

My all-business tone was wavering. "Yes."

He leaned forward and grabbed my hand. I had to hold in a sigh. My body missed him, and this tiny bit of contact was already making me feel so much better.

"I was an idiot. I was afraid of my feelings for you. And I didn't want you to leave town without knowing." His blue eyes shone as he talked, and all I wanted was to wrap him in my arms and get lost in him.

"Okay."

"I know I am the last person you want to see right

now, but I wanted to show you this." He slid a manilla folder across the table.

I opened it, and it was filled with official looking paperwork. I skimmed the first page. "These are incorporation papers." I kept reading. "For Quinn Beverages."

"I took your advice. I talked to my brothers, and we decided to start our own distribution company. To help Binnacle, but also other small brewers who are trying to get on their feet."

"This is great," I said, flipping through the paperwork.

"It's all because of you. You inspired me. I was a jackass who thought I knew everything, but your ideas and perspective are fresh and creative. You have completely changed my business in just a few short months."

This was not where I expected this conversation to go. But I was happy for him. Despite what had happened between us, I wanted him to succeed.

"And we would love to be your first client, if you are interested."

"What do you mean?"

"Well, you are the local Havenport marketing guru. I hear you do great work." He winked. "And we could use your help."

I flushed. "I don't know what you are talking about."

He grabbed my hand. "Cece, we both know how passionate you are about helping people grow their businesses. You did incredible things for the brewery and for me." How did he know? How did he know what I was thinking? I hadn't told anyone.

"Well, I am considering staying here and possibly working with some local businesses on marketing projects." I held my head up high. I had survived this pleasant, but awkward conversation, and now it was time to gracefully exit. I stood up and he grabbed my arm.

"Please don't go yet. I'm not finished."

He let my hand go and started nervously running his hands through his hair. "Cece, I am in love with you. I think I've been in love with you since the day you showed up at the brewery. This was never casual for me. I know you have a lot to figure out, but I want you to stay here with me so we can figure it out together. The brewery is not the same without you. My apartment is not the same without you. Hell, this town would not be not the same without you."

He continued, "I realized that I do need people. And that I need you so badly. I love the brewery, but I love you more. I don't want to be successful if I can't share it with you."

His words melted my icy heart. "I am in love with you too, Liam."

He looked up at me, surprised. "What?"

"Yes, you dumbass. I love you too. I am crazy in love with you, and the thought of leaving town makes me want to throw up. I am going to stay here, regardless of what happens between us. This place is crazy, but it's my kind of crazy." I took a deep breath. "And I want to be with you too. This wasn't casual for me either. As much as I tried to fight it I fell for you."

He stood up abruptly, spilling his coffee all over the booth. Next thing I knew he had yanked me up and was kissing me senseless.

I tried to break away. "Liam, we have a lot to talk about."

"Yes, we do. But let's make out first." And his lowered his mouth to mine, giving me what I had been desperately craving for the last week.

Jackie and Joe burst out from the kitchen, overcome with nosiness. "Joe, they are kissing," I heard Jackie squeal.

"About damn time," Joe replied.

I smiled at Liam, who called back, "Guys, she loves me too."

"Of course she does, sweetheart. We knew it would work out. Now get back to kissing. I gotta text all my friends about this."

"So how did you get Jackie and Joe to close the diner?"

"I asked. Nora said they owed her favors, whatever that means." He shivered. "And they were very happy to kick everyone out for 'true love' as Joe put it."

I smiled. I loved this wacky town.

"So how about we move this conversation to my apartment?" he asked, squeezing my ass.

"That sounds sensible," I replied with a sexy smirk. "You have a lot of groveling to do."

## 42

LIAM

*1 Month Later*

AND GROVEL I DID. I KNEW I HAD TO MAKE IT UP TO her. I had to regain her trust.

So we took it slow. Too slow for me, but I wanted to show her I had learned and was going to do better. I wanted to show her I was serious about a future with her. I wanted to show her she was worth making room for.

Apparently showing her included freezing my ass off on the pier in the middle of winter. We were standing with her sister, Maggie, her two kids, and Mrs. Leary. Her friend Emily joined us a bit later, with her husband, Derek, and their three kids. I currently had the middle one, Jacob, on my shoulders.

It was probably in the low twenties and the winds were brutal coming across the water. But we stood and waited along with hundreds of other families, bundled up and huddled for warmth. Next year, I would set up a tent and sell beer—several of the parents looked like they could use a drink.

After what felt like hours but was probably more like twenty minutes, we saw it. An enormous Coast Guard cutter cruised into the harbor, and on the bow were Santa and Mrs. Claus, waving to the throngs of screaming people.

I couldn't help myself. I got excited. I grabbed Cece's hand as we screamed and cheered. Jacob kicked me in the chest several times, but I didn't care. The high school marching band started playing Christmas carols and the crowd sang along.

Santa had been arriving in Havenport on a Coast Guard cutter for generations. It was a tradition I remembered fondly from my childhood. I hadn't been out here to see it in decades, but Cece insisted we go. She said she missed this kind of thing when she was in New York. And how could I say no to my girl?

And so here I was, freezing my balls off and screaming with a ton of little kids as Santa disembarked and started waving to the crowd. You could feel the kids in the audience positively vibrating with happiness, and I couldn't deny how fun this was. Cece looked gorgeous as usual, her wild hair shoved under a beanie and her brown eyes shining. I couldn't help but imagine bringing our kids to see Santa. Camping out for a good vantage point and bundling everyone up in their winter gear. Something that once seemed so far away was finally in my grasp.

I wanted this future with her. I wanted to be a dad and watch her become a mom. I wanted to raise our kids in this strange, quirky town and celebrate all our wacky traditions.

We had just gotten back together, but my heart did not want to listen to my brain. I wanted this future now. I wanted forever to start today. However, my brain kept fighting back, reminding me to take it slow.

But things were looking good. She had started joining Tuesday night beers with my brothers, and I had earned some brownie points with her mom by doing some projects around her house. Our families and friends were coming together, and we were building our own community in Havenport. Cece had decided to officially start her own marketing company and had already taken on a few clients. We were planning a trip to New York to clean out her old apartment next weekend. I wanted to drive that moving truck straight back to my place, but she hesitated about moving in so soon.

I wanted to wake up next to her every day, but I knew I had to earn that privilege. So we talked, and I listened, and together we built something beautiful and strong.

# EPILOGUE

## LIAM

*Two Years Later*

"Ugh." I let out a growl of frustration. "I hate ties."

Cece came over and took control, crafting the perfect Windsor knot while smiling at me. "I know. But you look so super hot in that suit."

"Thanks. I can't believe how gorgeous you look right now."

"Well, believe it, kid, because we need to leave in twenty minutes."

"Okay, okay. Do you need a zip?"

"Yeah, I do."

I gently tugged the zipper up Cece's charcoal-gray bridesmaid dress. Her hair was up in some kind of bun and soft curls escaped around her face and neck. She looked beautiful, as always, but today she just glowed.

When she turned around, I pulled her close and rested my hand on her stomach. "Are you going to behave, Maverick?" I asked, rubbing her belly and winking at her.

"Be a good *boy* and don't give mom too much trouble, okay?"

Cece smiled at me. "*She* will be fine. But I just have to make sure I find a bathroom before the ceremony starts."

Cece was seven months pregnant with our little surprise. We did not know the sex, but I was convinced it was a boy and had already named him Maverick because he was so stealthy. We didn't know she was pregnant until two months into the pregnancy. Cece thought I was crazy and was convinced it was a girl. Our families had set up a very complex betting pool, and we were getting closer and closer to the big day. My girl was usually right about most things, so I was really hoping for a win this time.

Pregnancy agreed with Cece. Although it was exhausting, she had never looked so beautiful. Her hair was fuller and curlier than ever and her skin glowed. Her body was ripe and lush, and she carried this baby with confidence. It was such a turn-on. We hadn't planned on kids so soon, but everything just fell into place. I was so excited for the next generation of Quinns to start running wild in Havenport.

Cece's mom decided to downsize and sold us the family house on Main Street. Although it was enormous, we were up for the challenge of filling it with love, family, and memories. We had rehabbed the carriage house in the back, and Cece was using it as an office for her marketing firm. Her business was growing every day, and she had become a bit of a local power player. Watching her build her business and gain confidence had been such a privilege. It was hard to even remember the timid woman who came in looking for a job a few years ago. We had a lot of work to do on the rest of the house, but we loved making it our own. I knew it made Cece so happy that our kids would grow up in the same loving home she did, filled with happy memories of her dad.

She still did marketing work for me at the brewery, but we had to hire a few full-time people to cover events and bartending and social media. My brothers and I had finally launched our distribution company, Quinn Beverages, and we had a few dozen clients so far—mostly other microbreweries, wineries, and even some non-alcoholic options as well. We had built a solid independent network in New England and were getting ready to expand into New York and New Jersey next. Being in business with my brothers was not always easy, but each of us brought vastly different skills and personalities to the table. Turns out, the three of us actually made a pretty good team. Since my attention had been diverted, Trent has become the manager of the Havenport brewery and is doing an incredible job. We had such a successful year we were considering opening a second location.

I wrapped my arms around her, resting my hands on her hips. I kissed the sweet spot where her neck met her collarbone, the spot that always drove her insane. I could feel her knees buckle slightly as I held onto her. She sighed. "We don't have time."

I continued kissing up her graceful neck. "But Cece, you look so incredible. And," I said, squeezing her ass, "you feel so incredible."

She pivoted and kissed me, deeply, wrapping her arms around my neck. "Liam, as much as I want to get out of this dress and my pregnancy Spanx already, we cannot be late for your brother's wedding." She kissed me on the nose and went back to getting ready.

I took a step back, admiring her. "Fair enough. I still can't believe this is actually happening. My brother is getting married. I never thought I'd see the day."

"Believe it. It's happening. And it's a miracle."

"It all happened so fast, but when it's right, it's right."

"Yes. They are really perfect for each other." She grabbed her tiny purse and took my arm.

I laughed. "What are the odds of finding your soulmate right here in Havenport?"

She wrapped her arms around me again. "I'd say they are pretty good, Mr. Quinn."

I kissed her deeply. "Yes, Mrs. Quinn, they are."

## WANT MORE CECE & LIAM?

Click here to get the Bonus Epilogue to see how Liam
proposed to Cece.
https://dl.bookfunnel.com/fbb4nwtc10
Be prepared to swoon!

# HAVENPORT BOOK 2

## SNEAK PEEK AT HAVENPORT BOOK 2
### Coming June 2021

*Are you in the mood for more small town romantic goodness? Do you love bearded, grumpy heroes and bitchy dogs? What about Type A heroines and makeover scenes? Then read on for a taste of my upcoming release.*

# PROLOGUE
## ASTRID

*March*

JUST MY LUCK. THE DAY I REALIZED I WAS IN LOVE was also the day I got arrested. When I woke up this morning, I did not expect this day to end with me getting my mug shot taken, but given how my life had been going, it was not a shock.

I was a planner. I carefully examined every decision and it's statistic implications before implementing and executing with precision. Needless to say, I had never imagined getting myself into a situation that culminated in my arrest. On the bright side, I was wearing a gorgeous evening gown and had professional hair and makeup done, so the odds were good it would at least be a decent photo. I wonder if I could get a copy of it? I could use it as my Instagram handle…

Getting arrested sucked. And I was pretty sure it would ruin my career and reputation. But damn, it also felt really good. After years of taking other people's shit and smiling politely, it felt good to finally fight back a little. To do what I wanted to do, what I needed to do. It was about time I reclaimed some of the dignity that had been stolen from me. And if a criminal record was the consequence, so be it.

The holding cell was pretty gross. There were a bunch of other women in here with me. Everyone kept to themselves. Yes, I was dressed like a beauty queen, but I was also pretty tall and years of being a lawyer had helped me develop an excellent 'don't fuck with me' face, so I was fine. I knew I would be bailed out soon. I was only going to get slapped with assault and battery, nothing crazy. Even murderers made bail sometimes.

If anything, the greatest tragedy of the night was the loss of my shoe. My new friends Christian and Dante had given them to me as a gift and they were sparkly Louboutin perfection. A four inch platform stiletto with a delicate sliver ankle strap, the toe box was covered with small crystals that created a purple and blue ombre effect. My toenails were painted a perfect purple to match and they set off my eggplant gown beautifully. They were the most perfect shoes I had ever seen. And now I only had one of them. Apparently my right shoe was evidence, so the odds of me getting it back were slim. Still, even with one shoe, and sitting in a grimy holding cell surrounded by criminals, this had turned out to be one of the most memorable days of my life.

# AUTHOR'S NOTE

Dear Reader,

Thank you for reading my first book! This was truly a labor of love, written in tiny stolen moments, late at night after my kids went to bed.

I started reading romance while suffering from postpartum depression. I fell in love with the genre and the community, and it gave me so much joy, hope, and laughter during a difficult time. I dreamed of one day writing stories that lifted people's spirits and made their days a bit brighter.

I wrote this story for anyone who needs a happy ending right now. I hope the few hours you spend in Havenport bring a tiny bit of joy into your day.

With all my love,
Daphne

# ACKNOWLEDGMENTS

Thank you to everyone who joined me in Havenport!

I wrote this book while locked down in my house due to Covid. I was trying to work my day job, homeschool my five year old, and keep my toddler from from setting himself on fire. I needed a creative outlet to help me get through some of the hard days. At the encouragement of my lovely friends, the world of Havenport was born.

There are so many people to thank.

To my husband, thank you for your patience and encouragement. You have been my real life romance hero for nineteen years.

To my mother, thank you for always having my back. I am so grateful for your support, encouragement, and child care.

Tatum Rogue, you were the first person to ever read this book. You are an incredible author buddy, and I appreciate all your notes and suggestions. You inspired me to keep going and tell this story.

To the ladies of HoCroWoHo, thank you for your decades of friendship, your continued excellence, and your constant encouragement.

To the amazing ladies who make up my Street Team, thank you for offering your time and hilarious memes. I appreciate the constant encouragement and the hilarity.

Leah, thank you for being a great beta reader and brainstorm partner.

Kari, thank you for the gorgeous cover.

Anns, thank you for your thorough editing.

The entire teams at Give Me Books Promotions and Enticing Journeys Book Promotions, thank you for helping me bring this book into the world.

Jennifer, thank you for jumping in and helping me with my blurb.

Thank you to my family for being hilarious and loving and silly.

# ABOUT THE AUTHOR

In High School, Daphne Elliot was voted "most likely to become a romance novelist." After spending the last decade as a corporate lawyer, she has finally embraced her destiny. Her steamy novels are filled with flirty banter, sexy hijinks, and lots and lots of heart.

Daphne is a coffee-drinking, hot-sauce loving introvert who spends her free time gardening and practicing yoga. She lives in Massachusetts with her husband, two kids, two dogs, two fish and twelve backyard chickens.

Find Daphne at:
daphneelliot.com
daphneelliotauthor@gmail.com

Stay in touch with Daphne:
Subscribe to Daphne's Newsletter
Like Daphne on Facebook
Follow Daphne on Instagram
Hang with Daphne on GoodReads
Follow Daphne on Amazon

Made in the USA
Columbia, SC
14 May 2023

16707117R00173